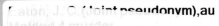

4 Murder

J.C. Eaton

KENSINGTON BOOKS
KENSINGTON PUBLISHING CORP.
www.kensingtonbooks.com

KENSINGTON BOOKS are published by

Kensington Publishing Corp.
119 West 40th Street
New York, NY 10018

All Kensington titles, imprints, and distributed lines are available at special quantity discounts for bulk purchases for sales promotion, premiums, fund-raising, educational, or institutional use.

Special book excerpts or customized printings can also be created to fit specific needs. For details, write or phone the office of the Kensington Sales Manager: Attn.: Sales Department. Kensington Publishing Corp., 119 West 40th Street, New York, NY 10018. Phone: 1-800-221-2647.

Kensington and the K logo Reg. U.S. Pat. & TM Off.

First Printing: September 2019
ISBN-13: 978-1-4967-1990-4
ISBN-10: 1-4967-1990-5

ISBN-13: 978-1-4967-1991-1 (eBook)
ISBN-10: 1-4967-1991-3 (eBook)

10 9 8 7 6 5 4 3 2 1

Printed in the United States of America

To the Sun City West Clay and Ceramics Clubs,
this mystery is all yours!
Just be happy our characters are fictional and
not signing up to join you anytime soon.

ACKNOWLEDGMENTS

Thanks once again to Larry Finkelstein, Gale Leach, Ellen Lynes, Susan Morrow, Susan Schwartz, and Suzanne Scher. Without your support, this book would still be in a file somewhere on our computer.

Special thanks go out to our dog park friend, Jeannine Phelps, who walked us through the complex processes needed to create designs in clay. We hope we got it right. Or close enough . . .

Of course, none of this would be possible had it not been for our incredible agent, Dawn Dowdle, at Blue Ridge Literary Agency, and Tara Gavin, our amazing editor at Kensington Publishing. From stellar advice to hand-holding, you have always been there for us. Ross Plotkin, production editor at Kensington, you deserve a big shout-out, too!

We genuinely appreciate all of the dedicated and tireless copy and line editors who must wring their hands at our mistakes. Thank you for helping us bring a quality cozy mystery to our readers.

Most of all, we thank you, our readers, for welcoming Sophie Kimball into your world and joining the antics in Sun City West, Arizona.

Chapter 1

Augusta, our receptionist/secretary at Williams Investigations, looked up from her computer and straightened her tortoiseshell glasses. "Hey, Phee, two ladies called while you were at lunch and wanted to schedule an appointment with you for this afternoon."

"With me? Did you tell them I'm the bookkeeper and not an investigator?"

Augusta sighed. "They already knew that and said it didn't matter. Said they met you on a plane a year or two ago. They couldn't remember."

Two years ago. That sounded about right. My mother was insistent I use vacation time from my job at the Mankato, Minnesota, police department and fly out to Sun City West, Arizona, because she was convinced the members of her book club were going to die from reading a cursed book. The only thing cursed was my trip.

I moved closer to her desk. "Oh my gosh, Gertie and Trudy from the Lillian. It's a residential resort hotel of sorts. Very elegant."

"Don't know about that, but those were the names they gave. No last name."

"I think it's Madison. Did they mention what they wanted to see me about?"

"Theft. They said someone's been pilfering things from their retirement complex. So much for elegance, huh?"

"That sounds like something they should be taking up with the Lillian's management company, not me."

"I got the feeling there was more to it. Anyway, I scheduled an appointment for two thirty. They want to be back at their place in time for the four o'clock seating for dinner."

"Four? That's almost as bad as my mother's five thirty. What is it with these people and their obsession about eating at a certain time? Sure, I'll see them, but only as a courtesy. Geez, when Nate retired from the police force in Minnesota and started this firm, I came on to do the books, not the investigations."

"And yet . . ."

"I know. I know. Things sort of happened."

"Uh-huh. By the way, Nate got called a little while ago to confer with the Maricopa County Sheriff's Office on a recent homicide. They didn't come right out and say 'homicide,' but you know that's what it is or they wouldn't have insisted he rush over to Sun City West."

"Sun City West? Yikes! That's where my mother lives. I'm surprised she hasn't called. She usually gets that news long before it reaches us."

"Yeah. About that . . ."

I let out a groan and waited for Augusta to continue.

"She called all right. I was just about to get to it. Good thing I remembered my shorthand from high school. Here goes. 'I left you more than one voice mail, Phee. Arlette from the Cut 'N Curl is going on vacation for three weeks. She didn't say anything to me when I was in last week. Myrna found out about it this morning when she went in for a trim. Three weeks! Who's going to touch up my hair? Are there any good salons near you in Vistancia? I refuse to have Cecilia drag me to one of those cheap seven-dollar haircut places. God knows what kind of color I'd wind up with. Call me. And don't forget to mark your calendar for the Creations in Clay on June thirtieth.'"

Augusta read the entire message without pausing to take a breath. For that matter, I didn't take one, either. I expected to hear some awful news that would link Nate's possible murder case to someone my mother knew. The last time that happened, my mother and her friends hired Nate to investigate because the sheriff's department was "moving like geriatric slugs." I prayed to the gods that whatever Nate was called to consult on wouldn't involve my mother or the Booked 4 Murder book club.

"So that was it? Hairdresser on vacation and the Creations in Clay?"

"Yep. That's all she said. You can breathe again. So, if you don't mind my asking, what on earth is the Creations in Clay? Some sort of exhibit?"

"Sort of, with tentacles. The Creations in Clay is the annual pottery and clay event in Sun City West. It always takes place right before the summer heat kicks in. It includes a juried art show and lots of booths where the clay club members sell their creations."

"That sounds nice. I didn't know your mother was interested in juried art."

"Up until a few months ago, she wasn't. Then one of her book club ladies read this article about people whose artistic talents don't begin to show up until they're in their seventies or eighties. Like Grandma Moses. Or that lady from the seventeen hundreds who discovered decoupage. Anyway, one of my mother's friends convinced her to join the clay club because, and I quote, 'Molding clay could be the conduit to our hidden artistic talents.'"

"Really? She said that?"

"Actually, if you want to know the real reason, I think my mother intends to make dog bowls for Streetman. Don't ask."

Augusta tried not to snicker, but we both started laughing.

I finally caught my breath. "It's only May, so she has lots of time to make that spoiled Chiweenie of hers a complete place setting. Well, I'd better get back to my accounts before Gertie and Trudy get here. And especially before Marshall returns from that missing person's case in Buckeye. I don't want him to think I stand around gabbing all day."

"So, how's it going between the two of you?"

"Geez, you're beginning to sound like my mother. Seriously, for someone dating in her forties, it's going great."

It was hard not to smile and get all dreamy eyed. I didn't want to jinx anything by saying it out loud, but boy, was I glad Nate hired him. Imagine, Marshall and I worked all those years for the Mankato Police Department and neither of us knew we were both interested in dating each other. Maybe Nate figured it out all along and that was why when it came time to hire another investigator for his firm, Marshall was his first choice.

"Glad to hear it." Augusta clicked the mouse and looked at her computer screen. "I'd better get back to work, too."

Within seconds, I was working on my billing and filing. The time went by so quickly I hadn't realized it was two thirty until Augusta knocked on my door frame.

"The ladies who called are here to see you. Do you want me to send them right in?"

I stood up and followed her out. "I'll get them."

Gertie and Trudy were facing the window and turned when they heard my footsteps. Their hairdos looked a bit

different from the last time I saw them. Short silver curls
with hints of blue. Perfectly styled. Same could be said for
their identical outfits. It almost looked as if the two of them
were standing at attention.

I rushed over immediately. "Hi! It's nice to see you again.
Can I get you some coffee or tea?"

Gertie shook her head. "No thanks. We'll be eating soon
and we don't want to ruin our appetites. The Lillian has a
marvelous master chef and tonight is tilapia night."

"It's always tilapia night, Gertie," Trudy said. "They
have that on the menu every night."

Augusta, who had returned to her desk, sat bolt upright
and gave me one of her unmistakable looks.

I turned the other way and ushered the sisters into my
office. "Please, take a seat."

There were two chairs in front of my desk, and I moved
my chair to the right of the computer so it wouldn't obstruct
anyone's view as we spoke. "So, tell me. What's going on
regarding the thefts? I understand that's why you came to
see me."

"It is," Gertie said. "It most certainly is. You show her
the list, Trudy."

Without wasting a second, Trudy opened a large floral
handbag and took out a folded piece of paper and began to
read it.

"Mildred Kirkenbaum, one spool of purple yarn, Emily
Outstrader, two cans of tuna, Warren Bellis, one jar of
olives. The green ones without those red things in them.
Mabel Leech, one fountain pen and some paper clips,
Norma O'Neil, a five-dollar bill, Sharon Smyth, a small
clay jar she bought from the last clay club art show, and
Clive Monroe, a box of tissues and his lifelong membership
pin to the Elks."

"Uh, is that it?"

Trudy nodded as she handed me the list. "As far as we know. And we've been asking. From the minute Mildred told us about the purple yarn."

"What about you and your sister? Are any of your items missing?"

"Not that we know of," Gertie said. "But sometimes you don't know if something's missing until you go to use it."

I had to agree with her on that one. I'd spent entire afternoons looking for stupid things like razor blades, the extra packet of dental floss I swore I had, and my reward card for a local restaurant that I only frequented once in a while. Most of the time the items in question turned up days, weeks, or months later, in places I never expected. I wondered if the same could be said for the residents of the Lillian, but I didn't want to sound as if I was dismissing the two sisters who had made a point of coming to our office.

"Is this the first time something like this has happened? Or the first time people felt it should be reported?"

Gertie and Trudy glanced at each other before Gertie spoke.

"The first time. We're certain. Those residents, who happen to be friends of ours, have lived there much longer than my sister and me. That's why we're so concerned."

I edged forward in my chair. "A theft is a theft no matter how small or valuable the item is, so why didn't your friends report it to the management?"

"They didn't want to get anyone in trouble," Trudy said.

Gertie gave her sister a poke in the arm. "Tell her the real reason. Go on."

Trudy started to fiddle with the strap on her handbag. "If we reported it, the manager would think the thief was one of the staff members. I mean, they have keys to our apartments in order to clean them and change the linens. Not to mention the regular maintenance. The staff members do all sorts of extra things for us like helping us put groceries away if we go shopping or move furniture around. Some of them even help residents with their hair if they have time. All of that will come to a stop if they get hauled in by the residence director."

"My sister's right," Gertie said. "I wouldn't go so far as to say the staff plays favorites, but those of us who remember them during the holidays or tip them once in a while get better attention, if you know what I mean."

I bit my lip and waited for a second. "Is it possible these thefts were committed by another resident and not a staff member?"

The sisters shrugged simultaneously.

"Maybe, if someone was careless enough to leave their door open or unlocked. That happens sometimes. But the people we mentioned, the ones on the list, were all insistent they locked up whenever they left their apartments, even if they were only going down the hall to get their mail," Gertie said. "And it isn't as if any new residents have moved in lately. The last one was Florence Shiver, and she moved in at least nine months ago."

"Well," I said, "this is troubling. Look, as you know, I'm the office bookkeeper and accountant, not an investigator, but I would be willing to speak discreetly with your residence director, without letting on you were the ones who called me. I'd be doing this unofficially. As a friend. Would that be okay with you? For all we know, maybe the director is aware of something going on."

"Do you have to show her the list of names?" Trudy asked.

I shook my head. "No. I'll type up a list of the items and go from there. How does that sound?"

Gertie opened her handbag and took out a twenty-dollar bill. "We're willing to pay you."

I honestly felt as if I was about to blush. Talk about feeling uncomfortable. "No. No. Please put that away. It's not necessary. I'll get in touch with the management and I'll let you know what I find out in a few days. Did you need me to call a taxi service for you?"

"Heavens no," Gertie said. "We told our residence driver to pick us up in a half hour. His car is probably out front."

Sure enough, a sleek white limo was parked a few feet from our entrance. I escorted the sisters to the door and reassured them I'd be in touch.

Trudy grabbed my arm and whispered, "There's one more thing."

Here it comes. Whatever it is, I can only imagine.

"Sharon Smyth is beside herself over that clay jar she bought. The woman was in tears."

"I know for a fact the clay club is having another sale on June thirtieth," I said. "That's coming up pretty soon. She can always buy another jar."

"That's what we thought, too, dear, but Sharon was still distraught."

Wait until she sees my mother's creations. It'll give a whole new meaning to the word "distraught."

"Yes," Gertie added, "you'd think that silly jar was worth a fortune the way that woman carried on. Wouldn't you say so, Trudy?"

"I would. Indeed, I would. She's still carrying on. And acting strangely, too. Refusing to go out on excursions like shows or shopping. If it keeps up, she'll be a regular recluse. So, you see, it's really important, Miss Kimball, that you find out who stole these items."

"I'll do my best."

The two sisters, with their matching teal capris and polka-dotted blouses, went directly to their limo.

"So, what did you find out?" Augusta asked when they left.

"Not much. Sounds like the usual stuff that probably happens in college dorms and all sorts of residences where there's a large population. Petty theft. I mean, if I were to add up all the stuff that was taken, it wouldn't even equal twenty-five dollars, but that's not the point. The residents are feeling very uncomfortable and one woman is taking it to the extreme."

"Yeesh. So I guess that means you'll be on the case, so to speak."

"Not a case. A favor for two elderly sisters. I've got Saturday off. I'll drop by the Lillian and have a word with their director. See what I can find out."

"You're a good soul, Phee. Just don't get too deep in the mire. Makes it hard to wipe your boots."

Just then the phone rang and Augusta grabbed it. I could hear her customary greeting of "Williams Investigations. How can I help you?" But instead of the usual banter that follows those calls, all I heard was, "Uh-oh. Okay. Okay, I will."

I hesitated to return to my office. Something was off.

"What's the matter, Augusta? What is it?"

"Looks like the mud you're going to be wiping off your feet is waiting for you in Sun City West. That was Nate. I was right all along. It *was* a homicide the sheriff's department was investigating. Some guy found dead in his garage."

Suddenly the corned beef sandwich I had eaten for lunch wasn't settling too well. "Not anyone I know?"

"I don't think so, but Nate wants you to call your mother and go over to her house."

"My mother? Why? What's she got to do with this?"

"The guy they found was holding a piece of paper with two names on it. Your mother's was one of them."

"Oh my God! Did he say who the other one was?"

Augusta shook her head. "No. All he said was for you to call your mother and go directly to her house. If she's not home, wait there for him."

"And here I thought the worst thing I was going to deal with today was a bit of filching."

Chapter 2

I raced to my desk and dialed my mother. It was one of those quick frantic calls that I made without thinking things through.

"Mom! I'm glad you're home. Are you alone?"

"No. Lucinda and Shirley are here. We're having a cup of coffee. Why? What's wrong?"

"I don't have all the details, but I'm on my way over. Don't go anywhere. In fact, tell Lucinda and Shirley to stay there until I get there. Or until Nate gets there."

"Nate? Now I know something's wrong. What? What is it? Is there a homicidal maniac in the neighborhood? Tell me. Tell me now!"

"Look, all I know is a man was found dead in his garage, and Nate wants to talk to you about it. I don't even know the guy's name."

"Then why does your boss want to talk to me?"

"Um, uh, well, because the dead man was holding a piece of paper with your name on it."

"What??? It said 'Harriet Plunkett'? Hold on a second. Lucinda! Make sure the door's locked. Shirley, close the shutters. Where's my Streetman? Oh, there he is, under the coffee table. Phee, are you still on the line?"

"I haven't gone anywhere, Mom, but I'm on my way over.

I'm sure you have nothing to worry about. Have another cup of coffee with the ladies and try to relax."

I hung up the phone before she got any more hysterical.

"I'm out the door, Augusta," I shouted as I raced across the office. "I'll call you later."

All sorts of weird and disturbing thoughts crossed my mind as I made the half-hour drive to Sun City West from our office in Glendale. Thankfully the traffic was light. It wasn't rush hour yet, with everyone leaving Phoenix for their bedroom communities.

When I pulled up to my mother's house, Shirley's Buick was parked in front and Nate's car sat directly behind hers.

Good. Nate's fielding the first blow.

"It's me!" I shouted as I rang the bell.

My mother opened the front door slowly and then the security door.

"Hurry up and get inside."

"Your house isn't under siege. Calm down. Did Nate explain what's going on?"

"Sure did, kiddo," came a voice from the kitchen.

"Great. Because I have no idea what's happening."

By now, I was standing near the kitchen table. Nate, Shirley, and Lucinda were all seated with cups of coffee in front of them and a platter of Pepperidge Farm cookies that may or may not have come from the freezer. Streetman was under the table and poked his head out once to acknowledge my presence.

"Grab a chair, Phee." My mother took her spot nearest the window. "This is a nightmare. A veritable nightmare."

I looked at each of their faces and only Nate appeared calm and collected. Lucinda, who usually had that frazzled hair thing going for her, was even more disheveled, as if she had been pulling at her hair. Shirley looked as stylish as always, but I swore, even with her dark skin, she was pale. As for my mother, it was hard to say. The combination of drama and genuine fear made it impossible to tell how upset she really was.

"So, will someone please explain what's going on? The only thing I know is a man was found dead holding a piece of paper with my mother's name on it."

Suddenly, Lucinda started gasping. "Not dead. He could have been murdered, for all we know. And your mother's wasn't the only name on that paper. Mine was there, too."

Murdered. The word itself had an ominous sound. I stood up, took a coffee mug from the cabinet, and helped myself to what was left in the coffeemaker.

"Yeah. Um, that's what Augusta thought."

Nate rolled his eyes and choked back a laugh. "Sorry, it's not funny, but lately Augusta's become a wealth of information and innuendo. Here's the real deal. First off, the news media will start out reporting a death. Then they'll tell the public the sheriff's department has evidence pointing to a potential homicide. In a day or so, the homicide will be verified. Law enforcement can't give away too much information or it will compromise the investigation. You all understand that, right?"

A collective "uh-huh" followed and Nate went on. "So, what I'm about to tell you stays in this room. Let me be clear. The only reason I'm sharing this is because two of your names were found at an active crime scene. And your help is needed."

Other than the sounds the dog was making from scratching himself under the table, no one made a noise, so Nate continued.

"Okay. The sheriff's department got a call midmorning from someone at the clay club who said Quentin Dussler was supposed to teach a clay class at eight in the morning and hadn't shown up. The caller was insistent something was wrong because Quentin wasn't answering his home or cell phones. So, since this is a senior community, a deputy was sent over to Quentin's house on Springdale Drive to do a welfare check. No one answered the door, but the garage door was off the ground by a few feet, so the deputy lifted it up and found the guy leaning back in a chair next to a potter's wheel. Dead."

"Why did they think it was a crime scene? Was he murdered?" Shirley asked. "Maybe he had a heart attack."

Nate groaned. "Because people who have heart attacks aren't usually found with large clay pots stuffed over their heads, waiting to dry. The clay was still moist in spots. The clay pot didn't smother him. It was an after touch. He was probably smothered by a plastic bag first and then clay was globbed in his nose and mouth."

Shirley fanned her neck with both hands. "Lordy! Lordy! That's the worst way to die. Someone molding the breath out of you."

"That *is* kind of gruesome," I said, "in a medieval sort of way. And why did he have a piece of paper with Lucinda's name and my mother's on it?"

Nate took a sip of the coffee and reached for a cookie. "That's what I'd like to know and that's why I came over here. I was just about to ask your mother and Mrs. Espinoza when you arrived."

I looked directly at my mother. "Is it because you're in the clay club, Mom? Were you and Lucinda in his class and he had to contact you?"

"No. We took our introductory class at Beardsley Recreation Center weeks ago. Besides, Quentin only teaches, I mean, *taught,* the advanced classes—specialty glazing and throwing pottery on the wheel instead of simple molds. Lucinda and I are discovering the early stages of our talents."

"I hate to say this, but you're sounding more and more like Aunt Ina."

"Hush."

I had hit a nerve with my mother. My aunt Ina was still living the hippie dream. A regular artsy-fartsy throwback from Woodstock, but with one difference. Aunt Ina came with a financial portfolio that could rival Donald Trump's. And that was due to her recent marriage to financier Louis Melinsky.

"Forget about Aunt Ina for a minute. Why would this Quentin guy have your names?"

"Oh Lordy!" Shirley said. "Was it a hit list?"

Lucinda all but exploded in her seat. "A hit list? My God, who'd want to kill us?"

Nate stretched his arms across the table, palms wide open. "Whoa! Slow down. No one said anything about a hit list. That wasn't even on the radar. There could be lots of reasons why this guy had your names. His garage was also some sort of studio for his clay projects. In fact, it looked more like a business. He had shipping boxes, those annoying popcorn stuffers, wrapping paper, and mailing labels all over the place. My take is he had a decent reputation for his clay pots or whatever they were and did a mail order business. So, did either of you ladies order anything from him?"

"I don't know about you, Lucinda," my mother said, "but I didn't. I've got enough tchotchkes all over the place. Plus, I'll be making my own."

"Well, don't look at me. I didn't order anything from him. I couldn't afford his stuff if I wanted to. Did you see the prices he charged last year at the clay show? I mean, yeah, his pots were phenomenal but still, who has that kind of money to spend on decorative items?"

Nate let out a slow breath and ran his fingers through his hair. In his mid-sixties, my boss still looked good. No sign of balding and a decent physique. I'm sure women found him attractive, but he'd been married to his job forever.

"Okay, ladies, let's think beyond the clay club. Does Quentin belong to any other clubs, churches, or organizations that either of you are in?"

My mother and Lucinda shook their heads as Nate scratched his chin. "The sheriff's deputies searched the house and there was no sign of any pets. Scratch off the dog club. And any other pet clubs."

"Not so fast," my mother said. "Cindy Dolton from the dog park knows everything that's going on around here. She's shared lots of information with Phee in the past. If I were you, and I'm not telling you what to do, but, I'd send Phee over to meet with Cindy." Then, she turned to me. "You can take Streetman for a nice early morning visit."

I can also go and jump in the nearest lake, but you don't see me rushing out to do that.

I gave Nate the "don't you dare" look and he winked.

"All right, Harriet. We'll consider it. Right now, I guess that's about it. If you or Lucinda think of anything, give me a call."

Shirley reached across the table and grabbed Nate's wrist. In addition to a gorgeous shade of yellow that accented her dark skin, someone had painted tiny daisies on each of her nails. "You're sure it wasn't a hit list?"

"The sheriff's department has no reason to believe it was anything of the sort and I tend to concur. They're checking the handwriting on that piece of paper to see if it was Quentin's. Maybe someone from the clay club gave him the names for another reason. Fund-raising, events, who knows?"

"Well, I know one thing," Lucinda said. "Until they find

out who killed Quentin Dussler, I'm not going anywhere without my screamer."

Nate flashed me a look and I tried not to laugh. "A while back, Myrna Mittleson purchased some handheld safety devices for the book club ladies. They're called 'screamers' and they emit a powerful scream if someone is being attacked."

"Really?" Nate raised his eyebrows. "I suppose if it makes you feel safe, why not?"

My mother bent down to look at the dog, who was snoring from under the table. "I accidentally bumped into my screamer a few weeks ago. I had it on one of the end tables when I was changing pocketbooks. It went off accidentally and poor Streetman peed all over himself."

At that point, Nate turned away from the table and squelched a laugh. "Remember, ladies, if you hear anything, call."

I stood up, gave my mother a quick hug, and told Shirley and Lucinda to have a nice day before hightailing it out of the house. I waited until we were at the foot of the driveway before I spoke. "What's your real take as to why our dead guy had those names?"

"Your guess is as good as mine. I was hoping your mother and her friend would know, but all I did was unnerve them."

"Don't worry about it. A change in the TV lineup unnerves them. So now what?"

"I'll see if the sheriff's department has gotten any further with this. I know they were pursuing DNA evidence, but that'll take weeks. Seems to me we'd move along much more quickly with old-fashioned sleuthing."

"Uh-oh. I see that look on your face."

"Come on, kiddo. How bad can an early morning trip to the dog park really be?"

"You haven't had to pull Streetman out of there when he decides to make amorous advances at the other dogs."

"Yeah, but it'll be worth it if this Cindy Dolton can give us more information."

"You're going to owe me big time, Nate."

"I always do."

Chapter 3

I had completely forgotten about my earlier meeting with Gertie and Trudy until later in the day when we were about to lock up. Marshall had just returned from his case in Buckeye and was helping himself to a cup of coffee before turning off the Keurig. Nate, who had been following up with phone calls I assumed were related to the Quentin Dussler murder, stepped out of his office and started to say something to Augusta.

I interrupted him. "Um, sorry to break in, but this is important. I need to let you know about something because I don't want you to think I'm overstepping my bounds. I met with two clients, well, not really clients . . . two elderly women I sort of know from Sun City West. They live in a senior residential resort community and wanted me to look into some petty theft going on in their residence."

"It's true," Augusta said. "I set up the meeting myself, so don't blame Phee."

"No one's blaming anyone," Nate replied. "I'm itching to hear the rest of this."

I took a quick breath. "The ladies, Gertie and Trudy, are in their nineties. That seems to be the average age for the people in the Lillian. Anyway, they came to me because I met them on the plane when I first came out here for that idiotic book curse. Anyway, they're afraid to report these thefts to the management for fear of repercussions. You know, if the staff decided not to treat them as nicely. So, I offered to stop by their residence this weekend and have a general chat with the director without mentioning any names."

Marshall gave Nate a quick glance before turning to me. "What kind of stuff was taken? Did they tell you?"

"They told me and they gave me a list. If I were to total up the monetary value, it would be around twenty-five bucks. Things like cans of tuna, some yarn, an Elks pin, a clay pottery jar, and a five-dollar bill."

Nate tried to squelch a laugh, but, unlike earlier in the day, he wasn't successful. "I don't mean to come across as callous, but really? A can of tuna?"

"It's serious for them," I said. "They've been living there for quite a while and nothing like this has happened."

"Maybe not that they're aware of," Marshall said. "But pilfering small items isn't unusual in places like that. Heck, I've heard of people stealing lunches from break rooms at businesses and even going so far as rooting through other people's desks."

"So, do either of you have a problem with me looking into it?"

The men shook their heads.

"I think it'll do you good," Nate said.

"What do you mean?"

Augusta stood up, grabbed her pocketbook, and turned off the copy machine as she headed to the door. "He means it will keep you out of his hair while he's investigating that murder. And if you ask me, that's a good thing, because the last time you got involved with a murderer, you were nearly killed."

I tried not to think about that horrific night a few months

ago when a deranged person tried to silence me because I knew too much.

"This is different. The only thing I'm doing in relation to the murder investigation is snooping around the dog park to pick up the local gossip from a lady who happens to be a wealth of information. Besides, Nate's the one who thought it would be a good idea."

Marshall gave my boss a quick look. "Really?"

"Underneath all that gossip and hearsay are some real facts. All Phee's going to do is ferret them out." Then he chuckled. "The worst that can happen is she'll step into something unsavory."

I locked gazes with Nate and didn't budge. "If I do step into something unsavory, you'll owe me a new pair of shoes."

The four of us left the office at the same time and Marshall walked me to my car. I told him a bit more about Gertie and Trudy, as well as the visit Nate and I had with my mother and her friends. Nothing seemed to surprise him.

"Hit list, huh? I can only imagine what's going through their minds. If I wasn't so inundated with that missing person's case, I'd jump right into this one, along with Nate. Seems we're picking up more and more of the retirement community crimes since the Maricopa County Sheriff's Office is stressed with drug-related killings, kidnappings, and arson. And here I thought the job would be a walk in the park, so to speak."

"Admit it, you're loving every minute," I said as he reached for my hand.

"I'm loving every minute we're together, but it seems as if I haven't seen you in ages. Since the weekend. That missing person's case has tentacles. First one lead, then another. I'll be heading south tomorrow to Maricopa and take it from there. I expect to be on the road for a day or so and will hopefully get this thing wrapped up. The family gets more panicked each day, and I don't blame them. Granted, their daughter's in her early twenties, so she's not a minor, but still. . . ."

"You don't have to say anything. My daughter's in her early twenties, and if she disappeared out of the blue, I'd be a basket case. So, you think you have some decent leads?"

"Yeah, I really do. Hey, getting back to us, how about if we take an overnight to Sedona this weekend? I've got some paperwork to wrap up Saturday morning, but we could take off around noon, check in to one of those spa hotels, and come back late Sunday afternoon. If not Sedona, then maybe Prescott. It's not even June and the heat's getting to me."

"Give it time. Your blood will thin. Actually, I think it has more to do with capillary action than actual thinning, but who cares. Hot's hot."

"So, is it a go? A weekend getaway?"

I looked at the impish grin on his face and smiled. "Sure. It sounds fabulous. It'll also give me time on Saturday to chat with the director of the Lillian regarding those thefts."

"Speaking of which, you might want to ask him or her if there were any changes in staff during the past few months or if any new residents moved in. Not that I'm telling you how to go about an investigation. You seem to have gotten that down pat."

My car was only a few yards away and I slowed my pace. I was still holding Marshall's hand and he pulled me closer for a quick kiss.

"I'll call or text you tomorrow. Same deal with the office."

"Wow. Hope I rank first."

"You do."

I closed the car door, started the engine, and pulled away from the curb. My thoughts bounced from one thing to another without lingering in any one place for long. One second I was wondering how I'd handle my conversation with the residence manager at the Lillian and the next I was thinking about the grueling schedule Marshall would have as he tracked down that missing woman. Then, out of nowhere, images of Streetman came to mind and I realized I'd better let my mother know when I planned to take him to the park. Not if, but when.

Much as I hated to admit it, I did have an "in" regarding the Quentin Dussler investigation, and to not capitalize on it would be downright stupid. I called my mother the minute I got home and told her I'd be picking up the dog on Friday.

"Friday? Why are you waiting until Friday? What's wrong with tomorrow morning? Or Thursday?"

"The talk about Quentin's death is going to escalate over the next two days, and I want to give Cindy Dolton enough time to hone in on all the buzz. Kind of like waiting for something to marinate."

"You're not barbequing a steak, Phee."

"No, but I'll be the one stuck serving the meal. I'll be by around six fifteen to get the dog."

"You'll let me know if your boss discovers anything new, won't you?"

"Relax. I doubt your name will turn up at any other crime scenes."

Unfortunately, I was wrong.

Chapter 4

Nate was right about one thing. In a span of three days, the news media went from reporting a suspicious death to confirming it was a homicide. The only detail they divulged was possible suffocation. The name wasn't released until the second day, but everyone in earshot of Sun City West knew who it was.

Meanwhile, Marshall's lead on the missing woman turned out to be a solid one, but as luck would have it, the situation was complicated. I didn't know any of the details, nor would I. All I knew was Marshall needed to involve the Pinal County Sheriff's Office. I just hoped they'd move fast enough so that he'd be back here for our weekend getaway.

The Friday morning bags under my eyes said it all. No one should have to get up at the break of dawn unless they were duck hunting. Or unless Harriet Plunkett was their mother. She had Streetman on his leash and "at the ready" by the time I arrived. That little Chiweenie was pacing back and forth by the foyer, one leg-lift away from creating a puddle. I'd barely said hi to my mom when she shoved the leash in my hand.

"Here, hold it tight. Loop your hand through the leash first and then grab it. Much safer. He pulls. Once you get to the park, don't let him chew grass. He throws up. And keep him away from that large gray schnauzer. They don't get along."

"Fine. Fine. I'm only going to be a few minutes in there. Long enough to ask Cindy some questions and get out. I've got to be at work before nine, and I planned to stop and grab a coffee."

"You'll have plenty of time."

Then she bent down and patted the dog on his head. "Go with your sister and be a good little man."

Your sister? Since when did I become the dog's sister?

I groaned and made a beeline for my car. Streetman was a decent passenger, provided he got to sit in the front. I once tried putting him on the backseat, and it was a disaster. He made all sorts of horrific noises until he finally managed to wedge himself through the middle console and onto the front passenger seat.

At six twenty in the morning, the dog park was bustling with at least nine or ten poodle mixes and one Boston Terrier. Streetman was like a maniac the second I released him from his leash. He charged over to the large date palms and began to irrigate them. Cindy Dolton was standing in her usual spot near the side fence. Bundles, her small white dog, was sniffing the ground a few yards away.

Cindy waved as soon as she saw me enter. "Don't tell me. It's about Quentin Dussler's murder. Am I right? Your office should put me on the payroll."

"Yeah, you're right. I was hoping, since you seem to have a good handle on what's going on in this community, you could tell me what you know about the guy and why you think someone killed him."

"How much time do you have?"

"Seriously?"

Cindy raised an eyebrow and grinned. "Quentin Dussler's been a fixture in Sun City West for years. Taught art at some college in New York City and retired here when his wife passed away."

"How do you know all of this?"

"He ran for the board a few years back and they printed his bio. It's probably still on file somewhere in the rec center office."

"I take it he wasn't elected."

"You take it right. According to the scuttlebutt around here, he wasn't the easiest person to get along with. Artistic temperament and all that."

"Um, can you be more specific?"

"A few dog owners were also in the clay club for a while. Quentin was a real bigwig over there. Supervised the workroom, the kilns, the pottery wheels . . . Anyway, if things weren't done to his specifications, he made life hell for those people. I once heard someone complain that Quentin read him the riot act because he didn't put the glazes back in the proper order. Takes all the fun out of a club, huh?"

"Could he have upset someone to the point where that someone wanted to kill him?"

"Nah. If people get pissed they usually leave one club and join another one. Besides, Quentin used to take off on long trips. Club members would mark their calendars and work on their clay projects when he wasn't around."

A few yards away, Streetman was still peeing or at least lifting his leg on various palms. So far so good. No interactions with other dogs. I turned my attention back to Cindy.

"What about family? Other than his deceased wife. Did he have children?"

"No children. At least not according to the board articles I've read. But I heard somewhere he has a niece who's a free-lance writer. Some sort of 'Gypsy journalist' who bounces from one country to the next—India, Israel, Belgium, China.

Don't ask me where I heard that because I can't remember. Anyway, it was a strange mix of countries, huh?"

I shrugged. "I suppose you go wherever the story takes you. I don't imagine you know where she lives or what her name is?"

"Sorry. No clue. I did hear some scuttlebutt about her living in New York City at one time, but I'm not sure. Say, you might want to check with the Melhorns—Lon and Mary. They used to come to this park when their dog was still alive. They knew Quentin. Their names are still listed in the dog club directory. You know, come to think of it, maybe it was Mary who told me about Quentin's niece. That's all I can tell you, I'm afraid."

"That's more than I knew when I came here today. Listen, if you hear anything whatsoever about the guy, please call me. You've got our number. Williams Investigations."

"I'll keep my ear to the ground. These unsolved murders have a way of making all of us feel vulnerable."

"Vulnerable in your case, hysterical in my mother's, so yeah, please give me a buzz if you hear the slightest thing because—"

"POOP ALERT! POOP ALERT! Brown Chiweenie near the date palm!"

"Oh no, Cindy. That's Streetman. Someone's pitching a fit. I'd better get to it quick."

Reaching for a plastic doggie bag from my pocket, I charged over to the dog and tidied up after him before the screamer went berserk again. Streetman glanced at me and proceeded to sniff around.

"You'd better appreciate what I do for you, little buddy." I clasped his leash to his collar. "Come on. If I don't get a cup of coffee soon, I'll be as on-edge as that screaming man over there."

The dog literally dragged me back to the car and jumped

in the front seat, where he sat like a statue until I dropped him off at my mother's.

She must have been standing by the front window because the minute I pulled up, she was at the door. "There's my little Streetman. Go inside and Momma will get you a treat."

The dog was out of sight in five seconds.

"So," my mother said, "was I right? Did Cindy know anything? Did she have any idea why Quentin Dussler would be holding a piece of paper with my name on it?"

"Um, er, we didn't talk about that. But I found out lots of other things. I'll tell you later. I've got to get to work."

"Does she have any idea who killed him?"

"No."

"Does she have any idea if he was into some shady business?"

"No."

"Well, good grief. I hope she gave you something to go on. Like witnesses. I can't live every second in fear. What if Shirley was right? What if it really was a hit list?"

"If it was a hit list, the person holding it would still be alive. I'll call you later. Oh, and by the way, your dog did his business in the park. If you need witnesses for that, I can procure them."

"Very funny. Talk to you later."

I was out the door when it occurred to me I needed a copy of that darned dog park directory. Drat. I knew it wouldn't be as simple as asking. My mother would insist on knowing why and I didn't want to waste an additional thirty minutes when I could be wrapping my hands around a cup of hot coffee. Granted, the canine directory listed names, phone numbers, and e-mail addresses, but so what? All I needed was a phone number, and if the Melhorns still had a landline, like most of the retirees in Sun City West, they'd be listed in the white pages. Easy to procure since Augusta kept one of those large tomes near her desk.

Nate was with a client when I walked in the door, and Augusta had only arrived minutes before me.

"You have that dog park look on your face. Am I right?"

"Uh-huh."

"So, did you find out what you needed to?"

"Sort of. I've got to look up a phone number first. Oh, and I almost forgot. I've got to confirm my appointment tomorrow at the Lillian with a Miss Kimberlynn Warren. The desk clerk at the residence penciled it in but told me to call back and make sure."

"Wow. Fancy-dancy."

"That's my take. I'd better hustle. I hate having so many early morning distractions. By the way, any word from Marshall?"

"I thought if anyone had heard anything, it would be you."

"Not since last night. I have this real uneasy feeling about that missing woman. Like it's not going to be as simple as locating her and driving her back to Maricopa. Marshall had to contact the Pinal County Sheriff's Office, so that could mean anything."

"Marshall's got a good head on his shoulders. He'll be fine. I'm sure we'll hear from him before the day's out."

"It's not that I couldn't call or text him myself, but I don't want to interrupt his investigation or take his mind off what he really needs to do. My gosh, that sounds so grown up, doesn't it?"

"It sounds sensible. That's a good trait to have. Got too many senseless folks wandering around here."

I chuckled as I opened my office door and booted up the computer. Kimberlynn Warren confirmed my appointment for ten thirty and told me she looked forward to meeting me. I felt a tad guilty. It wasn't as if I'd told a bold-faced lie, but I wasn't exactly specific with her, either. I had simply said I wanted to speak with her regarding the quality of life at the Lillian. I'm sure she thought I was a potential resident and therefore scheduled the appointment. Had she known I was the amateur sleuth/snoop acquaintance of two existing tenants, she might have felt differently.

The day seemed to drag with Nate in and out and no news on Quentin Dussler. I did manage to find the Melhorns' phone number and jotted it down on the "to-do list" for the office. I was tempted to call them myself, but if ever the expression "muddy the waters" came to mind, I would be the one knee deep in the muck. It was bad enough I kept finding myself sleuthing at the dog park. I really didn't need to spearhead the investigations.

Finally, at four fifty-three, I heard from Marshall.

"The woman I'm tracking is being held against her will. The sheriff's department is responding with their regional SWAT team. I'm meeting in a few minutes with one of their negotiators. Look, I hate to say this, but our holiday weekend is about to be postponed. I'm so sorry, hon."

"Oh my God. That's the last thing you should be worried about. Sedona and Prescott aren't going anywhere. We'll do it another time. Call me as soon as you're able. And be careful."

"You too. You know what I mean."

Marshall, and Nate, too, for that matter, were still rattled about how my sleuthing a few months ago almost got me killed. I promised them I wouldn't do anything as stupid again, and I swore I would keep them informed. Somehow, having a chat with the director of the Lillian didn't seem to fit into the category of "Danger Ahead," unlike Marshall, who was walking into God-knows-what.

Chapter 5

No sooner had I kicked off my shoes, turned on the TV, and helped myself to a glass of iced tea than I heard, "This just in from Casa Grande. Standoff in a residential neighborhood. Residents told to lock their doors and stay inside."

I immediately raced for the living room and jacked up the volume. Casa Grande. That wasn't too far from Maricopa, where Marshall was embroiled in that missing person's situation. He'd said something about a SWAT negotiator since the victim was being held against her will. Was this his case? It sure sounded like it. My right foot tapped automatically and a slight tremor shook my hands.

The camera zoomed to a close-up of a single-story beige stucco house with a SWAT vehicle off to the side. A few tactical responders approached the building, all of them hunched over and moving slowly. The only sound was the news commentator, but one of the responders held a megaphone.

My gaze panned the entire scene for Marshall, but, in a flash, the segment ended. "Disturbing scenario in Casa Grande" were the commentator's final words before reassuring the viewers they'd be kept up to date on "that changing situation." Rolling commercials for prescription

medicines, acne treatments, and investment options filled
the airspace as I reached for the phone.

Nate must've been expecting a call because he picked
up on the first ring. "Hey, kiddo, you beat me to it. I take it
you turned on the news when you got home."

"Casa Grande. Is that Marshall's case? He said something about a regional response team and meeting with negotiators. Oh my God. Please don't tell me he's in there."

"Calm down. It's his case, but he's not inside."

"How can you be sure?"

"Because he just called me from one of the deputy
vans. Apparently, the woman he was tracking down was
somehow involved with a known drug trafficker. When
she realized what was going on, it was too late. The guy
abducted her. Luckily your boyfriend is such a blood-
hound. He was able to piece things together with no loose
ends. The sheriff's department had no choice but to act on
Marshall's lead."

"He told me he had to speak with one of the negotiators. You don't think they're going to send him in there,
do you?"

"Hell no. Marshall had information that can be used to
get the perpetrator to reconsider. He's working with the
SWAT team, but in an advisory capacity."

No sooner did Nate finish his sentence than the TV
scene switched again to Casa Grande and the same commentator continued to speak. "If you've just turned on your
TV set, we've got a hostage situation unfolding in Casa
Grande. The Pinal County Tactical Response Team, in cooperation with the county sheriff's department, has surrounded
the suspect's house. Negotiators are pressing for release
of the hostage."

My gaze never left the screen. "Advisory capacity? That's

Marshall walking toward the front door. Why's he the one they're sending in?"

The pause at the other end of the line told me more than anything Nate could say.

My voice got squeaky and I kept repeating, "Why Marshall? Why Marshall?"

"Take a close look, Phee," Nate finally said. "There are two armed responders on either side of Marshall, who, by the way, has his hand on a gun, as well. My take is this—the suspect didn't want to speak with anyone from the sheriff's department or their response team. Marshall was privy to some information that he could use as leverage. Sit tight."

Again, stupid commercials. Last thing I needed to see were people dancing around because they liked their cholesterol medicine. I didn't remember what I said to Nate, but he was now insistent that he drive over to my place.

"No, no. I'll be fine. If something happens in the next five minutes, I won't be able to speak with you. Can you please stay on the line?"

"Sure thing, kiddo. I'm not going anywhere."

Everything on the TV screen seemed to happen in slow motion. More commentary. More snapshots of the area, only this time from different angles. I figured they sent in additional camera crews.

THE UNFOLDING SITUATION IN CASA GRANDE oscillated back and forth against a lineup of irritating commercials. I leaned back and turned my head to the kitchen. Seven fifteen, according to the clock on the microwave. It had been well over an hour since I'd called Nate.

"Hey, kiddo. I don't want to upset you, but my cell battery is getting low. I need to charge it for a few minutes and I'll call back. Promise."

"All right. You know where I am."

I put the receiver back in the cradle, relieved I had still kept my landline. Less than five minutes passed when the phone rang. It couldn't be Nate. Not so soon.

"Phee! It's your mother. I thought you were going to call me. What did Cindy Dolton know about Quentin Dussler?"

"I, um, er . . . listen, Mom, can I call you back? I'm in the middle of something."

"Shirley's going to be here any minute. We're going to the fish fry at Putter's Paradise. I know it's late, but on Fridays they drop the price after seven. Call me after nine. I'll still be up."

"Yeah, sure. Fine."

"Are you all right? You sound a little distracted."

A little distracted? My boyfriend's head could be blown off any second by some lunatic. Yeah, I'm distracted all right.

"It's fine. Like I said, I'm in the middle of something. Paperwork. Talk to you later."

Whoever invented the word "paperwork" needed to be congratulated. It served as the perfect excuse, any time, night or day, to hide whatever it was people were really doing. And the one thing I was doing, besides going out of my mind with worry, was hiding the situation from my mother. Last thing I needed was for her to traipse over to my house to offer moral support. And if Shirley Johnson came along with her, I'd be in double jeopardy. I could close my eyes and hear the both of them.

"Oh Lordy, those hostage situations never work out well. Crazy man back in the Carolinas wound up killing the entire family and their guinea hens."

"What about that nutcase on the roof back in Mankato? Oh, never mind, Phee's too young to remember."

Yep. The best thing I did was not say a word to my mother. Nothing changed on the TV regarding the matter.

The same loop was playing over and over again. I switched to three other channels and it was no different. Rolling my neck back and forth, I tried to relax my muscles. Just then, the phone rang again.

Nate's voice. "Only me. We should be good for a while. Battery's at eighty percent."

A commercial coaxing customers to switch their cell phone coverage ended and the news flashed back to Casa Grande. Only this time something had changed. Changed during the commercial. A man was being escorted out of the house, his hands behind his back, presumably in handcuffs. A woman, whose head was bent down, was also escorted out of the place. Off to the side stood Marshall and a response team member.

"So, there you have it, viewers. The standoff in Casa Grande has just ended with no casualties. More details on our ten o'clock report."

Although Nate had worked hard at keeping his voice steady and calm the entire time, I knew it was a practiced effort. I could tell the difference immediately.

"You can breathe again, Phee. Phee? You there?"

It was as if a hand had reached into my throat and grabbed it. "Yeah, uh . . . I'm fine. Really, I am. I'd better get off the line in case Marshall calls."

"I can guess what you must be thinking, but it's not like this all the time. You know that. Mostly interviews and boring stuff."

"I know. Um, before I forget . . . thanks, Nate, for being there. And next time, can you please send him to find a missing dog or something?"

"I'll take that under advisement. See you on Monday. It's the weekend. Try to have some fun."

Fun. It was the last thing on my mind. I was so mentally

exhausted from the last two hours I felt like throwing myself on the couch and calling it a night. It was horrible watching some nail-biting scene play out in front of me, knowing there was nothing I could do. Then it dawned on me. That was exactly how Marshall must've felt those times when I put myself in similar situations. At least I was certain of one thing—the Lillian wouldn't be one of them.

I was moving a few pillows to the side of the couch when Marshall called. "I hope you weren't watching the TV."

"From the minute I got home from work. Nate too. Thank God you're all right. I was scared out of my mind. Why did they send you in there? They should've sent armored guards or something."

"I offered to go. With what I knew about the case, I could leverage the suspect."

I gasped and didn't say a word.

"Don't be upset, Phee. Everything was under control."

"It sure didn't look that way on TV."

"You know the news media, they always blow things out of proportion to keep the viewers glued to the set. Honestly, I wasn't about to get myself killed."

"So, now what?"

"The suspect is in custody and the parents of the missing woman are driving to the sheriff's station in Casa Grande to pick up their daughter."

"What about you?"

"I'm drained. Completely fatigued. I'm going to check in to a motel in Casa Grande and head home tomorrow. Can I see you then?"

"You'd better. I have a short meeting with the residence director at the Lillian, but I'll be back by noon the latest. I'll pick up something for us to eat. You have a key. I gave it to you in case of an emergency."

"What's the emergency?"

"You'll find out when you get here."

Marshall might have been wiped out from all that drama, but once it was over, I was restless and edgy. Not to mention famished. I put together a tuna salad sandwich and complemented it with enough potato chips to keep Lays in business indefinitely. It was only later, when I started pacing around my casita, I realized I needed to keep occupied.

Unable to concentrate on anything that would tax my brain, I did something I hadn't done in years. I made cookies. Sugar cookies, to be exact, because I had the ingredients in my pantry and the recipe was as simple as could be.

Two hours later, I had dozens of sugar thumb cookies with jelly middles ready for consumption. Marshall wouldn't starve when he finally got here.

As I started to put away the last of the bowls, the phone rang and I nearly knocked over a Pyrex baking pan to get it.

"You should've told me Marshall was one of those hostage negotiators. It's on the late night news right now. Is he all right? That kind of thing can give someone PTSD. You should have called me. Shirley and I could've driven to your house."

"Thanks, Mom, but Marshall's fine. He's been trained for that sort of thing, and Nate was on the line with me until it ended. We didn't want to worry you."

"Next time, and I hope to God there is no next time, but if there is, you call me. Understand?"

"Uh-huh. Listen, it's getting late so—"

"So, tell me. What did you learn about Quentin Dussler?"

"Here's the abridged version, so listen carefully. Widower. Has a globe-trotting niece. Was a big shot at the clay club. Temperamental. I might have a lead on some people who knew him."

"That's all?"

"I'm afraid so. Anyway, I'll keep you posted. I don't know about you, but I intend to get some sleep."

"Make sure your door's locked."

"Love you, too, Mom."

Chapter 6

Elegant topiaries lined the circular driveway leading into the Lillian. Off to one side was a designated parking area for guests and another for residents. In addition, there was valet parking, should the resident opt for that amenity. A large waterfall and decorative pool stood in the center of the circle.

As I drove past the waterfall toward the parking area, I glanced at the main entrance. It rivaled most small castles and palaces. Ornate pillars, elegant scrollwork, and beveled glass doors. Fancy resort chairs and benches were tastefully placed on either side of the entrance. No wonder Gertie and Trudy raved about the place. I hadn't even walked inside and I was in awe.

It was a little past ten as I approached the doors. They slid open automatically and I stepped inside. No need to visit Versailles. It was right in front of me. Off to my right stood a marble reception desk that was manned by two young women. Blondes. Again, another waterfall feature in the center of the room, this one smaller and enhanced by flickering colored lights. Comfortable chairs and couches filled the welcome area. The flower arrangements were the freshly cut ones, and I stopped for a moment to inhale the sweet scent of roses.

I could see another room off to my left. A giant flat-screen TV was tuned to one of the local channels. A few residents, who were seated in overstuffed couches and chairs, appeared to be mesmerized by the program. On the adjacent wall stood another flat-screen TV that scrolled a continuous list of daily and weekly activities. Shopping trips. Casino trips. Restaurant trips. Day spas. The list was endless and I couldn't pull myself away from it.

"You look like you just fell off the turnip truck," came a man's voice from behind me.

I turned and stared at a white-haired octogenarian who was wearing a white button-down shirt and gray slacks. "Are you lost or something? You're too young to live here and too old to work here."

Too old to work here. Who's he kidding?

I started to say something but didn't get the chance.

"Now, don't go taking this the wrong way. You're damn good looking and probably not a day over forty, but they seem to hire twenty-year-olds who can't find their way out of a paper bag if you give them directions."

I wasn't sure if he was trying to compliment me or simply set me straight. "I, um . . . have an appointment with your residence director. Kimberlynn Warren."

"Hmmph. She'd need directions *and* a compass. They'll help you at the reception desk. By the way, I'm Vernon McWellan. I'm on my way to catch the morning movie. It starts at eleven. They make good popcorn. If your meeting turns out to be a snoozer, the movie theater is down the hall on your left."

"Uh, thanks. Oh, and nice to meet you, Mr. McWellan."

I immediately walked over to the reception desk. Vernon McWellan was right. The receptionists looked to be in their late teens or early twenties at most. They were both wearing uniform white tops and black slacks. They were sporting small drop earrings but, on close inspection, they had many more pierced holes that weren't currently in use.

"Hi! I'm Sophie Kimball. Phee, actually. I have an appointment with your residence director for ten thirty."

The blonde with the short-cropped hair looked up from her computer. "I'll let her know you're here. Meanwhile, you can help yourself to some coffee and snacks in the smaller reception area right behind me."

She ushered me into an elegant waiting room and returned to the front desk. Obviously, someone went to a lot of trouble to maintain their motto—elegant resort living. I had just started to peruse the cupcakes and assorted crackers when Kimberlynn Warren approached me. She was pretty much everything I expected. Tall, slender, and thirties, with a brunette bob that didn't have a single hair out of place.

"Miss Kimball? I'm Kimberlynn Warren. It's a pleasure to meet you. Frankly, I was expecting someone a bit—"

"Older?"

"Well, yes."

"Tell me"—I followed her out of the waiting area and into her office—"what's the average age for the residents at the Lillian?"

"I'd say in their late eighties, although we have people from their late seventies to their early hundreds. Each year we celebrate at least three or four birthdays for the folks who turn one hundred. The Lillian is graceful living at its best."

"I can see that."

"Please, take a seat. Can I offer you anything? Water maybe?"

"No, I'm fine, thanks. Listen, thank you for agreeing to meet with me. As you've probably surmised, I'm not here about acquiring a residence for myself or for anyone else. I'm here on an entirely different matter."

"Mmm. Now I'm curious." She seated herself behind a

white oak desk. "The message I received regarding your appointment was a bit vague."

"I work for Williams Investigations in Glendale, but I'm not here on official business. In fact, I'm not—"

"Oh my goodness. That was on the news last night. This morning, too. That long hostage standoff in Casa Grande. I'm glad no one was killed."

I took a quick breath. Last thing I needed was to be reminded of what I'd been through. "Yeah, me too. Anyway, I'm here on behalf of some of your residents who wish to remain anonymous at this juncture in time."

"Sounds serious. If something's wrong, we have a procedure for filing complaints, although we get very few of them."

"I don't think this would fall under anything procedural. The residents I'm in contact with are all quite contented with the Lillian. But recently, they've experienced some minor pilfering and it's upset them terribly."

"Minor pilfering? You mean petty theft?"

"Yeah. Petty theft."

"Why on earth wouldn't they report that directly to me? And what exactly was stolen?"

"Small stuff. Like cans of tuna, knitting yarn, a commemorative pin, and a clay jar."

"That's it? Any money?"

"A five-dollar bill. Worth five dollars. Not a rare bill. These were all things the residents had laying around their apartments. It's not the monetary value, it's about privacy and respect. They feel violated."

"That's understandable, but what I don't get is why they went to you and not to our management."

"Because they were worried about retaliation."

"Retaliation? Good grief. From whom? Certainly not the management."

"They believe the management would've discussed the subject with the staff and they didn't want to create any ill will. They also didn't want staff members to treat them differently."

Kimberlynn absently tore at a small piece of paper on her desk as she tapped her teeth together. "In a roundabout way, I can see their point."

"These incidents started a few months ago. Were any new staff members added since then?"

"No, the last hire was for a prep cook in the kitchen." Kimberlynn shook her head. "That was over a year ago. The staff who work at the Lillian have been here longer than that."

"Gee, the two receptionists out front look as if they're still in high school."

Kimberlynn laughed. "I wish I looked that good. Believe it or not, they're in their mid-twenties. Sisters. Lots of spa time on their days off and no kids to wear them out. They're both single. They've been with us a little over two years."

"What about new residents? Could a new resident, with say, a tendency to kleptomania, have moved in recently?"

"I'm afraid not. The only time we receive new residents is when one of our patrons needs assisted living, skilled nursing, or . . . well, there's no way to sugarcoat it, hospice and afterlife care."

"Afterlife care? That's a term I haven't heard of."

"Polite for burial or cremation."

I swallowed and nodded. "What about security? Do you have cameras in the hallways?"

"The entrances and common windows are alarmed and we do have security cameras on the outside of the building. But this is a residential hotel, not an institution. We're not a school or a hospital. So, to answer your question, no. Our hallways don't have security cameras. Besides, the residents would really consider that an invasion of their privacy. We do have security guards, though, but they patrol the perimeter."

It had to be an in-house job. But who? Or why?

Kimberlynn shifted in her seat and wrote something on the one piece of paper she hadn't torn. "As much as I'd like to use our daily bulletin to tell residents to be sure and lock their apartments, I don't want to create a stir. Things can get out of hand very quickly under one roof."

I stared directly at her and didn't say a word, waiting for her to continue.

"What I will do is mention this at our weekly staff meeting without divulging any names. Not that I could, since you haven't shared them, but I don't intend to mention yours, either. I'll simply use the familiar refrain, 'It's been brought to my attention . . .'"

"Won't that upset the staff?"

"The way I intend to present it is to ask their assistance in being vigilant should they notice something out of the ordinary. Like someone hanging around an apartment that's not on their floor or doesn't belong to one of their friends. Believe it or not, the staff is very in tune with the connections our residents have made. It won't solve anything, but at least it's a start."

And it puts people on notice. "I appreciate that."

"If the matter persists, Miss Kimball, you will contact me immediately, won't you?"

"Absolutely. And the same for you." I reached in my bag and pulled out a business card. "It's a small investigative firm and all of us are involved beyond the usual capacities. It was a pleasure to meet you and thank you for your time."

Kimberlynn stood to walk me out, but I motioned for her to stay seated. "It's all right. No need. I can find my way out. That is, if I can manage to walk past the snacks without going too crazy."

"Help yourself. It's one of the best perks around here."

I lingered for a minute or two in the small reception room before entering the large foyer. The two blondes were both glued to computer monitors as I walked past them. No sooner did I reach the front glass doors than I got a whiff of violet and lavender. Someone's perfume. I turned to find myself face to face with a short, stout, gray-haired lady dressed in a floral Mumu. She was definitely part of the octogenarian crowd.

"I overheard everything," she whispered. "I was in the next room making a photocopy of my driver's license. I'm Sharon Smyth. Come with me. We need to talk."

Sharon Smyth. Sharon Smyth. Why did that name sound so darned familiar? I opened my mouth slightly as she grabbed my wrist.

"Not here. Meet me outside in front of the waterfall. Act casual."

I wanted to say, "This isn't *The Bourne Identity*," but instead I muttered, "Okay." It wasn't until I was out the door and a few feet from the waterfall that I remembered where I had heard that name. She was on Gertie and Trudy's list. The stolen clay jar. The hysterical woman. Oh brother. I was in for a real treat.

Chapter 7

Sharon waited until I was standing directly in front of the waterfall before she approached me. I was facing the street, waiting for her to make the first move.

"Psst! See that clump of mesquite trees at the edge of the building? On your right. They're on your right. Past the topiaries. Walk over to the trees and take a seat on the benches. No one goes there. I think they put the benches in for decorative purposes only. We can talk there. You go first. I'll mill around here."

"I, uh, yeah. Sure."

Whatever it was Sharon had to tell me, she was certainly being covert. I walked to the benches, took a seat, and pulled out my iPhone. With my head down and my eyes glued to the small screen, I didn't think I could possibly be drawing attention to myself.

Within seconds, Sharon sat down next to me. "Sorry to make you walk down the block, but I couldn't risk being overheard."

"It's all right. I understand. So, what's this about?"

"Like I said, I overheard your conversation with Kimberlynn. And you're Sophie Kimball from Williams Investigations. I wasn't exactly snooping, mind you, but when I heard you talking about those thefts, I moved closer to the wall. The building may be gorgeous, but the walls are paper thin."

I gave a quick nod as if to say, "Hurry up and get to it."

Sharon leaned forward, glanced to her left and then her right, presumably to make sure no one was in hearing distance. "I happen to be a victim of those thefts as well and I want my clay jar back."

"Yes, the uh . . . clay jar. It's on my list."

"Well, it should be. It's probably the most expensive item that thief lifted, even though Clive Monroe will tell you his Elks pin is worth much more. Fiddlesticks. Listen, I've been living at the Lillian for over eight years and nothing like this has ever happened."

"Tell me, how did you learn about the other thefts? I mean, other than listening to my conversation with the residence director?"

"I dine at the same table as Clive and the Gertrudes. Gertie and Trudy. I call them the Gertrudes. Plus, word gets around. I found out about Mildred Kirkenbaum's yarn and Mabel Leech's pen from my neighbor. She plays cribbage with them. So, are you going to investigate? It didn't sound that way. You should, because this is an abomination. And if you don't mind my asking, which of my neighbors hired you?"

"Um, actually, no one hired me. I'm really not at liberty to say, but I do have some acquaintances at the Lillian."

"It doesn't matter how you found out. What matters is what you plan to do about it."

"Since no one wants to report anything officially and the thefts were really petty thefts, I'm afraid all anyone can do is be vigilant and alert. People talk. Eventually we'll find out who's responsible."

"Hurumph. By that time, my precious clay jar will most likely be in smithereens."

"I have to admit, I don't know one piece of art from the

next, but what makes you think your jar was valuable? I mean, according to what I know, it was made by a local Sun City West artist. Not a famous one."

"It was made by Quentin Dussler. And you know what they say about the value of artwork once the artist dies. The price tag goes way, way up. Not that I'm reveling in his death—heavens, how awful. And a possible murder at that. But now my piece is worth even more. And let me tell you, he never sells, I mean *sold*, those crimson glaze pieces. It was a miracle I was even able to purchase it at the winter Creations in Clay. That club only holds two of those events each year, one in the winter and the other right before summer."

Quentin Dussler. The murder victim. I felt as if I had stopped breathing for a second. "Did he sell you that jar himself?"

Sharon pursed her lips and thought for a moment. "I don't even know if he knew it was being sold. If you ask me, that piece got placed in the For Sale section of the event in error. It probably belonged with the exhibition pieces. And it didn't have a price tag, so they charged me the same price as a similar piece in brown glaze. Now it's been stolen and I'll never replace it."

"Did anyone know you purchased a Quentin Dussler original? I mean, other than the folks at the Creations in Clay who sold it to you?"

"Absolutely not. And I wasn't about to tell anyone for that very reason. It was an original design and it was valuable. As far as anyone knew, all I had was a new tchotchke for my kitchen."

"Can you describe the jar?"

"Certainly. It was about five inches high and six inches wide. It had a folded lip edge and a nice round opening. I knew it would fit perfectly in my kitchen niche. And the color matched my curtains and tablecloth. Now I have some hideous bowl from Walmart sitting in that very spot. I could just cry."

World hunger, unemployment, rising medical costs . . . and we're talking an ugly Walmart bowl.

I slipped my iPhone back in my bag and folded my arms in front of me. "Is there anything else about the jar? Anything that would distinguish it?"

"It was signed and numbered on the bottom. And, Quentin drew some wiggly little lines and arrows underneath his name. His trademark signature, I suppose."

"Signed and numbered? I've never heard of that for pottery. Not numbered, anyway."

"Well, this one was. And when I bought it, I wrote down the numbers and made a sketch of his little lines. I'll make a copy and mail it to you. I don't like to use e-mail. What's the address?"

I gave her my business card and she told me she'd have the information in the afternoon mail.

"Under normal circumstances, I would invite you back to my apartment and you could write it down yourself, but these aren't normal circumstances. I don't trust anyone anymore."

"Because of the thefts?"

"The thefts mainly, but there's something else. Something I can't quite put my finger on."

"Okay. I can't promise you anything, but I'll do what I can. And if you hear anything about additional thefts or anything disturbing, give me call. But complaints about the food and the service really should be taken up with the management."

"Understood. I'll start to walk back to the Lillian. Wait until I'm out of sight before you leave. And, Miss Kimball, I don't think it's petty theft. I think it's far more than that."

Again, Sharon looked in both directions before heading to her apartment. I checked the time on my iPhone and played around with a news app before walking back to my car. The usual Arizona headlines—altercations, road rage, robberies, and immigration issues. National and international headlines ran the gamut from global warming to an update on some diamond heist that had happened somewhere in Europe a few years ago. A never-ending stream of information went in one ear and out the other.

I stopped at a local sub shop on my way home and bought three different kinds of sandwiches, not knowing what Marshall would be in the mood to eat. The sugar cookies, although delicious, hardly constituted a meal. I also stocked up on chips and salads.

When I got home, no sign of Marshall, but the red light was flashing on my answering machine.

"It's me. I'll be over shortly. Less than an hour. I promise. I made a stop at the office. Someone sent you a fax. I'll bring it. Miss you like crazy."

I wondered why he didn't text me and then I realized I had turned off the phone when I left the Lillian. Sure enough, the text version of his message was waiting for me. I read it twice and muttered to myself, "Yeah, I miss you, too."

Not wanting my time with Marshall interrupted by phone calls from my mother, I decided to get it over with and call her first.

"You caught me just in time, Phee. I'm meeting the ladies at that new Greek restaurant for lunch. They better not put yogurt in everything. Anyway, who are the people who knew Quentin Dussler? Do I know them?"

"How on earth would I know if you knew them? Anyway, their last name is Melhorn. All Cindy Dolton told me was that they used to go to the dog park and they knew Quentin. How or why they knew him is anyone's guess at this point.

I'll let Marshall know when I see him this afternoon. I mean, it *is* their investigation, after all. I'm only gathering information to help out. Sort of."

"When you find out something, let me know. If there's a psychotic killer out there suffocating people in their garages, we all need to know about it. Of course, you don't have to tell me twice to keep the garage door closed. Last thing poor Streetman needs is to be confronted by a snake that wanders in."

"Good thinking, Mom. I'll give you a call this week."

"Unless you hear something first. And I'll call you if anything comes up."

Just don't let it come up in the next twenty-four hours. I need some alone time with Marshall.

I had enough time to check my makeup, change into jeans and a cute top, and fix my hair. I made a batch of iced tea and was about to settle on the couch when the doorbell rang.

"Boy, are you a sight for sore eyes!" Marshall pulled me close before I could even shut the door. It was one of the longest, sweetest kisses I'd ever experienced.

"My God. I was worried sick. Terrified, if you must know," I said.

"I know. I know. Got the whole rundown from Nate. I told him how that Casa Grande situation escalated from bad to worse in a matter of hours. None of us expected it. Not the sheriff's department down there, not anyone."

"At least it's over with. Come on. You must be starving. I got us three different kinds of subs. Also, salads for later, if we feel guilty about eating the subs."

"Smells like cookies in here. Were you baking?"

"Last night. After we got off the phone. I was so worked up I needed to do something. We've got enough sugar cookies to set an entire classroom of kindergartners spinning for hours."

"Oh, before I forget"—Marshall reached into his pocket— "I folded this. Hope you don't mind. It's the fax you got. Two pages."

I couldn't imagine who would send me a fax, but as soon as I saw the first page, I was dumbstruck. Sharon Smyth hadn't wasted a second. She must've seen the fax number on my business card. The message on the cover page said, "I decided to fax this from the office. No one saw me. I was careful."

The second page contained the numbers from the bottom of the clay jar and a rendering of the squiggly lines underneath Quentin Dussler's signature. Marshall peered over my shoulder as I studied the paper.

"What are we staring at? I didn't read the fax, other than taking a look to see who it was for. It's marked 'highly confidential.' So, what are these hieroglyphics?"

"It's a copy of an artist's signature and some numbers that may or may not mean anything."

"Go on."

I told him about my little sleuthing detail at the Lillian and how one of the stolen objects happened to be a Quentin Dussler creation.

"The lady who owns the jar said Quentin never sold the ones with the crimson glaze, but somehow it was for sale and she nabbed it. Now, of course, it's in someone else's possession. Probably another resident's or even a worker who didn't realize the jar had some artistic value. Look, you must be starving. Let's eat first and decipher pottery markings later."

"A woman after my own thoughts."

This time it was a quick kiss and an even quicker jaunt into the kitchen.

Chapter 8

Marshall wiped the sandwich crumbs from his mouth. "So, you've got yourself your own case, huh?"

"My own non-paying favor for two sweet ladies and their dining companions. Chances are the management will figure it out long before I come up with anything. Still, I did agree to look into it."

"Wish I could be more help, but I'm not familiar with artistic renderings."

"Don't worry. I know someone who is. Or at least I think she might know what those numbers mean." I reached for a kitchen towel.

Marshall had already cleared the remains from the table and was putting the last of the leftover sandwiches in the fridge. "Who?"

"Aargh. My aunt Ina, that's who. She's been collecting objets d'art for as long as I've known her. Only now, thanks to her second marriage, she can afford the good stuff like Limoges, Russian porcelain, and one-of-a-kind creations. I'm pretty sure she'll know what to make of the signature. I've seen that before, you know. One number over the other like a fraction. Usually on lithographs or serigraphs."

"Yeah, I've seen it, too. On other people's artwork. I'm more of a poster boy myself."

"A poster boy? Really?"

"Not me. The posters I have on my walls."

"Good, because I don't think poster boy is an actual term. Not like cover girl or pinup model. Anyway, the numbers don't make sense. On two-dimensional artwork the bottom number is the total number of prints made and the top number is that particular print. But a handmade clay jar? I could see it, maybe, if it was some sort of factory production, but not for something someone created in their garage or at the clay club room in Sun City West."

"Got to agree with you, there. So, an enjoyable visit with Aunt Ina?"

"I'll give her a call later. Right now, the only thing enjoyable I intend to do is crash on the couch with you."

The next twenty-four hours flew by. With the exception of an early morning walk on Sunday, Marshall and I didn't leave my casita the rest of the weekend. We ordered calzones and wings and vowed to eat light the remainder of the week.

"I really need to get back to my place at least for a change of clothing. Sure you don't want to spend the night there?"

It was a few minutes before eight and I was tempted. "I'd better not. We both need to be at work early and we should get some sleep in our own beds."

"Next weekend? Maybe we can actually make it to Sedona."

"Deal. By the way, has Nate mentioned what the next step is regarding the Dussler investigation? I meant to ask you sooner."

"Grunt work. Lots of it. Looks like he and I will be interviewing the members of the Sun City West Clay Club. There are thirty-six active participants, if I recall correctly, and a handful of others. We'll have Augusta make those arrangements. I'm not banking on too many people willing to drive to our office in Glendale, so I imagine Nate and I will be meeting at all sorts of places—coffee shops, restaurants, you name it. Can't really meet at the club room itself. It doesn't lend itself to privacy."

"Funny that the stolen clay jar was made by Quentin. You don't suppose—?"

"Nah. It's coincidental, I'll give you that much. But no, I'm thinking along the same lines as you probably are—a crime of opportunity. Maybe that Smyth woman left her door unlocked and didn't realize it. I hope she isn't putting too much hope on having her jar returned. Petty thefts are more than petty. They're pesky and nearly impossible to resolve. She'd be better off buying a new one."

"That's not going to happen. She was ecstatic when she saw the color of the jar. It matched her kitchen decor."

"And here I am, happy to own flatware and plates. Forget about decor." He put his arm around me and nuzzled my cheek. "Get some sleep tonight. I'll see you in the morning. Let's grab a bite after work. Got some smaller cases to deal with, so I'll be out and about."

I didn't say anything.

"Don't worry. It's just routine stuff."

Routine for Marshall, maybe, but I was still having a hard time dealing with the past hostage situation. The few spouses of the police officers I knew back in Mankato had always told me how stressful it was for them and their families. Now I understood.

Marshall left before eight thirty, and it felt like the air in the place left with him. Hell, I wasn't about to let myself become one of those awful clingy women. I had enough things to occupy my mind. Like the thefts at the Lillian.

Eight thirty was still early and I knew my aunt Ina would be up. I reached for the phone and dialed her number.

"Phee! How absolutely wonderful to hear from you. I missed you at the last Bagels 'N More brunch."

"Yeah, I've had a really busy schedule. Maybe next time."

I was genuinely afraid of asking how she and Louis were doing because it would result in a fifteen- or twenty-minute dissertation.

"I won't keep you long, Aunt Ina, and I hope you and Louis are doing well, but I really need your expertise with something."

I could picture my aunt puffing out her buxom chest and leaning back.

"My expertise? Certainly."

"Good, because I have a question about pottery."

"It's that murder in Sun City West, isn't it? The man worked with clay, didn't he?"

"Aunt Ina, you can't breathe a word of this to anyone."

"You can trust me. My lips are sealed. Now, what's this about?"

"Actually, it's about the way in which he signed his creations. It might give us a clue. Tell me, do pottery artists number their pieces?"

"Usually. If the piece is cast from a mold, they like to keep track of the numbers. And some artists number everything they do, even pieces made from a potter's wheel."

"What about one number on top of the other?"

"You mean like a lithograph?"

"Uh-huh."

"That wouldn't make sense. Even if it came from a mold. Pottery artists don't usually destroy their molds. Maybe what you're looking at is really part of the artist's signature. Some of those signatures are quite complex. And, some artists actually add a remarque on the bottom."

"Remark? Like a comment?"

"No, it's spelled with a *Q*. It's an additional etching. Makes the piece far more valuable."

Oh my gosh. Those squiggly lines with arrows. They have to be remarques. Maybe this Quentin Dussler is more famous than anyone realized.

"Hmm."

"I'll bet it was a robbery gone wrong, Phee. Someone killed him in order to steal one of his pieces. Did he keep an inventory? What was missing?"

Inventory? Why didn't I think of that? "Aunt Ina, I could just hug you. You've been a great help."

"Anytime, sweetheart. And, by the way, when you do talk to your mother, tell her I just finished reading the most scintillating book, translated from Swedish. *Whisper of Death*. Perfect for the book club."

"Um, sure. Again, thanks. Talk to you soon."

The only "whisper of death" I wanted to think about was Quentin Dussler's, and maybe my aunt was right. Maybe it was a robbery gone wrong. Unlike the one that had taken place in Sharon Smyth's residence. That robbery had apparently gone right. At least for the thief.

Chapter 9

I practically had to drag myself into the office the next day. That was what lack of sleep did to me. No matter how hard I tried, I was bombarded by all sorts of thoughts and connections that wouldn't shut off. The artist's signature. The Melhorns. Sharon Smyth's unexplained worries. Quentin Dussler's inventory. It wouldn't stop. And when I finally did fall asleep, the alarm clock rang. I was still yawning when I said good morning to Augusta.

"Looks like the weekend wore you out, huh?"

"Not the weekend, these crazy investigations. Are Nate and Marshall in?"

"Nate is. Marshall zoomed out of here about ten minutes ago. Said it was an easy errand for a fraud case."

"Thanks."

I opened my office door, booted up the computer, and returned to the outer office, where I made myself a cup of coffee before knocking on Nate's door.

"It's just me. Your friendly park gossip patrol checking in."

"Good morning, kiddo. Did you and my buddy have a chance to unwind? I knew Marshall would be all right, but I was worried about you."

"I think we unraveled, if that's what you mean. Hey, and

thanks again. If you weren't at the other end of the line, I don't know what I would have done."

"You're more resilient than you think, but we're a team around here. Remember that."

"Uh, speaking of teamwork, I did acquire a scant bit of knowledge at the dog park. I wanted to tell you on Friday, but you were in and out so much there wasn't time. That Quentin Dussler was a real prima donna. Club members actually avoided him. But I don't think that's what got him killed. I mean, not that I'd know, but . . . anyway, I got the name of some people who did know him. The Melhorns. Oh, and I found out he has a niece who's a freelance journalist. Travels to out of the way places. And according to Cindy at the dog park, Quentin used to be gone on long trips, too. She didn't know where."

"Take a breath. Slow down. And please, sit down. You're making me feel as if I should be standing at attention."

I pulled up the chair next to Nate's desk and put my coffee cup down. "There's one more thing. And believe it or not, it came from my aunt Ina."

"Dear God. Don't tell me you pulled her in on this."

"Heck, no. I'm not insane. I called her for something else, but it does relate to the murder."

Nate listened as I told him about the Lillian and Sharon Smyth's crimson glazed clay jar with the numbers etched into the bottom.

"Marshall and I talked about it last night. We weren't sure why a clay artist would sign something like that, so I checked with the only person I knew who collected that sort of thing."

"My God. Your aunt Ina."

"Who else?"

"And what did you learn?"

"That it could be a special signature and design that

makes the piece more valuable, but I don't think whoever stole Sharon Smyth's jar knew that. I think they were just pilfering. Which brings me to the next thing. Did the sheriff's department find any sort of inventory for Quentin Dussler's clay pieces? My aunt said keeping an inventory is something most artists do, especially if they're selling stuff and have to report it for taxes."

"You know, now that I think of it, it was the one thing the sheriff's office didn't mention. Good call, kiddo. I'll phone them and see if their deputies turned up anything. I do know they were trying to contact relatives. At least the guy had a cell phone and some contact numbers."

"I heard you and Marshall got stuck with the list of club members."

"Oh yeah. Should be a doozy. Augusta's setting up those appointments now."

"So, uh, about the Melhorns . . . Their names are Lon and Mary, and I was able to use the white pages to find a number and an address."

"Terrific. I'll have Augusta add it to the list. Whoever draws the short straw gets them. And don't tell Marshall, but I'm cutting all the straws we have. Oh, and if thirty-six-plus clay club members aren't enough to interview, the sheriff's office also e-mailed us a list of sign-in names from the club room. Friends . . . guests . . . The list dates back to a month before the murder."

"The list? There was a sign-in list? Oh, that reminds me of something. I'll, uh, catch up later. Got work to do."

"Sure thing, kiddo."

I could have kicked myself in the pants for not thinking of it when I was talking with Kimberlynn Warren. I never asked her if the Lillian kept a sign-in list for guests or visitors. Not wanting to have her think I was such a dunderhead, I decided to ask Gertie and Trudy. Besides, I knew they were probably anxious to find out how my meeting with their residence manager went.

It was a little past nine and I was fairly certain they'd be back from breakfast. I called Gertie's place first, but the phone just rang. Trudy was next. She picked up on the second ring.

"Trudy? This is Phee Kimball. I hope I'm not disturbing you."

"Heavens no. Do you have any news for us? About which wretched excuse for a human being has been going through our things?"

"Going through your things? You mean the thefts we talked about?"

"No. I mean going through our things. Well, the thefts, too. But someone has been going through our unmentionable drawers. Gertie's and mine. I always fold my things lengthwise first and roll them up. When I opened my drawer this morning, some of those rolls were loose. And Gertie said the same thing. Her drawer was tampered with."

Trudy's voice got softer until it was practically a whisper. "Between you and me, I don't know how my sister would know if anyone went through her drawers because she doesn't fold anything. She stuffs the clothing in there."

"I can hear you, Trudy," Gertie yelled. "And I know because everything was moved around."

The mere thought of an intruder rooting through someone's intimate apparel gave me the creeps. Petty thefts like a missing tuna can were one thing, but this was really disturbing.

"We're not the only ones," Trudy went on. "At breakfast this morning I overheard someone at another table saying he was certain his sock drawer had been rearranged."

"Um, listen. You really, really need to tell Kimberlynn Warren about what happened. She already knows about the thefts because I spoke with her on Saturday. I didn't give her any names, but I did tell her a handful of residents were victimized. The person who went through your things may or may not be the same one who stole those items."

The line went silent for a few seconds.

"Trudy, are you listening?"

"I can hear you, but if we say something, it will only make things worse. Gertie wanted us to buy mousetraps for the drawers, but I'm afraid we'll forget and wind up injuring ourselves."

"Good point. No mousetraps. I'll figure something else out. I called because I need to know something. When guests or family visit residents at the Lillian, do they sign in anywhere? Like the main desk?"

"Sign in? Of course not. You don't have people signing in to your house when they visit, do you?"

Only if my mother had her way. And they'd be vetted, too. "It was just a thought. If a sign-in sheet did exist, we'd know who was in and out of the Lillian other than the residents and the staff."

"I suppose that makes sense, but we're a resort retirement residence, not a jailhouse, and, now that you mention it, if we did report these incidents, next thing you know the management would insist on sign-in sheets. They'd say it was for security, but we'd all know otherwise. You give up a lot of things when you get old. You shouldn't have to give up your privacy."

Trudy was making a lot of sense, but none of it was getting me any closer to figuring out who the perpetrator was. I covered the receiver and let out a sigh. "Kimberlynn said she'd put her staff on alert. Not chastise them, but let them know something is going on. That may lead us to the responsible party or parties. If the staff has been around for as long as she says, they'll want the matter to be resolved quickly, too."

"And if it's not an employee?"

"Everyone makes mistakes. Thieves especially. Be on the lookout for anything out of the ordinary. And keep your doors locked."

"This undergarment Peeping Tom . . . you don't suppose he could be a killer? Sniffing us out?"

As soon as she said, "undergarment Peeping Tom," all I could picture was some silly cartoon character like Pepé Le Pew lifting up ladies' undergarments and admiring them. I had all I could do to stop myself from laughing.

"No, I doubt it. Besides, we don't know if it's a man or a woman. Not that it matters. Violating someone's privacy is beyond reproach. If anything else comes up, call me. And no mousetraps."

"Is this an official case now?"

"Um, for me, it's about as official as they get. Try to have a nice day."

When I got off the phone with Trudy, I walked to Nate's office and gave a quick rap on the door frame before walking in.

"The pilfering isn't the only thing going on at the Lillian. I just got off the phone with one of the Gertrude sisters. Seems their undergarment drawers have been disturbed. And they're not the only ones. Another resident was overheard telling people his sock drawer was rearranged, and not by one of those home organizers. Ugh. That kind of thing gives me the willies."

"Was anything stolen?"

"No. But it was really obvious to the sisters that someone had been rooting through their personal items. Do you think they were looking for something?"

Nate rubbed his chin and leaned toward me. "It's quite possible. Lots of people keep valuables in their underwear drawers. They think no one's going to look there, but that's usually the first place thieves go."

"Don't remind me. I still have nightmares about Louis Melinsky's underwear drawer."

"But it solved a case, didn't it? So, did the sisters say when they first noticed things were out of place?"

"In the morning. When they got up. So, it could've happened anytime the day before. Or even during the night. Eww, that's kind of scary."

"Thieves usually try to grab stuff when no one's around, so I doubt it happened at night. Most likely when the ladies were at meals or out and about. It's not as if people check their underwear drawers all day long. But I'll tell you what I do find odd."

"What's that?"

"If someone was stealing stuff or even going through stuff, they'd usually try to make it look as normal as possible so the victim wouldn't notice things missing right away. Why make it obvious they'd been rummaging through those drawers? Something else may be going on. Hard to say. How did you leave it with the sisters?"

"I wanted them to inform the residence director, but they refused. Can you believe it? They thought of putting mousetraps in their drawers."

"Did they talk to Augusta first? That's something right up her alley."

I stifled a laugh. "Seriously, all I could tell them was no mousetraps, and to be vigilant, keeping their eyes open for anything out of the ordinary."

"It's a retirement residence. Knowing how fast word gets around in those places, the management will probably find out about it before the end of the day."

"Yeah, I was thinking the same thing, too."

I went back to my office and spent the rest of the day at my computer. I had billing statements to send out and accounts to update. Other than a short break for lunch, I was the model of work efficiency. Then, at precisely four fifteen, my mother called.

Chapter 10

"I've given up calling that cell phone of yours. I hate leaving voice mail."

"Hi, Mom! Is everything all right?"

"You tell me. What were you doing at the Lillian on Saturday? I had lunch today with Cecilia and Louise. Cecilia said she saw you walking into the director's office on Saturday morning. Don't tell me you were looking into having me move there. I'm much too young. Cecilia was visiting someone from her church. Someone in his nineties. Do I look like a person in their nineties?"

"Oh, for heaven's sake. The last thing I would be doing is finding a resort retirement residence for you."

"Good. Because I'm barely in my seventies. And I stress *barely*. So why were you there?"

"If you must know, I met two sisters from Minnesota on that September plane ride. Since then, I'd been running into them on and off. Anyway, they contacted me regarding some petty thefts at the Lillian."

"You mean they hired you? To investigate?"

"Of course not. I only met with them as a favor. They didn't want to call attention to themselves and go to the management. So, I had a discreet conversation with their residence director on Saturday morning, that's all."

"What kind of thefts?"

"Small stuff. Cans of tuna, olives . . . oh, and, believe it or not, a clay jar made by that artist who was recently murdered."

"Quentin Dussler. I still don't know why he would have a paper with my name and Lucinda's in his hand. I haven't had a good night's sleep since I found out about it. I hope your boss is making some progress. Say, you don't think the stolen jar had anything to do with the man's murder, do you?"

"No, and neither do Nate or Marshall. The jar was sitting in some kitchen niche. Whoever snatched it did so as a crime of opportunity. They probably didn't even know how valuable it was. Listen, I really need to get back to work, so—"

"Call me this week. Will you be going to brunch with the Booked 4 Murder ladies on Saturday? They haven't seen you in a while."

"I, um, well, it depends on my schedule."

"Okay. Keep me posted."

As I hung up the phone, I thought about the book club ladies. Shirley, Lucinda, Myrna, Louise, Cecilia, and the snowbirds who arrived in October and left in April. Aside from their regular monthly meeting at the library, they had brunch every Saturday at Bagels 'N More across the road from Sun City West. It was a sandwich and bagel café that served as the central gossip hub for the community. Nothing went undisclosed at that place. Even my mother's neighbor, Herb Garrett, frequented the place with his pinochle buddies.

I switched the screen on the computer to my calendar and typed in "bagels" under Saturday. One of those women was bound to hear something regarding the thefts at the

Lillian and those rumors often had some truths associated with them.

Augusta was at the copier. "Hey, Phee. I forgot to ask. When did you and Marshall get into geocaching? One of you left your map on the copier this morning. This is the first time I've been at the machine, so I just noticed it. Why don't you use an app?"

"Geocaching? Map? I have no idea what you're talking about. Give me a second."

I got up and walked into the main office. Augusta handed me the original fax Sharon Smyth had sent me. I gave it to Marshall last night since he was going to ask our IT wiz guy, Rolo Barnes, if the markings meant anything. Marshall probably made a copy and, in his haste, left the original on the machine. Dealing with Rolo Barnes does stuff like that to you.

Rolo Barnes was an independent IT specialist who looked like a black Jerry Garcia. A Jerry Garcia who went from one wacko diet to another. Juicing. Grains. Paleo. You name it. "Independent" because he had so many quirks no one wanted to keep him on staff permanently. I should know. He used to work for the Mankato Police Department when I was doing the accounting. The guy only wanted special numbered checks but preferred to be paid with the latest kitchen gadgetry. If it wasn't for Rolo, half our cases would have gone unsolved and IKEA would've been out of business a long time ago.

Augusta held out the paper. "Sure looks like a geocaching map to me. Although that line's a little long for the longitude. Usually it's a minus sign for anything west of the prime meridian."

"I have absolutely no idea what you're talking about. Geocaching. Isn't that some sort of hide-and-seek game where people stash small objects in parks and recreational places so other people find them?"

"Sure is. Got a nephew back East who's really into that stuff."

"This paper's not a map. It's a copy of the artist marking for a clay jar that was stolen from one of the residents at the Lillian. And to complicate things, not that I think it had anything whatsoever to do with his murder, but the artist who made the jar was the one they found dead. Smothered with clay."

"Artist markings, huh? You could've fooled me. Sure looks like coordinates. Thirty-three point eight six over minus—and I still think it's a minus line—one hundred eleven point thirty is somewhere in Arizona."

"What? Are you sure? How do you know that?"

"Because I plotted the coordinates on my GPS when I drove out here from Wisconsin. Of course, the darned GPS is still in my car, but you can use a computer to figure out where your numbers are."

"Holy cow!"

I all but knocked her over running back to my office. "Sorry, didn't mean to hit your elbow. What do I do? What site do I go to?"

"Try NASA. They always have data tracking."

Augusta was literally at my heels as I sat in front of my monitor. A quick Google search and I landed at www.mynasadata.larc.gov. A few seconds later, I had typed in the coordinates and held my breath. "It's pointing west of Punkin Center, somewhere in the Tonto National Forest."

"Let me take a closer look. More like the Tonto Basin, if you ask me. Abandoned uranium and gold mines out there. I watched a TV special on that a few months ago. What else does that sheet of paper of yours have?"

"Squiggly lines and arrows. Oh my God, Augusta! What if the markings on the bottom of that clay jar were really maps to old mines?"

"Hold your horses. There are lots of maps to old mines. And no one's going to find anything without investing in more equipment than what the actual discovery will turn out to be."

I looked at the paper again and wished I was holding the actual clay jar. "Seems like an awful lot of trouble to put longitude and latitude coordinates on the bottom of a jar instead of a signature. And we're looking at a copy, not the real deal. Sharon Smyth might not have written everything down. Drat! Nate left the office an hour or so ago and Marshall's still out."

"If it is a mine, it's not going anywhere."

"No, but I am. As soon as I'm done for the day I'm heading over to the clay club in Sun City West to see what his other jars have on the bottoms. Maybe they *are* coordinates or maybe that's just the way the guy signed his pieces. Too bad we can't ask him. You know, up until this point, I was certain the theft of the jar had nothing to do with Quentin's murder. Now, I'm beginning to wonder."

"Well, I'm wondering, too. About my stomach. Should I stop and pick up a sub for dinner or fry up that hamburger meat?"

"That's what I like about you, Augusta. You always have your feet firmly planted on the ground."

As soon as we left for the day, I drove straight to Sun City West. My stomach was grumbling but my curiosity was even more demanding. If Quentin Dussler was as prolific with his artistry, the club was bound to have samples of his work on display.

I took the El Mirage cutoff to a crossroad leading into Sun City West. The recreation center, where the club was located, was only a few yards down the road. It was the original community center when Del Webb designed the place back in the seventies, but it had undergone numerous updates. There were two distinct structures, one that housed the aquatics area and another that resembled a large plaza framed by different club rooms. Large glass windows in front of each room showcased the artwork for that club.

It took me all of five minutes to find the clay club's room. It was large with a number of worktables in the front and at least six or seven kilns lined up against the back wall. Two potter's wheels took up a tremendous amount of space in the middle of the room. An entire side wall held cubbies. All were marked with people's names on them and quite a few held clay pieces in various stages of production from moist creations wrapped in plastic to some that looked nearly complete. I noticed a few members firing pieces in the kilns and others working on the wheels or at tables. I was surprised at how busy the place was for early evening.

"Can I help you?" a woman asked. "I'm Diane, the monitor for this evening."

Diane was short and extremely thin, with closely cropped dark hair. She was wearing a pinkish smock with a large name tag.

"Yes, thank you. I'm Phee Kimball. I work for Williams Investigations but—"

"Oh good Lord. The Dussler murder. You're here about the Dussler murder."

No sooner did she utter the words "Dussler" and "murder" than everyone seemed to stop what they were doing and look directly at me.

"Actually"—I tried to clear my throat—"I only came to look at something. The investigators, Nate Williams and

J.C. Eaton

Marshall Gregory, will be contacting members to interview them privately. Most likely sometime this week."

Diane seemed to relax for a second and, one by one, the club members went back to what they were doing.

"I was hoping to see a few of Mr. Dussler's clay pieces. Would that be all right?"

"Sure. A few of them are for sale and are in the glass showcase out front. I can point them out to you or remove them from the display for you to see. Most club members sell their pieces here or at the Sun City West Village Store. The club gets a commission as does the store. Remaining monies go to the artist. Or, in Mr. Dussler's case, I imagine, to his estate. I don't really know. In fact, I didn't know him other than seeing him work in here from time to time."

She motioned for me to step toward the small desk off to the right. "Frankly, he wasn't the friendliest of people, but he was a good instructor and a marvelous artist. Hold on, let me pull out a few of his pieces."

Behind me, a bearded gentleman wearing a navy blue T-shirt with a picture of a large jar on it was using the sink to wash up. Below the picture it said, "Just throw something." He gave me a quick smile and I nodded as Diane returned, holding two brownish jars, each one about five or six inches high.

"These are fairly typical of his work," she said. "Very fluid. It's really an art using that wheel. They sell for fifty-nine and seventy-nine dollars, respectively."

"Did he have any other colors for sale?"

Diane shook her head. "Not here. He only used the brown, yellow, and beige glazes, although many of his pricier pieces were made in his own studio."

"Studio?"

"Well, garage. Lots of artists in Sun City West use their garages as studios. Some to the extent where they no longer have room for their cars. That's where they found his body, isn't it? The garage?"

"Um, yeah." I tried not to think about how his body was found. "Do you mind if I pick these up?"

"No. Go right ahead. Take a good look. They *are* beautiful, aren't they?"

I wasn't much of a connoisseur where pottery was concerned, but I had to admit, the jars were really nice. Still, fifty-nine to seventy-nine dollars seemed awfully expensive to me. Slowly, I turned each jar over and studied the bottom. Since Sharon couldn't provide me with an actual copy of Quentin Dussler's artistic signature, I had no way of knowing if the one on the bottom of her jar was a match for the ones on these jars. And even if I had a copy of the guy's signature on a letter or something, it might not be the same as the way in which he signed his artwork. Aunt Ina told me some artists used a very stylized signature on their pieces.

What did stand out was the empty space underneath his name. No squiggly lines and no numbers. I ran my fingers over the bottom to make sure my eyes weren't fooling me. Smooth as glass.

"Diane, are these the only Dussler pieces you've got?"

"I think there's one more. Hang on. I'll get it for you."

As Diane walked to the showcase, the bearded man tapped me on the elbow. "You won't find what you're looking for in here. Only pottery Quentin made in this workshop was his cheap stuff. Common glazes, simplistic designs. His museum-worthy pieces were done at his place. He'd bring a few of those now and then for exhibitions. The crimson and cobalt glazes were worth beaucoup bucks."

"A lady I know purchased one of the crimson jars." I waited for his reaction.

"She must have money to burn. He only made one or two of those a year. They sell for close to a thousand dollars."

If it were possible for my jaw to hit the ground, it would have. I started to open my mouth when Diane placed another jar in my hands.

"Here you go, Miss Kimball. The remaining work."

The bearded man muttered "commonplace" under his breath as he left the room, but I don't think Diane heard him.

I turned the new jar over, but all I saw was a signature. I tried not to show my disappointment as she looked on. "Everything all right, Miss Kimball?"

"Yes. Say, I wondered . . . would it be all right for me to take a photo of the bottom of this jar? It might help my boss and his partner with their investigation."

"I don't see what harm that would do. Sure, go ahead."

I thanked her for her time and told her Nate and/or Marshall would be in touch regarding the club member interviews. Then, as I got to the door, I asked her one more question. "Did you ever hear anyone threaten Quentin Dussler?"

"If they did," she answered, "it wasn't when I was on duty."

Chapter 11

Marshall's easy errand took up the entire day. I finally heard from him at a quarter to nine.

"Can you believe it? I just got in the door. Had to run all over Phoenix today. At least I can put that fraud case to rest. Along with my body. I'm totally whipped. And dinner is going to be Rice Chex."

"Oh my gosh. That does sound bad. How's tomorrow shaping up?"

"Not much better, but at least I'll be in one place, or one neighborhood. Augusta got most of the interviews scheduled for the clay club members and left messages for the ones she couldn't reach. Nate and I will be at your favorite spot."

"Don't tell me, Bagels 'N More?"

"Nope. The posse office. They've got quiet rooms we can use, unlike our original plan to meet at a restaurant. Of course, a few folks agreed to come to our office later this week. I figure it's going to take Nate and me until the weekend to get through the list of people and the litany of questions we have for them."

"Next weekend still on?"

"You bet. But I'll need Saturday morning to catch up, so I figure I can drop by your place around one and we'll head out then."

"Sounds good to me."

I went on to tell him about the underwear drawer incident at the Lillian and Augusta's hunch about Quentin's markings on the stolen pottery jar.

"So, I went to the clay club this evening to see if I could find the same markings on the guy's other pieces. Nothing. Only the signature. Think Augusta's on to something?"

"I never discount Augusta's wisdom but . . . chances are those are specialty markings that might give the piece more value."

"Funny, but that's similar to what some guy told me at the club tonight. Did you know Quentin's specialty items were almost a thousand dollars? That makes it grand theft, regarding Sharon's jar, doesn't it?"

"Hmm, I suppose so if someone can show the jar was worth a grand. But it'll be hard, if not impossible, to prove. By the way, great call regarding the inventory. Nate told me what you said. He contacted the sheriff's department since they're scrutinizing Quentin's house for any forensic leads. Who knows, maybe if those deputies find an inventory, they may also find out where that niece of his lives."

"Maybe. Meanwhile, I really wish we could see what the signatures on his other pieces look like. The man I spoke with at the clay club said Quentin's really valuable pieces were made in his own studio, um . . . garage, that is."

"I'll see what I can find out."

"Wish I could say the same about what's going on at the Lillian. Nate seemed to think the management will find out soon enough and step in. I'm not so sure. Too bad I can't convince Gertie and Trudy to speak with Kimberlynn Warren."

"You know, that kind of stuff . . . rooting through drawers and the like, is not all that uncommon in college dorms and shared residences. It's usually some jerk getting his kicks. But at the Lillian? Tell your friends to make sure their doors and windows are locked."

"Already did."

Marshall and my boss were out more than in for the rest of the week with one exception. They had a few office appointments on Thursday. Marshall's began early, almost the moment he walked in the door, but Nate's first encounter wasn't until midmorning. At a little before ten, a stylish lady with tan slacks, a scooped neck top, and matching scarf breezed into the office. It looked as if she'd just had her shoulder-length hair curled and set.

"I'm here to see Mr. Williams. I have a ten o'clock appointment, and I want to get this over with. I'm meeting a friend at Home Goods."

I was standing near the copier when the woman walked in. Augusta had gone on a brief errand because we ran out of coffee.

"Sure," I said. "Welcome. Have a seat. Would you like some water?"

"No thanks. I really want to get going."

"Okay. I'll tell Mr. Williams you're here. And your name is?"

"Melinda Ranclid. I'm a member of the Sun City West Clay Club."

"Ohh . . . that. Give me one moment."

I knocked on Nate's door, told him his ten o'clock was here, and scooted immediately back to my own office. A few minutes later, Augusta returned with enough K-cups to keep us caffeinated for the remainder of the month.

"You missed a real hoity-toity." I grabbed a Donut Shop Coffee and plunked it into the machine.

Augusta laughed. "From what Mr. Williams and Mr. Gregory are saying, they're up to their elbows with kook-and-nut cases from the clay club."

Terrific. And this is the club my mother and Lucinda recently joined. "That bad, huh?"

"A few of them insisted there's a hit list out on them and one of them went so far as to demand twenty-four-hour protection."

"They'll have to wait in line. After my mother. What did Nate tell him?"

"Not sure, but I suppose he pointed the guy in the direction of the Maricopa County Sheriff's Office."

The phone rang and both of us jumped.

"If it's my mother, tell her I'm out on an errand. I was supposed to call her last night."

"Caller ID says Harriet Plunkett." Augusta gave the usual greeting and glared at me.

"Aargh," I groaned. "I'll take it. Hang up when I pick up the line in my office. My God, that woman must have ESP."

My mother's voice thundered into my ear. "It's a good thing I wasn't waiting for a meal or I would have starved to death."

"Um, hi, Mom. Yeah, sorry about that. I meant to call. Honestly."

"So, any news on the investigation or should I still be carrying my screamer around with me?"

"Nate and Marshall are talking with the clay club members, and the sheriff's deputies are tracking down Quentin's relatives. Or relative, I should say. And there's the usual crime scene investigation the sheriff's office is conducting."

"This would've been a done deal on *NCIS*."

"That's because they have to make it fit in an hour. This

is real life. Not television. Listen, I've got to get back to work, so—"

"So, yes or no? Are you coming to Bagels 'N More this Saturday? We're meeting at ten for brunch."

It was an opportunity I'd decided not to miss. Those book club ladies were constantly picking up chatter. Better than the National Security Agency. Maybe one of them had a clue about what was going on at the Lillian. I really couldn't get too involved in the Quentin Dussler case, but nothing was stopping me from looking into those unsettling goings-on at Sun City West's premier resort retirement residence.

"Um, yeah. Can I go now?"

"You're worse than the dog when he gets impatient. Fine. I'll see you on Saturday and call me if something comes up."

Nothing came up between Thursday morning and Saturday, except the unending interviews, each one more tortuous than the one before, according to Marshall. He was on his way to Sun City West for a few more rounds, and I had less than three minutes to speak with him. He popped in my office for a quick "see you later" but apparently really needed to vent.

"My God, Phee. Those clay people are something else. One of them gets murdered and they all suspect each other."

"I suppose that's not so unusual, is it?"

"Not if there's real evidence or any evidence, for that matter, but it's like sifting through river muck to catch a fish."

"Huh?"

"Bear with me for a second while I read you some of my notes."

He took out a small pad, rolled his eyes, and spoke. "Morris was sick of Quentin commandeering the new Olympic kiln, Sue Ann said Quentin hogged the work area, crowding her out, Marty was getting tired of Quentin signing up for the best work times. I'm telling you, the list goes on and on and on."

"Yeesh. I wonder if Nate's list is as bad."

"Worse, I think. Look, unless someone really lost it in a fit of rage, I doubt any of these characters were responsible for the guy's murder. And the way in which Quentin was killed doesn't fit the criteria for an act of rage. It seemed too deliberate. Frankly, I can't wait for Saturday to get here. That north county air will clear out my brain, if nothing else."

"Is that all?"

Marshall gave a quick wink. "It's a start."

Chapter 12

While I was buried in book work on Friday, Nate and Marshall were vigorously pursuing the Dussler murder. Other than a quick text from Marshall telling me he'd be at my place around one on Saturday, it was a relatively quiet prelude to the weekend.

That changed at Bagels 'N More Saturday when I arrived for brunch at a little past ten.

Herb Garrett, my mother's neighbor and the unofficial eyes and ears of her street, was at the cash register when I walked in. He sucked in his stomach the minute he saw me and ran his fingers through his semi-balding head. "Hey, cutie! Long time no see. The hens are clucking at the middle table. What's this about a hit list? Harriet said she and Lucinda are on some sort of list."

"It's not a hit list. Well, we don't know it's not a hit list, but I doubt it. And the sheriff's department doubts it, too. Apparently when they discovered Quentin Dussler's body, he was holding a piece of paper with their names on it. Most likely something to do with the clay club since they both joined recently."

Herb made some sort of guttural sound. "I told your mother not to worry. I'm right across the street if she needs me."

Across the street and sacked out in front of the TV with a bowl of potato chips in his lap. "Thanks. I'm sure she appreciated that."

"No problem. Hey, looks like the ladies are waving you over. I'd better get going."

"Sounds good. Nice running into you."

I walked directly to the middle table and took a seat next to my mother. The waitress was just coming around with coffee, and everyone was preoccupied making sure their cups got filled. It was the usual crew—Cecilia, Myrna, Louise, Lucinda, and Shirley. And the usual shouting.

"Mine's decaf."

"Same here."

"Regular for me. Is it fresh?"

My mother gave me a nudge. "Hold out your coffee cup. God knows when she'll be back. I can't believe how crowded it is in here today. I swear, those snowbirds are staying longer and longer."

"Um, sure. Regular."

"I'll be back to take your orders in a few minutes." The waitress scurried off before anyone could bombard her with questions. Obviously, she knew this table.

Cecilia, who was seated two chairs away from me, leaned forward. "I saw you at the Lillian last week. I was visiting an elderly gentleman from my church. Lost his wife not too long ago. Thought he'd enjoy some company."

"Phee was on business," my mother said. "Investigative business. She had to see the director."

Cecilia looked as if someone had slapped her wrist. "I didn't say anything."

My mother went on. "Before any of you get any ideas, I'm not moving into the Lillian. Not for another two decades at least. And certainly not with all the problems they're having."

"What problems?" Myrna asked. "Does it have anything

to do with bedbugs? Because I heard it was a problem in hotels and residential resorts. And why was Phee investigating? I thought she was the bookkeeper."

"She is the bookkeeper. I mean, I am the bookkeeper." Two minutes at the table and I was already flustered.

Cecilia clapped her hands twice as if she was calling a few preschoolers to attention. "I know what the problem is and it's very upsetting. Mr. Aquilino told me all about it. Someone's been stealing things from the residents. He wasn't missing anything, but when he came back from lunch the week before, his two small paintings on the wall had been rearranged. Their positions had been reversed."

Shirley let out a gasp. "Lordy, it's a ghost. One of those mischievous kinds. What do they call them?"

"Nonsense is what they call them," Louise said. "That man probably imagined it."

Cecilia dismissed Louise with a wave of the hand. "I'll tell you what's not imaginary. A missing Snickers bar. That's right. You all heard me. Mr. Aquilino's neighbor bought three candy bars and put them in his cupboard. When he went to get one, there were only two. So, it's the thefts, isn't it, Phee? That's why you were there. Did your boss decide to make you a detective?"

"What? No. You can't make someone a detective. And Williams Investigations didn't send me. I went as a favor to two nice ladies I met when I first came out here."

Everyone seemed to quiet down. I thought it was because of what I had said, but I realized it had nothing to do with me. The waitress was standing over our table waiting to take our orders. By the time she had finished, we moved from thefts to theories. The most notable included disgruntled employees, residents with kleptomaniac tendencies, or my personal favorite, gaslighting. Shirley couldn't wait to introduce that one.

"They're making the residents believe they're going crazy. Just like that movie with Ingrid Bergman."

Lucinda was indignant. "How can you say that, Shirley? People's things are really missing. It's not like they're showing up elsewhere. And don't start telling me it was a ghost."

"Sometimes people don't consider petty theft a crime," I said. "They think it's no big deal to take something that doesn't have a lot of monetary value or something they don't think is worth much, even though it might really be valuable. And so far, that's only two objects as far as I know. An Elks Club pin and a handmade clay jar by Quentin Dussler."

Shirley and Lucinda continued their own conversation while the rest of us sat there like mutes.

"The murder victim? The dead man? That Quentin Dussler? Lordy, it could be *his* ghost."

"Don't start that nonsense, Shirley. Besides, what would he want with one of his own clay jars in the afterlife? It's not as if he was decorating his house."

"How do you know what gets decorated in the afterlife?"

I felt like pulling every strand of hair out of my head, but instead, I tried to get the ladies to focus. "I'm sure the management is taking this seriously. True, it's unsettling, but it's minor. It's not as if the residents are in any real danger."

In retrospect, I should've kept my mouth shut. Our meals arrived a few minutes later and the conversation shifted to calorie counting, gluten, and genetically modified organisms. Something that didn't give me indigestion.

It was a quarter to twelve and I needed to drive home and wait for Marshall. I had already packed a small overnight bag. At least I was walking away with one new piece of information. A name. Maybe this Mr. Aquilino knew

more about the thefts than he cared to share with Cecilia.
I could always check.

"Well, ladies," I said, "it's been nice visiting with you,
but I've got to get going. Lots of things on my docket
today." *And some that I'm not sharing with my mother.*

Just then, my phone rang. I had actually remembered to
charge it and keep it turned on.

"Excuse me a sec. I've got a text message."

I turned away from the table, fully expecting to see a text
from Marshall. I was right. Only it wasn't what I expected.
The message was short and disturbing.

**Murder at the Lillian, plans cancelled. Call u later.
XXs**

It was the first time I ever got a text with the word "murder"
and "kisses" in the same message.

"What's the matter, Phee?" my mother asked. "Don't tell
me you have to go back to work?"

"As a matter of fact, I do. Something just came up. I'll
give you a call later."

Marshall and Nate might've been called to consult on
the latest homicide, but nothing prevented me from paying
a visit to two very dear sisters. At least I hoped there were
still the two of them. I had no idea who the latest victim
was. Or if it had anything to do with Quentin Dussler.

I paid my bill at the cash register and headed across the
parking lot to my car. An ear-piercing shriek, which I recognized immediately, made me stop dead in my tracks.

My aunt Ina had just slammed the door to her car and
was waving frantically at me. "Phee! Have they all left? I
would've been here forty minutes ago if they didn't have
half the streets in Sun City West closed down. Everything
was fine when I went into the nail salon this morning, but

as soon as I stepped out the door, I saw a zillion deputies rerouting traffic from the strip mall. I thought maybe there was a fire or something, but I didn't smell anything. Then, sirens. Enough of them for an air raid. It's either something at the Lillian or maybe even at the Camino del Sol Plaza."

"You're fine, Aunt Ina. The ladies are still talking. Chances are they'll be in there for at least another hour. No one seems to be in any hurry."

"Good. Because all I had to eat this morning was a croissant. So, tell me. Were you able to figure out those markings on that pottery jar?"

"Not yet, though you've been a tremendous help. But I don't want to keep you. Something came up at work. I've got to go. Say hi to Louis for me."

I didn't wait for an answer. I hurried off, got into my car, and headed in the general direction of the Lillian. My aunt had confirmed what I already knew. The sheriff's department would have the major intersections blocked off. I meandered all over the place until I found myself directly behind the residential resort on a small side street. Fortunately, the Lillian was in the opposite direction from my mother's house. At least she wouldn't be driving past a barrage of emergency vehicles. Plus, I was banking on the fact my aunt would keep those book club ladies pretty steeped in conversation for quite a while. I could hear it now. Aunt Ina insistent that they read another one of her deadly European tomes and my mother ready to shove a bagel in my aunt's mouth.

I knew what I would be facing at the Lillian, but I couldn't help laughing when I thought about the table conversation. I parked my car in front of a small beige house and walked around the block until I reached the front of the building. Marshall's text had said "murder" but, given the number of response vehicles, it looked more like a massacre.

Telling the deputy sheriffs who were manning the main entrance that I was with Williams Investigations wasn't going to work this time. Marshall was already on the scene and, for all I knew, so was Nate. I decided to try another tactic.

"Hi! I can see there's some sort of emergency here, but Gertie and Trudy Madison are expecting me. They'd be very distraught if they knew I wasn't allowed inside."

"Go to the front desk and have one of the receptionists call them. We've blocked one of the corridors on the second floor, but if their apartment isn't in that area, you should be okay."

"Um, do you mind telling me what's going on? I mean, are you at liberty to tell me?"

"All I know is our department was called to respond to an emergency."

Judging from the look on his face and his no-nonsense demeanor, the heavyset deputy wasn't about to divulge anything.

"Thanks."

I did as he said and had the receptionist phone Gertie. It was a different receptionist from my last visit. Not one of the two blondes from the other day. This lady was also young, probably early twenties, but with shoulder-length dark hair. Like the blondes, she was tall and slender. Same black and white ensemble.

"This must be very upsetting for the residents." I leaned over the counter. "Especially the witnesses." Then I did something not quite kosher. I flashed my Williams Investigations card and covered my name as well as the part that read "bookkeeper."

The woman looked up from the computer and opened her mouth slightly. I could see the bronze name tag she wore. It read "Taylor."

"I didn't think there were any witnesses. I thought

Mrs. Smyth was already dead when the housekeeper found her in the second-floor laundry room. My God. Those screams. You could hear Marie, that's the housekeeper, all over the building."

Oh my gosh. Sharon Smyth?

The receptionist whispered and I kept my voice low, too. Gertie was going to be at the front desk any minute now. I had to make the most of my conversation while I could.

"Sharon Smyth? How? Shot? Stabbed?"

"Suffocated. They found a pile of linens over her. And towels. I overheard one of the deputies saying something about a towel stuffed in her mouth, but that's not what she was suffocated with. It was a plastic bag. Not the kind from the grocery stores. More like a boutique bag. The house-keeper found a torn part of it. I guess the murderer didn't realize a piece of it had ripped off."

"When did the murder take place?"

"I'm not sure. When the housekeeper went into the second-floor laundry room this morning, that's when she saw Mrs. Smyth."

"Is that laundry room for the residents?"

"No. Only the staff. Linen and towel service are pro-vided for all the residents. Clothing too, if they wish to pay for it. We do have a laundry facility on the ground floor for resident use. And not the coin-operated kind, either. There's a laundry chute on every floor. Huge. You could stuff a person in it. So much easier with one of those things. The residents can drop their dirty wash right downstairs. The whole operation is automated, sort of like a conveyer belt so, once the laundry lands in a bin downstairs, the bin moves forward. Otherwise you'd get stuck with someone else's dirty things. Once the laundry is done, residents can roll the bins into the elevators. They think of everything here. It's definitely an inclusive residence."

Yeah, including murder. "Poor Sharon Smyth. I imagine the director, Ms. Warren, must be extremely upset."

The woman glanced at the office behind her as if to verify what she already knew. "Ms. Warren isn't in today. She doesn't work every Saturday. Neither do Tina and Tanya."

"The other receptionists?"

"Uh-huh. The L'Oréal mascots. Oops. I really shouldn't've said that. It's so catty of me."

I was beginning to like this new receptionist more and more. "Sounds like you know the staff pretty well. How long have you been working here?"

"A little over three years. The hours are great, it pays well, and the residents are really nice. Well, most of them."

"What about Mrs. Smyth? Naughty or nice?"

"Definitely a sweet lady. I don't know why anyone would have killed her. Shh. I'm not supposed to know it was murder, but honestly, with a population of octogenarians and nonagenarians, it's not a shock to find a deceased person in their bed or living room. And the housekeepers don't scream their brains out when they encounter someone who's died."

"Um, er, you wouldn't have any idea who would've wanted to kill her, would you?"

"None whatsoever. I imagine those deputies will be questioning the staff, but right now, the crew is upstairs, along with two other private detectives."

So Nate did go with Marshall. "Are you sure about the private detectives?"

"Oh yeah. They were the only ones who weren't in uniform."

Just then, Gertie approached the desk. She grabbed me by the elbow and pulled me toward her. "Trudy's on her way. Slow as molasses. I would've been here sooner but that darned elevator wouldn't budge. Come on, we can talk in the garden area."

Then, as if she suddenly realized I wasn't standing by myself, she greeted Taylor and asked her to let Trudy know we were in the garden area.

Taylor smiled and nodded. "Certainly, Miss Madison. And it was nice chatting with you, Miss . . . ?"

"Kimball. Sophie Kimball. I should've introduced myself. And it was nice talking with you as well."

Chapter 13

Gertie hustled me off to a large atrium with a koi pond and lounge seating. Bougainvillea and oleander seemed to fill every corner. Oddly enough, we were the only ones in the garden area.

"No one comes here," Gertie said. "They complain about pollen, but I don't think there's any pollen. What did Taylor tell you about the murder? I know someone was murdered. The sheriff's department doesn't show up with the cavalry for nothing. Or did you know about the murder ahead of time? Is that why you came? To warn us?"

"To warn you?"

"Yes. Aren't you listening? In case there's a serial killer loose. It's not bad enough we have some lunatic thief running around; now we have a psychopathic killer."

"Whoa. Whoa. Slow down. No psychopathic killer. We don't even know if someone was murdered or if it was natural causes."

"But someone's dead, aren't they? And they don't send the sheriff's department out in full force if one of us kicks the bucket. So, who died?"

"I, um . . ."

"I'm going to find out sooner or later. If you were talking to Taylor for more than two minutes, she probably told you.

That girl can pick up gossip quicker than a black sweater picks up lint."

"Well, if you must know—"

"Oh good Lord. Here comes Trudy."

"What must we know? What did I miss? They've got to do something about that elevator. The down arrow flashes and all of a sudden the thing's going back upstairs."

Trudy immediately took the lounge chair to my right, ensuring I was cornered on both sides by her and her sister. I felt as if I was sitting between two owls that were about to peck out my eyes.

"All right," I said. "I received a text message from one of the investigators in our office informing me the Lillian was a crime scene."

Trudy poked me in the elbow. "Well, we all know that. It's been a crime scene. All those thefts. The tuna cans, the purple yarn—"

"She doesn't mean the stolen goodies, Trudy," Gertie said, "She means what we already figured out. There's been a murder. So, who got the one-way ticket?"

It was no use hemming and hawing. The Madison sisters were going to find out no matter what, and maybe they'd have an idea regarding motive.

"You can't say a word to anyone. Understand?"

The sisters stared at each other for a second and nodded.

I finally spoke, making sure to keep my voice low. "It was Sharon Smyth."

"Sharon Smyth?" Gertie shouted.

Trudy leaned over and shushed her sister, blowing hot breath right into my face. "Phee just told us not to say anything and you're announcing it to the whole world."

"Look around you. We're the only ones here."

Trudy stamped her foot on the ground. "The way you're yelling, they could hear you in Cleveland."

Then she turned to me. "Sharon was going on and on about that clay jar of hers. You'd think it was from the Ming Dynasty. Maybe she accused someone of stealing it and they killed her."

Gertie shot up in her seat and motioned for us to lean forward. Bending her head down, she whispered, "Maybe she found out who the thief was and he or she had to shut her up for good."

"Over some tuna fish and olives? That's crazy," her sister said.

It seemed unlikely to me, too, but maybe someone in the Lillian had a stronger motive for killing Sharon Smyth. I tapped my teeth for a second, hoping to make the most out of my next question. "Okay, what exactly did you know about her?"

"I really don't feel comfortable saying it," Gertie said.

My God! The woman is dead. Say it! Say it! For God's sakes just say it! "Um, look, anything you can tell me would be really helpful."

Gertie looked at Trudy for what seemed to be the longest time. Meanwhile, I found myself gesturing with both hands to get them to speak.

"All right. All right. I'll tell you," Gertie finally said. "The woman moved in here with her husband a few years before we did. He was much older. Died not too long ago. Anyway, she's one of those women who is always on the prowl. Flirting with men in the dining room, that sort of thing."

"There's more," Trudy said. "Tell her the rest. Tell her the rest."

"Enough, Trudy. You know I don't like to gossip."

Trudy scrunched her face and gave her sister one of those looks from hell. "Since when? Just tell her."

"Fine. But you didn't hear it from me. I heard this from a very reliable source. Mario Aquilino from the third floor was seen leaving Sharon's apartment at a very, very early hour a few weeks ago. That's some social call, if you ask me."

Aquilino. Mr. Aquilino. That was Cecilia's friend from her church. "Is that all?"

"Isn't that enough?" Trudy asked. "Maybe she jilted him and he killed her."

I'd heard of things like that, but not with the geriatric crowd. Somehow it didn't seem likely.

"Is there anything else I should know about Sharon Smyth?"

The sisters shook their heads. At least I had another lead—Mario Aquilino. I had planned on speaking with him regarding those thefts. Now I was even more anxious to have that chat. Nate and Marshall couldn't really blame me if I inadvertently managed to pick up some information related to this new homicide.

"Thank you so much for speaking with me. I came here this morning because I heard something had happened at the Lillian and I wanted to make sure both of you were all right. I'm sure the management is still looking into those thefts but—"

Trudy grasped my wrist. "What if the management is behind those thefts? You know, to throw everyone off course so they could get to the real business at hand, murdering the residents."

I look a breath and placed my other hand on top of Trudy's. "I think that's really—"

"Absurd," Gertie said. "Absolutely absurd. Not to mention idiotic. Why on earth would the management want to murder its own residents? They need our money, for crying out loud. And believe me, the residents at the Lillian pay a very commanding fee for the lifestyle here."

The three of us walked out of the atrium into the large reception area. The elevator chime rang and Trudy said,

"Good. Let's grab it before it closes. The darn thing has been acting so strange."

As the elevator door opened, Marshall stepped out and I froze.

"Phee! How'd you get here so fast? I swear I just sent you that second text."

"Um, fast? Text? I, uh . . ."

Gertie and Trudy weren't about to miss out on my conversation with Marshall, so they let the elevator door close without getting on.

I cleared my throat and smiled at the sisters. "Gertie, Trudy, this is my, um, I mean, our, I mean, the—"

Marshall chuckled and held out his hand. "I'm one of the private investigators at Williams Investigations, where Phee works."

"So how did that Smyth woman die?" Gertie asked. "Bludgeoned to death? Shot? Stabbed? What?"

My mouth opened slightly and I closed it, swallowing a few times.

"The sheriff's department hasn't made a positive identification yet. How did you—?"

Please don't tell him you heard it from me. Whatever you do.

"It's buzzing all around the building," Trudy said. "Those sheriff's deputies might not have made a positive ID, but the people here can recognize a dead resident. We may be old but we're not senile."

I touched Marshall's arm and whispered, "Word gets around fast in this place."

Then I turned to the sisters. "The cause of death won't be made public for a while. It's protocol in an investigation."

Just then, the elevator returned to the ground floor and a heavyset woman stepped out, her shoulder brushing against

Trudy. I rushed over and pushed the button to hold the door open for the sisters.

"Tell me," Gertie said to Marshall as she got in the elevator, "is the sheriff's department going to provide protection for us?"

"Yes. That much I can tell you. They'll post a deputy or two at the Lillian until this is resolved."

"Have a nice day," I shouted as the elevator door closed. Then I told Marshall I hadn't had a chance to check my text messages since reading the first one.

"When I got your original text, I made a quick escape from Bagels 'N More and drove here. I was concerned about Gertie and Trudy, hoping one of them wasn't the victim."

A second elevator opened and this time a sheriff's deputy stepped out. Middle aged, heavyset, and balding. He acknowledged Marshall and me with a partial nod. "We were finally able to reach the director. She's on her way in. My partner told her she needed to inform the residents of the situation before all hell breaks loose. What am I saying? All hell *is* breaking loose. In the past five minutes, even more residents are lining up outside the corridor demanding to know what's going on. If I hear one more senior citizen shout, 'We've got rights!' I think I'll jump from the nearest ledge."

Marshall and I both laughed as the deputy walked to the reception desk.

"This isn't exactly the e-mail crowd," I said. "And forget about smartphone messenger alerts."

"No kidding. What the sheriff's department had in mind was a simple statement that could be photocopied and delivered to each of the apartments. I imagine that lucky deputy will be dictating it to Kimberlynn Warren as soon as she gets here. Listen, I need to talk to you about that second text I sent. Come on. No sense standing here when there are chairs all over the place."

We opted for two large floral accent chairs that faced the fountain. Marshall pulled his closer to mine and clasped his hands. "When the coroner's staff went to move the victim, something fell out of the pocket of the housedress she was wearing."

I didn't say a word and waited for him to finish.

"It was a piece of paper with a handwritten note. The top part had been torn off. We looked around the laundry closet, but it wasn't there. Anyway, the note said, 'Would appreciate your help with this.'"

"With what?"

"We don't know, but underneath that sentence were two names—your mother's and Lucinda's."

I became light-headed. "My God. Just like that other piece of paper Quentin Dussler was holding. Same handwriting?"

"No. It was in cursive. I wanted you to know because we need to find out if your mother or Lucinda knew the victim."

"And you're afraid they'll go off the deep end?"

"I'm afraid they'll get into a full-blown panic. That's why we can't be the ones to talk with her. But you can. Look, the second note may indicate the murders were linked somehow. Like it or not, you've got to find a way to get some info from your mother."

"Aargh. There's no easy way. You know that. My mother will be convinced it's a hit list and the book club ladies will only make matters worse. You can't tell her what you found. Not yet. But we can tell her about Sharon Smyth's untimely demise and see if she knew her. I guarantee she'll start calling all her friends to find out if any of them were acquaintances

of Sharon. If I know my mother, we'll have our answer before
Arizona News at Five."

"That's what I adore about you—you've got the right
amount of deviousness to balance that sweet disposition
of yours."

He reached over and gave my hand a squeeze. "I came
down here to get a list of Sharon's neighbors' names from
the receptionist, so I'd better do that. Nate and two more
deputies are upstairs waiting for me. So, are you up for
having that conversation with your mother?"

"Right now?"

"Uh-huh."

"You realize once I give her the victim's name, I might
as well post it on social media."

"Believe me, I know. And even though Kimberlynn
Warren isn't going to divulge the name, you can bet your
bottom dollar every resident in this place will know it was
Sharon Smyth. The sheriff's department is aware of that, too,
and they've got someone tracking down the next of kin."

"Okay. I'll get to it."

"I'll call you later. At least we can do dinner."

I glanced at the large ornate clock that hung over the
reception desk. One fifteen. My mother had to have left
Bagels 'N More by now. She wouldn't go off someplace
else without first heading home to check on Streetman.
*Or the multitude of infractions he might have committed
while she was out of the house.*

Chapter 14

There were no other cars parked in front of my mother's house, so that meant she had to be the only one in the house with the dog. I walked directly up the driveway and rang the bell. No barking. No nothing.

My mother opened the interior door and peered through the heavy metal security one.

"It's okay, Streetman," she called out. "It's only Phee. You can come out from under there."

I stepped inside as the dog scurried across the room and positioned himself under the coffee table.

"What's wrong?" my mother said. "I thought you were going back to work."

"Um, actually, that's why I'm here. I needed to ask you something."

"Sit in the wing chair. Streetman doesn't use that one."

I closed my eyes for a nanosecond, afraid I might begin to roll them.

"Before you ask me anything, I simply have to tell you how annoying your aunt Ina was at brunch today. Insistent we read another of her deadly books."

"Yeah, I ran into her in the parking lot."

"Did she tell you about the big commotion on the other

side of Sun City West? You know, we still haven't been able to figure out what was going on."

"It's another murder investigation. Marshall sent me a text."

"Another murder? The Quentin Dussler one wasn't enough?"

"It happened at the Lillian. And since you know so many people around here, I wondered if perhaps you might have known the victim. That's why I stopped by."

My mother gave me that "I think you're not telling me everything" look of hers. "You know who the victim is? They told you? Usually you have to wait for hours, sometimes days. So, who was it?"

"A Mrs. Sharon Smyth. Does that name ring a bell?"

My mother plopped herself on the couch and sat there for a minute. "How does she spell her last name? The normal way or the snobby way?"

"Snobby?"

"With the *Y* instead of the *I*, as if they needed to impress someone."

"*Y.*"

"Figures."

"What's that supposed to mean?"

"Maybe she was as stuck-up as her name."

"That's a terrible assumption to make. So, I take it you don't know who she is."

"And a good thing, too, considering she was just murdered. I don't need to be next in line if some lunatic decides to go after her friends. So, how was she killed? Did someone poison her?"

"What makes you think that?"

"Because it took place in the Lillian. Those people are too old to wield a knife or shoot a gun without injuring themselves. Unless it was the management. Or the staff.

Maybe it was her aide. Did she have a personal aide? Some of those aides kill their clients in order to get the insurance money. Nancy Grace did a story on that not too long ago."

I hated to say it, but my mother had offered up a theory I was sure the deputies as well as Nate and Marshall hadn't considered. But it still wouldn't explain why my mother's name and Lucinda's were on that torn piece of paper.

"I don't know the cause of death." *And don't give me that look.*

Then I paused and said the one thing I knew would have the opposite effect. The last thing I needed was for my mother to get suspicious. "Listen, you can't breathe a word of this to anyone. Especially Lucinda. Shirley too. You know how they talk."

"I'm meeting them tonight for dinner at the Homey Hut. What if it slips out?"

"Make sure it doesn't."

"By tonight it will be all over the news. And maybe one of the ladies will have heard about it already. I can't help that, can I?"

"Fine. Fine."

Streetman had moved from cowering beneath the coffee table to snuggling under my mother's feet. She bent down to pet him. "Do you think those two murders are related? Maybe this Sharon woman was having an affair with Quentin Dussler and the jealous wife killed them both."

"It's always an affair with you, isn't it? Quentin was a widower. I thought I'd mentioned that."

"What about Sharon? Maybe it was her husband."

"I happened to find out she was widowed, too. So there goes your affair theory."

"How about blackmail? Maybe she was blackmailing him."

"He couldn't have killed her. He was already dead!"

"Not him, maybe someone close to him."

As if to validate what my mother just said, the dog sat straight up and looked directly at me.

"Affair. Blackmail. I'll take that as a hint I should be going. If you think of anything, other than going down the alphabet for murder motives, call me." *Or Google the late Sue Grafton . . .*

My mother walked me to the door. "I used to feel so safe around here. Now it's becoming a regular combat zone."

Combat. That makes three. "It'll be fine, Mom. Those murders don't appear to be random."

"Since when did you become the expert?"

"You told me yourself that 'working all those years at the Mankato Police Department must have rubbed off on me.' Now you have to eat your own words."

"Very funny."

"Try to have a nice time at the Homey Hut. Talk to you later."

The security door closed behind me, and I walked directly to my car. I knew it couldn't possibly have been an affair gone wrong, but my mother's comment had gotten me thinking. Two dead bodies. Both holding a piece of paper with her name on it. If that wasn't a reason for me to start piecing things together, I didn't know what was.

It was a little past three when I got home. The answering machine light was blinking and I realized I'd left my cell phone on mute. Marshall and Nate had already figured out it was best to leave me landline messages coupled with voice mail.

Sure enough, it was Marshall. I chuckled when I heard his message.

"Do you have any idea how many residents live in this place? I'll be ready to move in myself by the time we get done interviewing them. The sheriff's department is adding some extra deputies, but it will still take us the rest of the weekend. Talk about spoiling our weekend plans. Again, no less."

I immediately called back and left my own message.

"Hey, don't worry about the weekend plans. The rocks aren't going anywhere. We can always sneak off for a romantic weekend once the murders are solved. You *do* think you and Nate will be able to figure it out, don't you?" Then I realized how demanding that sounded and quickly added, "I have confidence in you. This won't turn out to be one of those thirty-year-old cold cases. Catch you later."

I felt badly for my boyfriend and my boss. Not only were they stuck questioning the Lillian's residents, now they had a new murder to contend with. And all of us were thinking the same thing, only none of us would say it out loud: *What if the killer is just getting started?*

My throat was parched and I desperately needed something cold to drink. No sooner did I grab bottled water from the fridge when the phone rang again. I figured Marshall had forgotten to tell me something, so I quickly picked up the receiver.

"Phee! It's your Aunt Ina. I'm so upset I could spit. I simply had to talk with someone, so I figured it might as well be you."

"Um, sure."

"Your mother has become as obstinate as a stone wall when it comes to book club selections. She won't consider anything that remotely stretches the imagination. At this rate, we'll all be stuck reading Nancy Drew's *The Secret of the Old Clock.* And she's not the only one, mind you. Shirley doesn't want to read anything upsetting, Lucinda refuses to read anything where there's blood, Louise said—"

"I understand, Aunt Ina, I really do, but I don't think I'm going to be much help."

"Oh, I don't want any help. I just wanted to get that off

my chest. But speaking of help, did you get anywhere with those pottery numbers?"

"Not really. In fact, it may be something completely different. The secretary in our office thinks they may be coordinates."

"Like GPS? Longitude and latitude? I haven't thought about that since grade school."

"It's probably nothing."

"If I know you, you've already tracked a location for those numbers. I'm right, aren't I?"

"Um, well, yeah."

"Where's the location? Someplace exotic?"

"Not unless you consider an old Arizona mine enticing. And I'm not sure it really leads to one, although there are lots of them in that area."

"What area?"

"The Tonto National Forest, near Roosevelt Dam."

"That's about two hours from here. Phee, I have a marvelous idea."

Anytime anyone had ever told me they had a marvelous idea, it ended in disaster. I tried to change the subject, but it was no use. Aunt Ina was going to shove her marvelous idea down my throat, no matter what.

"Louis is going to be in Prescott all day tomorrow. Playing at a bar mitzvah. The saxophone player for the band came down with the flu and called Louis. Those musicians all seem to know each other. Anyway, Louis wouldn't let anyone down. I don't expect him back till late in the evening."

Oh dear God, no. Here it comes.

"Let's drive to that location of yours and see where it is. Unless, of course, the roads aren't paved. It's bad enough this state doesn't believe in guardrails. I hate to think of what horror we'd come across on a dirt road. So, are the roads paved?"

"The main ones are. Yes."

"Then it's settled. We'll take a nice scenic drive tomorrow and see if those coordinates of yours can tell us if that Quentin Dussler was up to some nefarious business."

"Huh? I think all we're going to be looking at are rocks." *Oh my God! I accidentally told her we'll be going.*

"Pick me up at nine thirty. We can get a bite to eat on the way."

"Um, Aunt Ina, I don't think this is such a great idea."

"Nonsense. We'll be fine." *Of course we will. I'll have to bring enough water for an army and a fully stocked first-aid kit.*

I couldn't believe what I had just agreed to, and I certainly wasn't about to tell anyone. Especially Marshall. Not yet, anyway. Lots of people took scenic drives to Roosevelt Dam. And technically, it wasn't the real hot summer yet. But lots of people weren't going with their loony aunt.

Chapter 15

As things turned out, Marshall was so exhausted by the end of the day that he called to beg my forgiveness and went home to crash in his own bed. He said Nate was equally wiped out. Unfortunately, both of them had no choice but to return the next morning to the Lillian, even though it was Sunday.

"If I'm not too pooped, maybe we can get a bite Sunday night," he said.

"Sure. Call me when you get out of there. Even if you're crawling."

Aunt Ina must have heard my car pull up because the front door was wide open. For a moment, I wondered if she had understood we were taking a drive and not climbing the Austrian Alps. Her outfit stood out, even for my eccentric aunt. She was decked completely in Tyrolean attire, and I didn't mean one of those cute dirndl dresses. Oh no. She was sporting black lederhosen with white knee-high socks. If that wasn't frightening enough, it was offset by a white blouse with billowy sleeves. The last time I saw anyone wearing a shirt like that, it was Johnny Depp in one of those pirate movies. At least she wasn't wearing open-toed shoes. And no matter what, those heavy hiking boots of hers were bound to protect her in the off chance she decided to get out of the car to "scope out the desert." She shouted to me, "Can you give me a hand with the cooler? Louis dragged it as far as the door. He left a little while ago to meet up with the other musicians in Prescott for a rehearsal."

The cooler? What did she need a cooler for? I had picked up a half-dozen bottled waters and made sure my car's first-aid kit was fully stocked. I also remembered to charge my phone.

"My God, Aunt Ina. That cooler's the size of a small house. I've got water and we're stopping for breakfast. You can leave it at home."

"I've packed all sorts of provisions in case we need something between the West Valley and Roosevelt Dam."

"We're taking Route Sixty to Mesa and then Eighty-Seven North. A major highway and a state road. They'll have convenience stores at every exit."

"I don't want to take any chances."

Ten minutes later I had hoisted the giant cooler into the hatchback of my car and took off. We were on Grand Avenue (aka Route 60) in a matter of minutes when I realized something. While my aunt knew about the Dussler murder, she had no idea the lady who owned the clay jar was killed as well. Come to think of it, my mother didn't call to tell me she had seen it on the news. Maybe the sheriff's department was holding off until they had more information. Or, most likely, until they found Sharon Smyth's next of kin.

As far as anyone was concerned, there was an unexplained death at the Lillian. Unexplained didn't necessarily add up to suspicious. Still, I felt compelled to say something about it to my aunt. Especially since it was Sharon's jar sending us on this little trek.

I cleared my throat and gave her a quick glance as I drove. "The coordinates we're tracking down were etched on the bottom of a Quentin Dussler jar."

"I know. You don't have to remind me. I'm not going senile."

"Um, there's more to it. The jar belonged to a lady at the Lillian and it was stolen from her residence a few weeks ago."

"Not from Quentin's place?"

"No."

"Ah-hah. Maybe someone was in her apartment, saw that jar, and realized exactly what they were looking at."

"Which is?"

"Well, one of two possibilities—a very valuable signed jar with a remarque, or secret coordinates to some scandalous thing Quentin Dussler was up to. Goodness, Phee, this is better than any of the books we've been reading. Why, I'm beginning to feel like Baroness Orczy."

"Who the heck is that?"

"Hungarian mystery author. She wrote *The Scarlet Pimpernel*."

Of course she did. "Um, about that lady from the Lillian . . . it's kind of complicated, but she was murdered. Someone from housekeeping services found her in an upstairs laundry room."

"Murdered? So I was right. It was a robbery gone bad. How long was the body sitting in that laundry room?"

"The body wasn't exactly sitting. And it happened yesterday. It couldn't have been a robbery. Like I said before, the clay jar was stolen weeks ago. And who would carry a clay jar into a laundry room?"

My aunt made little clicking sounds with her tongue. "True. True. Too much of a coincidence, I'd say. It has to do with that other murder. Funny, but there was no mention of it on the news."

"You know how those things are. Notifying next of kin and all."

"I suppose. What was that lady's name anyway?"

"Sharon Smyth. With a *Y*."

"Nope. Didn't know her. She had to be pretty long in the tooth if she was living at the Lillian."

Long in the tooth? By God, she sounds more like my mother each day. "Her husband was quite a bit older. He passed away, but she continued to live there."

"I don't blame her. When you get a taste of luxury, there's no turning back."

I continued to drive down Route 60 through central Phoenix while my aunt dozed on and off. The traffic was steady but not as bad as on weekdays.

"Did you have any preference where you'd like to get a bite to eat?" I said as we approached Mesa.

"Pick a well-known quantity like Cracker Barrel or Panera Bread. It's hard to ruin eggs."

We settled on a Panera Bread a few miles south of Route 87 so we could be in and out of the place without wasting a whole lot of time. And while I considered my aunt's clothing to be outlandish, apparently no one else seemed to bat an eye. That was one of the things I liked about Arizona. Anything went as far as one's wardrobe was concerned.

Breakfast was the last relaxing interlude I had before getting on the road again. State Route 87, also known as the Beeline Highway, was a serpentine that wound around a number of canyons.

With each curve, my aunt became more and more agitated. "Slow down, Phee." *Gasp.* "Stay away from the edge." *Gasp.* "Watch for rocks."

"It's fine, Aunt Ina. We're only going forty-five." *And that's because it's an uphill climb.*

If I thought my aunt was nervous with the uphill portion

of the drive, it was nothing compared to her reaction when I crossed over to Route 188 and headed south.

"Louis and I haven't finalized our wills. If we go off a cliff, they'll never find our bodies in that canyon."

"Don't worry. The state has helicopters."

"That's not funny. Use your brakes! Use your brakes!"

"I *am* using the brakes. But I can't slam them on. There are cars behind us."

The road continued to curve dramatically, culminating with a hairpin turn right before our Punkin Center exit. Fortunately, my aunt had closed her eyes and was busy reciting some sort of mantra.

"You can open your eyes now, Aunt Ina. This is where we get off the road."

Punkin Center was an unincorporated community in Gila County, which was a nice way of saying it was an out-of-the-way place in the boondocks where no one in their right mind would spend the day. With the exception of a small grocery store and a bar, there was nothing there. Not even pavement. It was as if someone had plunked down those buildings in the middle of the high desert. Off in the distance were two mountain ranges—the Mazatzal and the Sierra Ancha. In between were miles of scrub brush, rock, and saguaro cacti.

If there was an old mine, the locals would probably know where it was. I drove a few yards past the buildings and parked the car. Other than an old Jeep, ours was the only vehicle near the storefronts. I figured both places must have parking out back for the employees.

The rush of cool air felt absolutely glorious as I stepped out of the car. Less than a two-hour drive from Greater Phoenix and we were in another climate zone. I leaned my neck back and inhaled the fresh air.

"I suppose someone in the grocery store or that bar

might know if we are near a mine or something out of the ordinary, but we don't want to call attention to what we're doing."

"Then go into the bar. People who're drinking don't care."

My aunt was right. No one even noticed we had walked in. Maybe because it was so dark in there.

"Listen," I whispered, "let's order a couple of Cokes and take it from there, all right?" My eyes slowly became accustomed to the darkness.

Two people were sitting at a table in back and an older man with a scruffy beard sat at the end of the long wooden bar. An antique mirror spanned the length of the bar and served as the backdrop for all sorts of postcards and old photos. I motioned for my aunt to take a seat at the bar.

Within seconds, a slender woman with a long strawberry-blond ponytail came out from the back and headed our way. She appeared to be my age—forties. A few wisps of blond curls framed her forehead. "What can I get you?"

"We're driving, so make it two colas," I said.

It was impossible not to notice my aunt's garb, even in semidarkness. The bartender smiled slightly and began pouring our drinks. "We don't get many tourists out this way, only off-roaders and dirt bikers. You two don't seem to fit that category."

She placed the glasses in front of us and I picked mine up. "Yeah, we figured as much. We've seen the usual tourist places in Arizona and thought we'd take a drive to someplace more remote."

The bartender laughed. "This is about as remote as it gets. In the summer we get campers who have cabins around here, but in early spring, there's not much going on. Except, of course, the dirt bikers and four-wheelers."

"Are there any points of interest around here?" I tried to sound casual.

Before the woman could respond, my aunt chimed in. "Like maybe an old mine or a secret burial ground?"

The woman shrugged. "There are lots of old abandoned mines in these hills, but I wouldn't go near them on a bet. Some might have toxic waste and all of them are probably teeming with desert critters."

"See, Aunt Ina," I said, "let's just snap some photos of the terrain and continue on."

The bartender walked to the table in back, pulled up a chair, and chatted with the two people seated there. A man and a woman. In the semidarkness all I could really see were their silhouettes. My aunt got up to use the restroom, and as I watched her walk across the room, I noticed the bartender taking a cell phone from her pocket and texting someone. The man and woman looked on.

When my aunt returned, I left some money on the bar, thanked the bartender, and walked out with my aunt.

"There are no nail salons around here," she said.

"What? Please don't tell me you want to get your nails done."

"Don't be silly. I had them done a few days ago. But that bartender . . . did you notice her nails?"

"Um, no. Why?"

"Because she had to have them done in a more cosmopolitan place than Punkin Center. Her nails were done in that new iridescent holographic glitter coat. Very specialized. Not like the everyday French manicure you've got going."

I held my hands up in front of me and looked at my nails. They seemed perfect to me. "What are you getting at?"

"That woman's not from around here."

"I doubt many of the employees are. This place is only about an hour to Payson and that's a pretty large city."

"Well, someone's mother certainly got around."

"What do you mean?"

"She sent a postcard of the Grote Markt van Antwerpen. Scrawled 'Mom' all over it. It was tacked to the wall next to the other postcards of rattlesnakes, elk, and coyotes. The Grote Markt. Imagine that. It's a famous square in Antwerp. Louis and I were there on our first European visit."

I couldn't believe my aunt was so observant. "Well, maybe whoever she was, she took a tour and sent a postcard back to one of her kids. Maybe they tended bar or something."

"If I had to live around here, I'd drink myself to death. They should've gone to Europe with their mother. So many wonderful things to see in Europe . . ."

My aunt's reminiscing came to an abrupt halt when I unlocked the car and ushered her in.

"I should really reenter the coordinates on that app I installed, just to be sure."

Surprisingly, the app worked beautifully, unlike some of the others that sent me into tailspins.

"We'll have to drive about a quarter of a mile and walk," I said. "But only if there's a marked path. Otherwise, we'll take a look from a safe distance. No toxic waste or rattlers for me. If there's an old mine, maybe we'll spot it."

We didn't.

"Check those coordinates again, Phee."

I stared at the small screen on my iPhone before shutting it down. No sense wasting the battery. "According to this map, the spot we're looking for is off to the left."

My aunt reached in her bag and pulled out a folded canvas hat. As she pulled the brim over her forehead, I heard a faint noise in the distance.

"What's that buzzing noise?" she shouted. "They don't have crop dusters out here, do they? It's getting louder. Sounds like cars that have lost their mufflers."

"Four-wheelers. See for yourself. They're bouncing all over those hills. There are at least four or five of them."

"What kind of crazy sport is that?"

"Off-roading."

"We pay all kinds of highway taxes for asphalt. You'd think they could just drive on a road. So, did you figure out where we're going?"

"Looks like it should be that way." I glanced at the four-wheelers in the distance. "According to our location and the numbers on the bottom of that jar, we're less than an eighth of a mile from the location."

"Where? Where? I don't see a road. I don't see maps."

"I think it's ahead on that footpath. It's definitely a footpath. The car will never be out of our sight. We'll grab some bottled water and start walking."

"If it's so close, why do we need bottled water?"

My aunt had a point. Still, every time I pulled up the news, someone was always in trouble in the desert because they ran out of water.

"Desert protocol."

It was as good an answer as any. As I started on the path, something else came to mind. Snakes. The desert was known for all sorts of them. Rattlesnakes. King snakes. Coral snakes. Not to mention the other possibilities—scorpions and lizards. Last thing I needed was for something to happen to my aunt.

I came prepared with decent hiking boots that went well above my ankles. And even though Aunt Ina's boots were probably substantial, I didn't want to take any risks.

"Um, listen," I said. "I'm thinking it's probably better if one of us stays with the car. I'll only be a few minutes. All I'm going to do is walk up that path and see if it leads to anything. Too many small hills and boulders to tell if there's an old mine."

"Fine. I'll stand here and guard the car. Hurry up."

The path was narrow and strewn with lots of small rocks and pebbles, but it was certainly walkable. I moved steadily, listening for the slightest sound of a rattle, just in case. I had read somewhere the best thing to do in case of an encounter with a rattlesnake was to back off slowly and let it slither away.

A few more steps and I was on a small knoll. The four-wheelers were still cruising all over the place, the hum of their engines echoing off the hills. Behind me, Aunt Ina was leaning against the car. Minutes later, all I could make out was her silhouette. Around me were small knolls, prickly pear cacti, and lots of rocky outcrops. I kept going.

I looked at my iPhone map. I'd need to step off the path and work my way toward one of those outcrops. Certainly not an entrance to an old mine. If I was going to encounter a snake, this would be the place.

Against my better judgment, I took the first step off the path. That was when the roar of those four-wheelers got louder and, next thing I knew, two of them were headed straight toward me. If they meant to scare me, it was working. Last thing I wanted to do was start running in case that rustled up a rattlesnake. But it wasn't as if I had many choices.

The two four-wheelers were now a few yards from me. They fanned out and came at me, one on each side. Whoever they were, they wanted me out of there and now. Unfortunately, their move had the opposite effect. Usually when people were frightened, it was that "fight" or "flight" thing. For me, it was more like "Freeze in your steps and pray you don't wet your pants."

Thank goodness my aunt was at the car. I stood perfectly still as the four-wheelers circled around me. Not once, but twice before taking off.

What the heck! I didn't drive all this way with my aunt to be scared off by a couple of yahoos.

I took a slow breath and continued to follow the map on my phone. Too bad it didn't coincide with what I was actually seeing—rocks, cacti, and occasional Joshua trees. I looked at the map again. This time it read, "Destination four yards to the left."

What was four yards to the left? All I saw was another outcrop. I shrugged and took a step. That was when the four-wheelers returned. Again, circling me. I tried to get a good look at the drivers, but it was impossible. They were wearing helmets with visors and their vehicles didn't slow down. In fact, one came so close I thought it was going to knock me over.

Then I remembered something my cousin Kirk once said. "The next guy doesn't want to get into an accident any more than you do." Maybe he'd heard it from his mother, my aunt Ina. In any case, he was right. Whoever was driving that four-wheeler didn't want to risk an accident by getting too close to the boulders. Within seconds, they had driven off.

Directly in front of me something glistened in the sun, enough to catch my attention. My imagination went wild. At least for thirty seconds.

Chapter 16

I inched my way toward the object and felt like spitting on the ground the minute I realized what it was. Not gold from some mine or any mineral, for that matter. What I had seen reflected in the sun was nothing more than an empty water bottle someone had tossed on the ground.

It was unlikely it had come from the four-wheelers. No one could drive one of those things and drink water at the same time. Unless the bottle fell from a backpack or something. I bent down and picked it up. Sure enough, there was enough dirt caked on it to tell me it had been laying around for a while. I'd stash it into a recycling bin when I got home. Then I took a closer look.

The bottle was a custom design, like one of those specialty ones for weddings and graduations. The purple and white logo was unmistakable, and the bottle read, "The Lillian, Forty Years of Graceful, Elegant Living."

This was no coincidence. Those markings on Sharon Smyth's clay jar *were* coordinates and someone from the Lillian had to be behind her murder and Quentin Dussler's. I turned the bottle over in my hand and groaned. Damn. It was evidence and now my fingerprints were probably the only viable ones.

I don't even think like an investigator. The least I could have done was to pick it up with a tissue.

The grinding hum from the four-wheelers was getting louder. These guys didn't give up, did they? Well, I wasn't about to give up, either. I had to take a quick look at that outcrop and see what the fuss was about.

At first glance, it looked like a ledge, but there was something odd about it. Too many of the rocks looked as if they had been placed there. I squinted and took a closer look. It was as if I had seen a picture of this in a magazine or maybe even a tour book, but I couldn't recall when or where. Most of all, I was struggling with the "what" or "why."

No time to hash it out. Maybe my aunt would have a clue. Aunt Ina! I told her I'd only be a few minutes and God knew how long I'd been here. At least I was fairly certain those off-road yahoos wouldn't be plaguing my aunt. She wasn't the one about to find . . . what? What was it I was stumbling on? It had to be important enough to upset those guys.

Clutching the plastic bottle under my arm, along with the full one I brought, I got back on the footpath and wasted no time getting to the car.

"Come on, Aunt Ina. Buckle up and let's get out of here."

I started the engine like Mario Andretti.

"What did you find? Was it another body? Is that why you're in a hurry?"

"No body. Maybe a clue. Check out the empty water bottle I put in the console. Oh, and use a tissue. Don't get your fingerprints on it."

"What am I supposed to be looking at?"

"The label. The label. It's from Sun City West. The Lillian, to be exact. Someone from the Lillian was here."

"Here? Where? Did you find an entrance to a mine?"

"No. Not a mine. Something else. An outcrop. Only it

didn't look like the others. Too many rounded boulders all stacked up."

"Oh, like those Indian burial grounds?"

"Indian burial grounds?" *It's like everyone else is doing all the thinking and I'm just along for the ride.*

My mind was processing everything at once. "I don't think it's the bodies beneath those boulders that Quentin Dussler was pointing out with those coordinates of his. And someone from the Lillian knew what he was trying to do."

My aunt rubbed her back against the seat. "What was he trying to do?"

"Um, well, that's the thing. I don't know. No one does. If we did, maybe we'd know why he was murdered. And that other lady, too. Sharon Smyth. Anyway, I want to put some serious miles between us and Punkin Center."

"I know. I'm getting hungry, too. A panini is hardly a meal."

"It's not the food, although I could eat. It's those four-wheelers back there."

"Annoying monstrosities, aren't they? My ears are still buzzing from the vibration. How can anyone stand that as a form of recreation?"

"In this case, it was more of a form of intimidation. Two of those vehicles tried to run me off the path."

"Shameful hooligans. It's drugs, I tell you. Those teenagers are all on drugs."

"I don't think they were teenagers, and I don't think they were messing around. It was deliberate. The drivers didn't want me to go near that outcrop—I mean, burial ground."

But how did they know I would be in the area? Then I remembered the bartender texting someone. Either I was letting my imagination get the upper hand or that woman knew more than she was willing to say.

"You think that bartender tipped someone off?" I asked.

"Like a conspiracy?"

"I don't know if I'd go that far, but yeah. Maybe whoever killed Quentin Dussler and Sharon Smyth was trying to find the same thing we are. Whatever that is. Not that I'm about to go back and find out. There could be all sorts of snakes and who-knows-what in those rocks."

"We could come back next weekend with some large rakes or shovels and poke around."

Or we could take a drive to Mexico and cliff dive. "I don't think that's such a great idea. Besides, we're holding on to a decent clue. One Nate and Marshall will want to see."

My thoughts immediately switched to Marshall. I pictured him shaking his head and muttering about me taking chances. But taking a scenic drive with my aunt hardly constituted sending up a red flare. And how was I supposed to know about those off-roaders?

My aunt babbled on and on the entire way back. From lunches she had packed my cousin Kirk thirty years ago to replacing wallpaper, there wasn't a topic she didn't cover. And that included the book club and my mother. By the time we'd reached the Greater Phoenix area, I was ready to wave a white flag out the window.

Unfortunately, the one subject we needed to talk about didn't cross my mind until we stopped for an early dinner at a diner in Mesa.

As my aunt scooped some chicken salad on her fork, she said, "We really should've figured out what those squiggly lines and arrows under the numbers meant."

"Oh geez, you're right. I should've looked closer at that outcrop burial spot to see if anyone had carved something similar on the rocks. There was no graffiti, but I really didn't take a close look. And I should've snapped some photos. I have the iPhone, for heaven's sake. But honestly, how could I? Especially with those off-road drivers gunning for me."

"I wouldn't worry about it if I were you. If something was scrawled on those rocks, someone else probably saw it first."

"We really have no idea what this is all about, Aunt Ina, do we?"

"It has to be something to do with money. It wasn't as if that Smyth woman was involved with Quentin Dussler. All you have to figure out is why anyone would kill them."

And why they were both found with pieces of paper with my mother's and Lucinda's names on them.

"I think the real answer is back in Punkin Center," I said.

"Then what are you waiting for? It's only five and it won't be dark until eight."

I'd been talked into doing stupid things before. Mainly by my cousin Kirk, and that was when we were kids. He'd have a fit if he knew I was letting his mother coax me into driving an hour back to Punkin Center.

"If you're worried about it getting dark and all those desert animals coming out, you don't have to worry," she went on. "You've got lots of time."

"I wasn't even thinking of that until you mentioned it. Are you sure you're okay with the drive back? I mean, the winding road sort of freaked you out."

"Go slower this time and I'll be fine."

Slower? We'll never get there.

Sure enough, my aunt Ina didn't complain the second time around, although she did close her eyes a few times. I swore I heard her say the Hebrew "final words," but then again, it could've been one of her mantras. We arrived back in Punkin Center a little before seven.

"See, plenty of time. Take out that phone of yours and get some pictures of those rocks. We didn't come this far just to get that empty water bottle."

"That empty water bottle's a major clue." I pulled off

the road in the same general area where we had been before. "I don't hear any noises, so those four-wheelers must be gone."

My aunt leaned on the car and gazed at the hills while I reached for my phone. As I turned it on, I saw there were three voice mails. Two from Marshall and one from my mother.

Marshall's first call was left at 4:43. "I'm totally wiped out but I should be at your place around eight. Call me. I've got a few more interviews left. It's like extracting teeth or herding cats. Miss you."

His second call was left a few minutes ago, at 6:33. "I left you a message on your home phone but haven't heard back. My brain's turned to mush. I'll try you at your mother's."

Oh God no! Oh hell no!

While my aunt adjusted her canvas hat again, I took a deep breath and listened to my mother's message.

"Phee! Where are you? Marshall called. He's been trying to reach you. Call me the minute you get this message. I also called your home phone."

I groaned. "Got to return a call to Mom before she reports me as a missing person."

"That would be like Harriet. You know, she could benefit from a nice meditation class."

"Uh-huh. Give me a second. I'll make it quick."

I stepped away from the car and pushed the "call back" command.

"Phee! Where on earth are you? Did you call Marshall?"

"No. I called you first. You sounded pretty frantic."

"Of course I'm frantic. I might be on a hit list. So, where are you?"

"Um, actually, I'm with Aunt Ina. We're east of the valley on a nice—"

"What? Don't tell me she's taken you to one of those

sweat lodges of hers. Or worse yet, those tribal mud baths. Is it a mud bath? Tell me it's not a mud bath. That stuff is laden with bacteria."

"No. No sweat bath, I mean no mud bath or sweat lodge. We decided to take a nice scenic drive, that's all."

"You're not telling me everything. Ina doesn't take nice scenic drives. What's she up to? Put her on the phone."

"I can't. I don't want the battery to get low. Look, I'll call you later tonight. Everything's fine. Honest. Okay?"

"It'll have to be. What should I tell Marshall?"

"Nothing. I'll call him."

"What about the battery?"

"I'll talk fast. Love you, Mom."

The next call was going to be trickier. My fingers tapped the "call back" command and I waited for him to pick up.

"Phee, I've been trying to reach you. Where are you?"

"Um, uh . . . I'm with my aunt and I won't be home for at least another two or three hours."

"Two or three hours? What are you doing?"

"We took a long drive to—"

"Please don't tell me you followed those coordinates."

"It was a scenic drive, that's all."

"So, where are you now?"

"About an hour from Payson, not too far from Roosevelt Dam."

"It's pretty remote out there. Those numbers on the bottom of that stolen jar could be just that—numbers. Let's talk about it when you get back. We can always have the sheriff's department check it out if it comes to that. Don't go traipsing around. Stay in the car."

"Don't worry. I'll call you as soon as I get home."

"Be careful. That goes for your aunt, too."

"We will. And relax. I already spoke to my mother so there's one less headache you'll have to deal with."

"Hah! Get home safe."

"So you can yell at me?"

"No, so I can kiss you."

I tapped the delete button to end the call. My aunt had walked a few feet from the car and was looking at something in the distance. "What kind of birds are those? The wings are enormous."

"Turkey vultures. There must a dead animal out that way. Listen, whatever you do, stay right here by the car. I'll only be a few minutes. I'm going to follow the path back to that burial mound, or whatever it is, and take a few pictures."

"Vultures. They only eat dead things, right?"

"Uh-huh."

"I'll make sure to wave my arms around once in a while so they'll know I'm alive."

"I don't think you have to worry about vultures, and I'll only be a few minutes. And you were right, by the way."

My aunt gave me a funny look. "About what?"

"Driving back here. It would've plagued me all night if we didn't come back to take those pictures. Those squiggly lines might be the real clue."

"Look, Phee. A third vulture joined the other two."

"Wonderful. That means the dead thing is way over there and not where I'm headed."

Chapter 17

I didn't need to hold the map in front of me in order to find the location the second time. Still, I kept my cell phone in my pocket in case I mistook one footpath for another. Occasionally I turned my head to make sure Aunt Ina was visible within a yard's radius of the car. A few more yards and she'd be out of sight. I bit my lip and sighed. At least she could lock herself in the car if she had to.

Although dusk was still a good hour away, the sun was starting its descent, turning the sky into a long ribbon of pink and blue. In other, normal circumstances, I might have paused to admire it, but all I could think of were those creepy desert sounds. I figured they had been there all along but I hadn't noticed due to the noise from those four-wheelers. Thankfully, those jerks had gone home for the day.

A few more yards on my left and I had returned to the outcrop. I wasn't sure why, but my fingers were shaking slightly as I reached for my phone to tap the icon for the camera. There was nothing unusual about the rocks, but maybe there was something I was missing.

I made sure to take at least three panoramic shots of the area before zeroing in on smaller sections. No visible graffiti. No carvings. Only rounded boulders that formed a rock ledge. I wasn't about to get any closer, but what if I could skirt around it?

The time on the phone said 7:08. Lots of daylight. I took my chances and walked a good fifteen yards or so past it. From that distance and direction, the ledge looked like squiggly lines. Quentin had drawn squiggly lines and arrows under his name on that jar. The squiggly lines made sense, but what on earth were those arrows supposed to be? I snapped another two photos and stepped farther back. Darn. I should have taken a picture of the drawing Sharon Smyth made.

Grumbling to myself, I took more photos before shoving the phone back in my pocket. It was now 7:17 and the sun was getting lower in the sky. Aunt Ina's vultures had moved on or maybe they were on the ground eating something. I tried not to think about it as I walked back to the car. Those unsettling desert sounds seemed to be getting louder. Maybe because there were no other noises to drown them out. First, a crunching sound, then something a bit more subtle. Rabbits? Coyotes? Nothing that would pose an immediate threat.

It was only when I heard something rustling behind me that I turned my head. All I saw was scrub brush, cacti, and rock. It had to be a harmless desert animal like a kangaroo rat or something similar. Still, I moved quicker, taking longer strides. If I didn't think I'd trip over a stone or rock, I might have decided to jog.

Aunt Ina was clearly visible by the car. But instead of standing there with her arms folded across her chest or her body leaning back against the hood, she appeared to be stomping her feet and motioning for me to hurry. Maybe Louis had called and she was in a rush to get home. I forced myself to quicken the pace. As I got closer, I could hear her yelling.

"Hurry up, Phee. Move it! Move it!"

I could hear her screaming from a good twenty yards.

"What? What's the matter?"

She had already gotten into the car and slammed the door. I flung open the driver's side door and literally threw myself in the seat: "What's going on?"

"Start the motor and drive."

I shrugged and pulled back on the road. "Now will you tell me what's going on? It's not those turkey vultures, is it? Oh no, did my mother call you? Is that why you're in such a state?"

"Of course not. There was someone behind you. I didn't see them when you first headed to that burial mound, but on your way back, I could see someone following you. I'm sure it was a person."

"What do you mean you're sure it was a person? As opposed to what? Anything else that would've been on four legs?"

"Don't get upset. It was a person. Taller than you. Thin."

"Man or woman?"

"I couldn't tell. It was shadowy. But I did see one thing."

"What's that?"

"They were holding what looked like a gun."

"A gun? You could see something like that from far away? It could've been anything. A cell phone, a candy bar, a—"

"People don't hold out cell phones or candy bars like they're going to shoot them. He or she was pointing that thing."

I looked in the rearview mirror and held my breath. This was always the scene in those police movies where the innocent victim was being followed. All I saw was empty road.

"Are you sure your eyes weren't playing tricks on you?"

"Of course I'm sure. We may be in the desert, but that was no mirage. If I was going to see a mirage, it would be a lovely turquoise pool with a nice cabana and some wine."

Only my aunt could think of cabanas and wine at a time like this.

"Okay, okay. Suppose it was a person—"

"No suppose. It was a person. A person with a gun."

"Fine. A gun-toting person. How do you suppose he got there? No one's going to hike that far. And I didn't hear or see those four-wheelers just now."

"The bartender told us about dirt bikes. You know, those nasty things that always need to be hosed off?"

I laughed. "Yeah, I know."

Then I realized something. It was quite feasible someone could've been in the area on a dirt bike and set it on the ground behind some rocks or scrub brush when they saw me. But to follow me with a gun?

My aunt reached across the console and patted me on the knee. "I think something strange is going on here and I, for one, am even more convinced those clay jar markings were coordinates. But what that has to do with a bunch of old coots at the Lillian and some hoity-toity clay artist is beyond my scope of reasoning. But I do know one thing. . . ."

"What's that?"

"You may be the next victim."

"What makes you say that? There's no one following us and no one knows who we are."

"Your car was parked in front of that bar long enough for someone to write down the plate number."

Leave it to my aunt Ina to string together a bunch of unrelated incidents and have them come out sounding rational and, worse yet, ominous. I checked the rearview mirror again. Nothing.

"Why would anyone write down the plate number?" I

asked. "That's nuts. The only people who bother to drive here are those bike riders."

"With water bottles from the Lillian?"

"Oh holy hell! You're right, Aunt Ina. Marshall isn't going to like this one bit."

"Marshall? I'd be more worried about your mother, if I were you."

As if I didn't have enough on my mind, now I had to add my mother to the mix. I pushed that thought to the back of my mind as I concentrated on the road. Thank goodness it was still daylight. The twists and turns weren't as bad going uphill on Route 188, but to listen to my aunt, one would think we were making our way through Tibet. At least there were no cars behind us. That changed once I got on the Beeline and headed south.

There were vehicles all over the place returning to the valley from Payson—RVs, small campers, trucks, SUVs, sedans, and motorcycles. Probably weekend campers or casino gamblers headed to Fort McDowell, in Fountain Hills. Sunday nights were apparently popular gambling nights.

I hugged the right side of the road and let anyone and everyone pass me. I figured the last thing I needed was to go careening off a cliff because I was unfamiliar with the hairpin curves. It wasn't until we reached Mesa that I was able to pick up speed on Route 60.

We made a quick stop at a Circle K, where my aunt and I grabbed some ready-made hot dogs before I filled up the car with gas. An hour or so later, we arrived at her house. Louis must have just pulled into the garage, according to Aunt Ina, because the outdoor motion sensor lights were still flooding the area.

"Come inside, Phee. Louis would love to see you."

"He's probably exhausted from that bar mitzvah. Besides, it's almost ten and I really need to get home."

Then, for no apparent reason, all sorts of bizarre and worrisome thoughts entered my mind. What if it wasn't Louis? What if someone else was in my aunt's house? I knew I was being irrational, but irrational trumped dead any day of the week.

"Um, on second thought, maybe I'll just come in for a minute and say hi."

My aunt used her key to unlock the front door and shouted for Louis. Within seconds, I heard his voice. "I hope you're alone, Ina, because I'm buck naked. I threw my clothes in the washer."

"Never mind, Aunt Ina." I raced out the door. "Another time."

At least she was safe and sound at home. With my uncle in his birthday suit. I tried not to picture it as I drove to my own place. It was ten thirty when I finally walked into my casita and kicked off my shoes. The answering machine light was blinking and it didn't take Sherlock Holmes to figure out who left the messages.

"Call me the minute you get in. Scenic drive my patootie! What godforsaken place did that sister of mine take you to? Some sort of native witch doctor to make her look twenty years younger? What? Call me. And, by the way, I left Ina a message, too."

Then there was Marshall's message. "I don't care if it's midnight. Call me the second you get in. It's no fun worrying about you on those winding roads."

I knew if my mother didn't hear from me in what she considered to be "a reasonable amount of time," she'd be likely to call the county sheriff's department. Marshall, on the other hand, would exercise some restraint. I called my mother first.

"I'm home. Aunt Ina's home. We're all fine. I'll tell you

about it tomorrow, but I need to call Marshall. Talk to you later."

"Fine. Call me on your break tomorrow."

It wasn't going to be as easy explaining things to Marshall. He'd be relieved my aunt and I made it back in one piece but, deep down, he was probably fuming I decided to trace those coordinates.

"Hey, we're back in the land of fast food and twenty-four-hour gas stations," I said.

"Phee, you have no idea how worried I was about you. And before you say anything, I know. I know how your curiosity can get the better of you, but the high desert? My God. Anything could have happened. Geez, I'm sounding like a broken record."

"You're sounding dated. It would be an iPod."

"Don't change the subject. I'm still pretty miffed. Oh, what the hell. All I really want to do is pull you close to me."

"Trust me. I want to be pulled, too. Um, about those numbers on the bottom of that jar . . . I think they really *are* coordinates."

"Why? What did you find?"

"Some sort of outcrop in the desert that might be a burial mound. But here's the thing—I found an empty water bottle on the ground next to it. And not any old water bottle. One with a special logo from the Lillian."

"I'm waking Nate up. He deserves to hear this. It's the best clue we've had all weekend. Heck! It's the only clue."

"It's covered in dirt, and I think I compromised it with my fingerprints. I should've known better."

"Relax. If there are any additional prints, the sheriff's department will be able to isolate them."

"What about DNA?" I asked.

"First off, I don't think any of that evidence is going to be viable. It's probably been compromised. And, it's not as if the bottle was found at an active crime scene. It would've been different had it been found next to one of the bodies. But don't get me wrong. Like I said, it's the best clue we have."

"Good. Because I had to put up with my aunt Ina all day in order to find it."

"I'll give you an extra hug tomorrow. All right?"

"Yep. And thanks for worrying."

"For that, you'll owe me at least half a dozen more."

I couldn't wipe the idiotic smile off my face for at least five minutes. Even while I was putting the evidence in a Ziploc bag. This time I remembered to use a tissue.

Chapter 18

I made it a point to get into the office early the next day. As the first person through the door, I turned on the copier, got the Keurig all set up, and even did Augusta a favor by booting up her computer as well.

No sooner did I flip on the lights in my office than I heard someone come through the door.

"Get over here and give me that damn hug before the rest of the crew arrives! Wait! Better still, I'm heading into your office."

Marshall reached for my hand, all but swung me around, and planted a kiss on my lips before I could say a word. "Next time can you please keep your sleuthing to the dog park or your mother's neighborhood?"

"If I did that, you wouldn't have this."

I walked to my desk where I had tossed my bag and pulled out the empty water bottle from the Lillian.

Marshall eyeballed it carefully through the Ziploc bag. "I'll show this to Nate as soon as he gets in. One of us will get it over to the sheriff's department so they can process it. Looks like the circle got a whole lot bigger."

"Tell me"—I leaned over to boot up my computer—"what were you and Nate able to find out from all those weekend interviews?"

"When we left the Lillian yesterday, Nate was shaking his head and mumbling to himself. Honestly, it was absolute torture."

"You mean the residents didn't want to talk with you?"

"Oh, believe me, they wanted to talk, all right. Only it wasn't about the murder investigation. One guy relived D-Day for me and three others had war stories about Korea. I didn't have the heart to stop them. It was worse for Nate. Somehow, he wound up with most of the women, and when they found out he was single, they immediately rattled off the names of their unwed children or grandchildren."

"Yikes."

"I don't think it was much better for the sheriff's deputies who were conducting interviews as well. They left the place looking like the cast from *The Walking Dead.*"

"So now what?"

"As soon as Nate gets in, we're heading over to the sheriff's station in Sun City West. All of us need to compare notes, look for commonalities, and see if there are any realistic leads. It'll be like sorting through a decade of taxes."

"Were the interviews with the staff more productive?"

"They were more succinct, but it's too early to tell until we piece together the information they shared. All I can say is thank God for technology. Imagine what it would be like if we didn't have laptops. We'd be sorting through handwritten notes for weeks."

The door opened and Augusta marched in. "I'm not late, am I? What time is it?"

"Good morning, Augusta," Marshall said as we walked into the main office. "It's ten minutes to nine. We've only been here a few minutes."

With that, Marshall gave my hand a quick squeeze and headed into his office.

Augusta eyed me with one of her "I know what's going on" looks. "*We've* only been here?"

"Not what you think. Well, not today anyway. I got in early and Marshall breezed through the door a little while after. Listen, remember the drawing of those numbers and markings on the bottom of that stolen clay jar? Numbers you thought were GPS coordinates. Well, I think they were. I drove to that spot yesterday."

"By yourself?"

"Of course not. My aunt Ina went with me."

"Hells bells, Phee! That's worse. So, what happened? Find anything?"

"It's a remote spot in the high desert south of Payson. Lots of outcrops, cacti, and scrub brush."

"Get to the point."

"The spot was a strange-looking outcrop but with rounded boulders. My aunt thought it might be an ancient burial ground. Of course, she didn't actually see it up close since I made her wait at the car."

"Good move."

"And I found something—an empty water bottle. And get this, the place was teeming with off-roaders who kept circling around me. Either they were a bunch of idiots or they wanted me to get the hell out of there. So, we left. But we came back later. After we drove all the way to Mesa."

"You're kidding me? You drove back? What on earth for?"

I told her about my stupidity in not snapping any photos the first time around.

"Yeah, I suppose that makes sense. So, what about the water bottle?"

"Oh, that's the best part! It's one of those commemorative ones they use for special occasions, and this one was from the Lillian."

"Holy cow! You really did find a clue."

At that moment, my boss walked in. "Morning, ladies. Don't mind me. I'm still reeling from yesterday's delightful sojourn at the Lillian. Marshall in yet?"

"In his office," I said.

"Guess he told you we're about to spend the day with the sheriff's department. I'm going to make myself a cup of coffee, check my e-mails, and head over there with him. Anything comes up, call me."

"I found a clue, Nate. Not any old clue but one that proves those numbers on the bottom of Sharon Smyth's stolen clay jar were really GPS coordinates."

My boss looked as if I had sprouted wings. "Don't tell me you did something stupid or dangerous."

Augusta took a step forward and held up her palms as if she was stopping traffic. "She had her aunt with her. It was fine."

"Oh brother. *This* I need to hear. But coffee first."

By the time I was done telling Nate about the encounter at Punkin Center, the four-wheelers, and the water bottle, he was absolutely speechless. The one piece of information I did leave out, however, was that bit about being followed by someone who might or might not have been holding a gun. No need for him or Marshall, for that matter, to get into a tailspin.

"Marshall has the water bottle," I went on. "Guess the sheriff's department will be glad to get it. I mean, it wasn't as if they were about to trek all the way to that spot on their own."

Nate didn't say a word but smiled and shook his head.

"I have the photos I took of that outcrop. I'll send them to your e-mail."

"Promise me you won't go out there again. With or without your aunt Ina. That's something for the sheriff's department. And not the one in our jurisdiction. The Gila County

Sheriff's Office. Lucky them. These two murders are like a net that just keeps getting wider and wider."

"But Phee caught you a fish in that net, didn't she?" Augusta asked.

"She was lucky that's all she caught." Then he looked right at me. "Can you please keep it to Sun City West? Surely there's enough there to occupy that inquisitive mind of yours. Okay, kiddo?"

"Yeah. Sun City West."

Marshall and my boss headed off to the sheriff's station a few minutes later. Augusta and I got right to work.

Around midmorning, as I was preparing to take a break and have my third cup of coffee, Augusta knocked on my door frame.

"Your mother's on the phone."

My mother. I had totally forgotten I'd told her I'd speak with her during my morning break. There was no escaping it.

Her voice boomed the second I said hello. "I'm glad you're in one piece, Phee. I talked to your aunt this morning and all she would say was that the two of you took a scenic drive. If that's the way you want to be about it, fine. But don't call me if you wind up at some New Age retreat with a bunch of crazies."

"Don't be upset with Aunt Ina. She was only covering for me."

I went on to tell my mother about Sharon Smyth's drawing and how Augusta thought the numbers might've been coordinates. When I was done, I got the third version of "don't drive there again."

Then she changed the subject. "I ran into Cindy Dolton at PetSmart yesterday. In the grain-free section, where I get Streetman's special food. She's changing Bundles's diet.

Anyhow, she asked if you ever contacted Lon and Mary Melhorn about Quentin Dussler."

"Me? No. It's on Nate's list. Anyway, I should get back to work. Don't worry. Everything's fine."

"Sure it is. Two people have been murdered and no one has any idea why Lucinda's and my name wound up at one of those crime scenes. Light a fire under that boss of yours. And your boyfriend, too."

Whew, at least she doesn't know her name wound up at both. "Love you, too, Mom. Catch you later."

As I hung up the phone, I thought about what she said regarding the Melhorns. Nate and Marshall were way too busy to interview them. After all, it wasn't as if the Melhorns had witnessed anything. All Cindy told me was that they knew Quentin Dussler. But what did they know? And more importantly, would it help solve his murder? I turned my attention back to a spreadsheet I was working on when Nate's words sprung to mind. "Keep it to Sun City West."

Fine, so it wasn't as if he'd asked me to probe further with my contacts in Sun City West, but he didn't tell me not to do so. Surely a little chat with Lon and Mary Melhorn couldn't be considered anything more than mild snooping. *Oh my God! I'm sounding like my mother.*

I went back to the spreadsheet and tried not to think about it. That lasted all of five minutes. I got up, rummaged through my bag, and found the original pad where I had written down their number for Nate. Picking up the phone before I had time for second thoughts, I called them. Mary answered on the third ring.

Getting right to the point, I told her I was an acquaintance of Cindy Dolton and worked for Williams Investigations.

"I'm not an investigator," I said, "but I do help out when I can, and this might be one of those times."

I went on to explain how little details and seemingly

insignificant observations could result in solid leads for a
murder investigation.

"I'm not sure what we can tell you," she said, "but if it
can get your office closer to finding out who killed Quentin,
we'd be happy to try. Lon and I are going to be at the Kuentz
Courtyard this evening around seven for their jazz night. It's
the recreation center on Stardust Boulevard. Maybe you
could meet us there for a few minutes."

"That's perfect. Um, how will I recognize you?"

"Good point. At a certain age, we all begin to look alike.
Bald men and gray-haired women. Tell you what, I'll wear
a red scarf around my neck. Lon and I usually get there
early and sit in the back near the water fountain."

"I'm in my mid-forties with highlighted brownish hair
and I'm wearing tan slacks and a blue cowl-neck top with
sequins."

"You'll be the youngest one there. We'll notice you."

"Great. See you around seven. And thanks so much."

Augusta and I called out for lunch and had hot subs delivered. At a little past four, Nate phoned to ask us to lock
up. Apparently he and Marshall were going to be stuck at
the sheriff's office for the remainder of the day, sifting
through interview notes. With so many residents from the
Lillian, I figured it would take more than one day. Marshall
confirmed that when he called me around four thirty.

"Looks like we'll be here tomorrow as well. Nate's
having Augusta move our Tuesday appointments to later in
the week. Thank goodness today was a clean slate as far as
office appointments. Uh, would you be really disappointed
if we got together tomorrow night instead of this evening?
I'm dead on my feet and it's not even five."

"Actually, that works for me, too. I'll talk to you later
tonight. How's that?"

"You'd better."

Whew! I was off the hook considering I'd agreed to meet the Melhorns around seven. Marshall would learn all those salient details, if there were any, when I phoned him later. Technically, I had Nate's permission. But was it a technicality?

Chapter 19

The Kuentz Courtyard was an atrium nestled in the middle of the smallest recreation center complex. It featured overhanging trees and a lovely fountain surrounded by resort-style furniture. Tiki torches added to the ambience. For special events, like this evening's jazz session, additional chairs were placed along the perimeter.

I spotted Lon and Mary Melhorn immediately. No one else was wearing a red scarf. Or a gold Hidalgo bracelet and matching enamel ring. Way out of my price tag. The Melhorns had saved a chair for me next to the couch they shared.

"You must be Phee." Mary's bracelet glimmered as she reached out to shake my hand.

It was barely seven, so the music hadn't started yet, only instrument tuning. The people were still streaming in. I prayed none of them were from the Booked 4 Murder book club. Keeping my voice low so Mary and Lon would follow suit, I asked them to tell me anything they could about Quentin Dussler.

"Lon and I used to be in the clay club years ago," Mary explained. "That's how we met Quentin. Once in a while we went out for coffee if our clay club schedules coincided. The man was an absolute artistic genius. Especially the way he sculpted those jars of his on the potter's wheel. Not to mention the glazing. His technique was unparalleled."

"Is that what made his pieces so valuable?"

"Some of them. The rare colors."

"I see."

I had heard that before, but somehow I thought there was more to it.

"How did he find a market to sell those expensive pieces? From what I've heard, some of them sold for close to a thousand dollars."

"Close to? Try thousands. Quentin once told Lon that if he could sell a few more pieces, he'd be set for life."

"It still doesn't explain how there was a market for them," I said.

"I think his niece handled that part of the enterprise."

"The journalist?"

"That's the one. I suppose she took care of the marketing when she wasn't flitting all over the world on one of her assignments."

"You wouldn't happen to know how to reach her, would you?"

"Sorry. We haven't a clue. Not even her full name."

I shrugged. "Someone told me Quentin taught art at a college in New York. Did he ever say what his wife did?"

Mary bit her lip and looked at her husband. "Not directly, but I got the feeling she worked in the diamond industry in New York City."

My eyes about popped from their sockets. "The diamond industry? What makes you say that?"

"Remarks here and there Quentin made. Nothing specific."

I glanced at the courtyard. It had filled to capacity in the few minutes I had been speaking with the Melhorns. The jazz musicians were still tuning up their instruments, so I had a bit more time.

"I have one more question before I take off. Do either of you have any idea who might have wanted to kill Quentin Dussler?"

Both of them answered without hesitation and, even though their voices overlapped, the response was clear as could be: "Someone who was looking for something."

"Like money or credit cards?"

Again the Melhorns locked gazes, but this time only Mary spoke. "Like information. If it was one thing Quentin knew how to do well, other than create pottery, it was conceal information."

By now I was hearing more than I could process. "You mean like a spy? Like espionage?"

"Let me be really frank," Lon said. "Most people around here are like puppies. Wagging their tails and telling you everything about their life stories. Quentin was more like a cat. Secretive and cagey as could be. He never answered anything directly when we got together. Almost as if he was hiding something. Then again, he might have simply been one of those nonobtrusive quiet people."

"Fat chance," whispered Mary just as the first piece began.

"Thank you both," I said. "Enjoy your evening. If I have any more questions, can I contact you?"

Both of them nodded and I slipped out of the courtyard as quietly and unobtrusively as I possibly could.

Since the only thing I had eaten since lunch was a quick salad at Wendy's, I headed home to make myself something more substantial. But not before making a stop at the first Walgreens I saw. It was time for poster paper, markers, and string. Maybe real detectives had Smart Boards, but fourth-grade artwork always seemed to come through for me.

I made two charts that basically resembled outline webbing for an essay. The easy webbing that looked like a sun with spokes coming out of it. One of the posters had Quentin Dussler in the center and the other one had Sharon Smyth. I filled in the spokes with the tidbits of information I had gathered, trying to stick to the facts and not my theories. Somehow, it wasn't working. That's when I got the brilliant idea to use one color ink for fact and another for supposition.

By the time I had finished, I had a fantastic plot for a murder mystery thriller spanning Europe and the Western Hemisphere. Totally disgusted with myself, I sat on the couch, picked up my phone, and called Marshall.

"I'm glad I'm not a detective. It's too darn frustrating."

"Whoa. What brought that on? I thought I was the only one mentally and physically exhausted. As if the Lillian interviews weren't enough, we're still patching together the information we got from the clay club members. And it's worse for Nate."

"What do you mean?"

"At least I can sit here in peace and quiet. He's still babysitting his aunt's African parrot."

"Eww. I forgot about Mr. Fluffypants."

"He'd like to forget, too. Seems the thing talks nonstop."

Nate's elderly aunt lived south of Tucson in Sierra Vista and last year, when she broke her hip, he agreed to babysit her parrot. Apparently recuperating from a broken hip could take an epoch amount of time. Being a kind and dutiful nephew, it was no wonder he offered to help her out, even if it meant temporarily acquiring an obnoxious roommate.

I giggled while Marshall continued. "So, what did you mean about it being frustrating?"

"I knew you and Nate were piled high and deep, so I called those people Cindy Dolton told me about. The ones

who were acquaintances of Quentin. The Melhorns. I met
them tonight. Nate had them on a list for interviews but—"

"You couldn't resist. Hey, I'm not going to get all
worked up. It wasn't as if they were bona fide witnesses to
anything. Truth is, I'm glad you saved us some time. So,
what did you find out?"

"A smattering of possibilities. We talked at the Kuentz
Courtyard in Sun City West. Jazz night. Very safe. Do you
want to hear the facts by themselves or my theory?"

"The facts. Please. Then we'll get to your theory. Good?"

"Uh-huh."

I proceeded to tell Marshall about the real cost of Quentin's
special pieces, his niece's travels, and his late wife's possible, albeit remote, connection to the diamond industry.

"Now, do you want my theory?"

"Oh sure, why not."

"The niece was, probably still is, some sort of agent. She
stashed some information at her uncle's place and that's
what got him killed. Someone was looking for it."

"Wow. And all this time I thought Lee Child was the
only one with a handle on that stuff."

"I'm serious, Marshall. Listen for a sec, will you? Nothing of value was stolen from Quentin's house. Not even his
credit cards. And we can rule out an affair gone bad because
women usually don't murder their victims by stuffing clay
in their faces. No matter what those book club ladies tell
you. A person has to be pretty strong to do something like
that. If we can figure out what Quentin was really up to,
we'd find his killer. Unless . . . oh my gosh, I hadn't thought
about this until just now—what if the niece killed him?"

"Seconds ago you said a woman wouldn't be that strong.
Which is it?"

"Oh heck. I don't know. And what about that niece? Has
anyone been able to track her down?"

"Nope. The sheriff's deputies haven't been able to find anything about her at Quentin's place."

"Ah-hah. My theory's still in play. She's an operative. Whoever she is. Too bad the Melhorns couldn't give me more information. At least you and Nate probably have something to go on where Sharon Smyth is concerned. I feel as if I'm wadded up in some ball of yarn and can't even knit myself out."

Marshall laughed. "Relax. Cases aren't solved by a few facts and some theorizing. Unless it's a TV series. Then they can do it in less than an hour when you factor in the commercials. We've got another day at the sheriff's station to compile and analyze what we learned from those interviews. Then maybe we'll be able to get somewhere."

"I hope so."

"Hey, I almost forgot to tell you this. The sheriff's department found Quentin's inventory log. It was a plain old notebook, one of those marble composition ones. The guy had it stashed in a small pull-out drawer in this desk. If it wasn't something your aunt said, Nate never would have mentioned it to the sheriff's office. Their department thought they had everything when they took Quentin's laptop. Apparently that didn't yield any information, but the inventory did."

"Wow."

"Yeah, 'wow' about sums it up. They've got the information all right, but none of their deputies can figure it out. So, it wound up in Nate's lap. Literally."

"Yeesh. You know what that means, don't you? Get out your wallets and find out what kind of diet Rolo Barnes is on now."

"Already done," Marshall said. "Something with biblical grains and cage-free eggs."

My body twinged. "Um, this log of Quentin's, I take it there are no names or e-mail addresses."

"Correct. Lots of codes. Probably bank routing numbers."

"Yep. That'll be right up Rolo's alley. So, uh, I guess I don't get to see you tomorrow, huh?"

"Not during the day, but I'll be damned if I spend the night sifting through those interview notes with your favorite deputy sheriffs. Let's say I pick you up at seven thirty. We'll get dinner somewhere and then—"

"Oh yeah. I like the 'and then.'"

Chapter 20

Unfortunately, the "and then" never happened. Not on Tuesday night, anyway. I was getting ready to leave work when Marshall called.

"You won't believe this. Hell, I don't believe this. A few minutes ago Nate got a call from the residence manager at the Lillian. She called him because she didn't, and I quote, 'need a scene with the sheriff's department.'"

"Huh? What's going on?"

"Apparently our weekend of interviews created so much stress for the residents that now some of them are threatening to leave. A few have already packed overnight bags and headed to relatives' or friends' houses. Kimberlynn Warren asked if we could please go over there and try to calm the rest of them down. A major exodus, according to her, 'is going to shut this place down like an epidemic of bedbugs.'"

"Poor Gertie and Trudy. They must be wringing their hands. Do you think I should head over there, too?" I asked.

"Truthfully, we don't know what the heck we're walking into, so maybe it's best if you stayed put. I'll give you a call once I know what's really going on."

That was at four forty-five. I didn't hear back from Marshall until well past eight.

"One more minute in that place and I swear I would

have poked my eyes out with a fork. Do you have any idea how fast those people can go from cranky to psychotic?"

"Yikes. That bad?"

"Kimberlynn thought it best to have them all sit in the dining room while Nate and I tried our darnedest to reassure them. I've seen prison cafeterias that were less threatening. It seemed our questioning regarding Sharon Smyth stirred up a number of other issues. The residents are convinced they're being watched by secret surveillance in their rooms. The director tried to assure them it wasn't the case, but they weren't buying it. Add that to the fact a few of them had their belongings rifled through and we all but had a revolution."

"What finally happened?"

"Nate promised he'd have the sheriff's department discreetly check their rooms for any electronic bugs and Kimberlynn said she'd hire security personnel to walk the corridors. Hopefully to end any concerns about unwanted intruders."

"Do you think someone at the Lillian is orchestrating all of this to shift the attention away from the investigation?"

"Funny, but Nate and I asked ourselves the same thing."

"Hmm, it's getting late for them or I'd give those sisters a call. Maybe they haven't told us everything. Think Nate would mind if I dropped over there tomorrow?"

"I think he'd be delighted if anyone, other than he, dropped over. Still, you might want to run it by him."

As things turned out, Nate was fine having me visit the Gertrudes, as Sharon Smyth had referred to them. Marshall and I had postponed our evening together for later in the week, so when I got out of the office on Wednesday, I decided to make an impromptu stop at the Lillian.

It was a little before six and the residents had already finished their evening meal in the dining room. As promised, Kimberlynn had added additional security. And while she told Nate it would look seamless and unobtrusive, it didn't. Pairs of thirty-something men and women in light pastel tops and khaki slacks were everywhere.

The blondes were at their usual places, manning the reception desk, and were more than happy to page Gertie and Trudy for me.

"They'll be right down," one of them said as she picked up her phone and thumbed through it.

"Thanks. I'll grab one of those seats by the elevator."

A few minutes later, both sisters emerged from the elevator and motioned for me to follow them outside.

"All of a sudden this place has become the Pentagon. I've never seen so much security," Gertie said. "And I don't like the fact someone can listen to my private conversations."

I slowed my pace to keep in time with her as we walked out the front door. "It's just the residence's way of protecting its tenants and staff."

"That's what you think," Trudy said. "I call it snooping."

The evening air was still warm, but a light breeze made it perfect for sitting outdoors. We found an empty table and chairs in a small courtyard near one of the parking areas. With the exception of an elderly man walking a small white dog, we were the only ones in the vicinity.

I clasped my hands together and leaned toward the center of the table. "I came here tonight because I was concerned the recent series of events might tempt you into doing something you'd regret later."

Gertie crinkled her nose and gave me a funny look. "You mean like saying something to that stuck-up Kimberlynn Warren?"

"Well, no. Actually, I was afraid you'd want to leave the

Lillian. And I wanted to reassure you that whatever's going on, I mean, besides Sharon Smyth's murder . . . that, um . . . my boss, his partner, and the sheriff's department will get to the bottom of it. These investigations take time."

"If they take any longer, it won't matter," Trudy said. "We'll all be dead."

Gertie shot her a dirty look. "We're not leaving the Lillian."

"Good. Glad to hear that," I said. "So, other than all those interviews this past weekend and the additional security, is there anything else going on that you want to tell me about?"

They shook their heads.

"Fine. I've got another question for you. Do either of you remember special commemorative water bottles being used here?"

Trudy gave a quick nod. "The purple logo ones for the fortieth anniversary?"

"Yes. Purple."

"That anniversary was around Thanksgiving. Huge celebration. Or was it Christmas? Anyway, it was months ago. Carving tables with steamship roast, glazed ham, and turkey. And a Viennese table with all sorts of desserts. That logo was on the bottled waters as well as the napkins. Very classy."

Thanksgiving. Christmas. It meant that water bottle had to be at least six months old. Not likely. The paper logo that was wrapped around it wouldn't last in the desert for months. Weeks maybe, but not months.

"Um, are they still using those bottles with the special logo?"

"No. We're back to using the regular ones. Been using

the regular ones for months now. I think they stashed the leftover logo ones in the office somewhere for staff."

"What makes you say that?"

Gertie glanced at her sister. "Because we'll see one of those specialty bottles once in a while on the reception desk next to the computers. And sometimes we'll see one of the cleaning ladies or maintenance men with them. It's the same thing with the holiday candy and other seasonal stuff. The management gives the residents the newest, freshest amenities. And that's the way it should be. Gracious. I wouldn't want to be drinking water on Memorial Day from a bottle that said, 'Happy Halloween.'"

Then Trudy held up her hand as if to shush her sister. "Why are you asking us about the water bottles? Are they contaminated? Is that what's going on?"

"No. No. Absolutely not. I, um, happened to see one and thought it was very unique. That's all."

Gertie cleared her throat and sat up. "I'll tell you what should've been unique. Someone should have taken one of those water bottles and dumped it over those deputies' heads this weekend. Questioning us as if we were suspects."

"We *are* suspects, Gertie," Trudy said. "Everyone is."

"Not everyone. Some people more likely than others. Mario Aquilino's name springs to mind. Maybe it was a crime of passion."

Mario Aquilino. From Cecilia's church. The man whose paintings had been reversed. I knew I was forgetting something. I meant to chat with him days ago.

"Uh, what can you tell me about this Mr. Aquilino? Other than what you mentioned a few days ago. You know, about him leaving Sharon Smyth's place at a really early hour of the morning?"

Trudy made a tsk-tsk sound and tapped the table. "That's all I know. Isn't that enough?"

"It's very helpful," I said. "Very helpful. Anyway, I should be going. I've kept both of you way too long. I'm sure you have other activities or things you'd rather be doing. Remember, if you hear anything that upsets you or, worse yet, if you see something questionable, call me. You have the office number, right?"

As I stood up, I recited a line that every physician's office, dental practice, and optical place used ad nauseum. "If it's an emergency, hang up and call nine-one-one."

"Hummph, it must be seven already," Gertie said. "Tina and Tanya are leaving for the day."

I glanced to my right and the two blondes walked to a small parking lot reserved for employees. Must be they worked a ten-hour day. I'd met Taylor, the weekend receptionist, but I wondered who manned the reception area at night.

"Say, who takes over the front desk when the regular receptionists are gone for the day? Is someone there all night?"

Gertie was still eyeballing the blondes. "No. They have a sign that says 'Call the house manager in case of emergency' and phone calls go into his apartment."

"The house manager?"

This was the first time I had heard of such a person. Did Nate and Marshall know there was a house manager?

"It's more like a twenty-four-hour maintenance person. You know, if someone's toilet gets clogged in the middle of the night or someone locks themselves out. The maintenance manager gets to live here rent free plus a salary and meals."

While it sounded like a cushy job, I knew it wasn't. That poor guy probably hadn't had a decent night's sleep in years.

"What's his name?"

"Good question," Gertie said. "Everyone just calls him Tiny Mike."

"Anyway, have a nice night, ladies, if you can."

When I got home, I called Marshall and told him about Tiny Mike. It turned out they did have his name on the staff list under maintenance—Michael Melroy. He'd been with the Lillian for over a decade. Ex-army, divorced, no priors. So much for that tidbit. The next revelation was more promising.

"I found out something about that water bottle."

"Really?"

"Yep. It was for a celebration that happened months ago. Residents aren't being served water in those bottles anymore, but guess who's still using the leftover ones? The staff. Gertie and Trudy said they've seen the receptionists and the cleaning staff with those commemorative bottles. So, you know what I'm thinking, don't you?"

"One of the staff members took a fairly recent drive to Punkin Center?"

"You bet. And you're probably thinking the same thing I am. Whoever stole Sharon Smyth's clay jar figured out what those numbers on the bottom really meant. Or maybe they knew all along and that's why they took the jar in the first place. According to the Gertrudes, Sharon was bragging all over the place about her special find from the Creations in Clay. Suppose, for a minute, that someone at the clay club realized the mistake that had been made in selling Sharon that jar and had to find a way to get it back. Sharon never would have resold it, so—"

"It was an outside job with some inside help?"

"That's my latest theory, and I'm sticking to it."

"It's a solid theory for the theft, all right, but it doesn't explain her murder. The jar was stolen way before she was killed."

"Hey, I can't be expected to figure out everything."

"You're still one step ahead of most of us."

Chapter 21

"Stop fussing and meet me at the clay club room when you get out of work today. It should only take you ten or fifteen minutes to see what I've done. Lucinda wants to show you her pieces, too. Right now, they're greenware. That means they're unfired, but we're putting them in the kiln for their first firing tonight. When they come out, they'll be bisque and we can glaze them."

That was the gist of the phone conversation I had with my mother during my afternoon break. I made the mistake of calling her to find out if she thought Cecilia would be willing to share any information she had about Mario Aquilino, especially since she knew him from her church. My mother said she'd ask and then immediately tried to rope me into rendering an opinion about her clay artwork.

"I decided to do hand-building for my first piece rather than use a mold. You'll have to tell me what you think."

It was a trap and there was no way out. The closest I'd come to seeing my mother's art was when we played a game of Pictionary. "A stalk of celery?" "No, Phee! It's a monk praying. Can't you see that?"

The thought of having to say something about her first creation in clay was giving me a case of mild indigestion.

"Fine. Fine. Ten minutes. I want to get home in order to take a quick swim. The weather's perfect this time of year."

"Good. By the way, tonight's clean-out night."

I am not going to allow myself to get coerced into cleaning out anything. "Huh? Clean-out night?"

"Yes. A few times a year, club members clean out the old pieces that have been gathering dust on the shelves or, worse yet, cobwebs in those storage cabinets. They're pieces that were made by members who are no longer active. That's a nice way of saying dead. Well, not all of them have died. Some have moved, others decided not to stay in the club. . . ."

"I get it. I get it. So, do you just throw them out? The pieces, I mean."

"No. If they're greenware, we fire them. If they're bisque, we glaze them. Then we donate them to the Empty Bowls in Phoenix for their annual fund-raiser."

"Empty Bowls. I seem to have heard of that."

"It's a national thing now. The bowls are either sold as is or sometimes the organization holds a dinner and fills them with soup. People eat a meal and take the bowls home with them. The proceeds go to feeding the homeless."

"Hmm. Sounds like a neat charitable thing but, like I said, I'm only staying for a few minutes."

So much for that. I should've known better.

At five forty-six, I walked into the clay club room. It was the second time I'd been there. The first was a week and a half ago when I had the tour from Diane, the monitor on duty. This time there was a different monitor on duty, a heavyset man who appeared to be in his sixties. I introduced myself and told him I was looking for Harriet Plunkett and Lucinda Espinoza.

"Hold on a minute," he said. "They're in the back room cleaning out some cabinets."

One person was seated at a potter's wheel and another at a workstation. Two ladies were in the back of the room sorting through items on some of the shelves. I figured they were cleaning out the old pieces.

Lucinda burst through the doorway from the back room, followed by my mother. Both of them were wearing work aprons over their clothing, and, while my mother made sure the outfit she had underneath that apron was stylish, Lucinda looked as if her apron was being used to cover up a crumpled paper bag. My mother immediately walked to one of the workstations and came back holding her objet d'art.

"Well, what do think?" she asked. "You won't see many of these around."

Thank God. "Um, yeah. It's very original. It's a bowl of sorts, with handles. Right?"

"It's a serving platter, and look closely at the handles."

I bent down to study the piece, hoping she'd explain what I was looking at. "Uh-huh. Very unique, Mom."

"I thought so, too. I think it's a good likeness of him. You don't come across handles shaped like a dog's face, do you?"

Goodness. So that's what it is. Streetman's bust incorporated into the grips for the platter. Yikes.

I smiled and nodded. There were no words that came to mind. At least none I dared use. Lucinda showed me one of her creations, too. It was a jar. A lopsided, ugly jar. At least it was easily recognizable.

"Once these are fired," she said, "your mother and I will glaze them. To be honest, I was really nervous coming back to the club room once our names were found on that note.

But this place is always so busy, I don't think anyone would commit a murder in here."

My mother gently placed her platter back on the work-station table. "Did Nate or Marshall ever find out where that note came from? We've been wracking our brains out with this."

"They're working on it. That's all I can tell you."

My mother grunted. "That's all the sheriff's department says, too."

"You called the sheriff's department?"

"Ever hear the expression about the squeaky wheel? I don't want those bumbling deputies to stick that note in some file and forget about it."

"I don't think you have to worry about that."

"No, I have to worry about lunatic killers."

Just then, a petite woman with bluish hair poked her head out from the back room. "Harriet? Lucinda? Can either of you give us a hand moving some of the larger pieces to the front room?"

"It would go so much faster if you give us a hand, Phee." My mother grabbed my arm and ushered me into the back room. "This should only take about ten minutes, tops."

"I, er, um . . ."

Lucinda all but shoved me into the narrow, musty-smelling room. "You're an angel to help out."

Ten minutes. I am only going to be here for ten more minutes.

The petite woman tottered off to the front room, leaving my mother, Lucinda, and me to deal with moving the large pottery pieces. We removed them from the open metal shelves in back to an area reserved for them adjacent to the kilns.

"Whew! That looks like we're about done." I placed some sort of urn on the counter.

My mother blocked the only path between me and the

front door. "Don't go yet. There's a walk-in closet in the back room, and it may have some heavier pieces. Five more minutes isn't going to ruin your evening."

No, it's probably ruined already. "Five minutes. I really want to get in a nice swim."

Lucinda propped the closet door open with her foot as my mother and I stepped inside. Stale air and dampness permeated the area.

"When was the last time they used this space?" I asked.

Lucinda leaned forward and took a whiff. "Not in a while, I'd wager. Hang on. I'll move that heavy wastebasket over and use that to keep the door from shutting."

The second she walked off, I expected the door to slam behind her, leaving us in darkness and mold. Thankfully, that didn't happen. The door remained open on its own. I found the wall switch and flicked on the overhead light.

Most of the shelves had pieces that were still wrapped in plastic, but there were a few chalky grayish bowls and jars. All they would need was some glaze and another firing. The "hot" firing, according to my mother.

"If we move at a steady pace, we can grab something, march it out to the front and line up to get another piece," she said. "This will be over in no time."

And it would have been, had it not been for Lucinda, who decided to read the markings on the bottoms of the bisque pieces and recite them out loud.

"E. Stevens. I wonder if that was Edith. She passed away two years ago."

"Audrey Manger. I don't know her."

"F.S.M. Who could that be?"

It went on and on until most of the pottery had been removed from the walk-in. The two ladies who had been at the workstations in front had gone home for the night and, other than the three of us, only the monitor and the diminutive woman remained.

"Looks like we're done," I said. "Or at least I'm done."

"We've got four more pieces, Phee. Just grab that large bisque bowl and put it near the kiln on the right."

"Fine, Mom. One large bowl coming up."

I don't know what prompted me to do so, but, for some inexplicable reason, I picked up the bowl, set it down next to the kiln, and then picked it up again to see if anyone had signed it. If nothing else, Lucinda would have another name to announce.

It took me a few seconds to process the name beneath the bowl. Mainly because the person who inscribed it into the soft clay had pressed down so hard as to create rough ridges along the sides of the letters. The date underneath the name was easier to read. The artist created the bowl four years ago.

At first I couldn't believe what I was reading, but there was no mistaking it. The name inscribed on that pottery piece was none other than Sharon Smyth's.

"Mom! Lucinda! Take a look at this bowl!"

I held the thing upside down and all but shoved it in their faces. "See what it says? It says Sharon Smyth. How many of them could there be? It had to be her. She never once indicated she used to belong to this club. And check the date out. It was four years ago. Four years. Who stops coming to a club in the middle of a project?"

Lucinda gave my mother a poke. "Maybe something happened four years ago. Maybe something to do with Quentin Dussler. What do you think, Harriet?"

"Hmm. An affair gone sour . . ."

"Oh no," I shouted. "Not the affair thing. And if it did go sour, why did she wait four years to do him in? Because that's what you're thinking, isn't it? That Sharon Smyth killed Quentin and then someone killed her."

"Do you have a better theory?"

"No, not yet. Come on, look at the bowl, will you? It's her name all right, isn't it?"

My mother studied the signature like an Egyptologist would study hieroglyphics. "Take a picture of this with your phone, Phee. Hurry up. You've got to see if the signature matches her handwriting."

"And how am I supposed to do that?"

The only sample of her writing I'd seen was her rendering of the Quentin Dussler signature with the squiggly lines beneath it. Aka—the coordinates. Hardly a match for comparison.

My mother put her hands on her hips and shook her head. "By now those deputies have been through Sharon Smyth's apartment. Not to mention your boss or that boyfriend of yours. One of them can compare the handwriting with some grocery list she wrote or notations in her address book."

I had to give her credit. She was as astute as she was exasperating, and it made me feel as if everyone had better deduction skills than I did.

"I'm going to e-mail this to Nate and Marshall as soon as I'm done." I placed the bowl with the other pieces of pottery.

Lucinda immediately snatched it up and headed back to the closet with it. "Maybe we shouldn't put it on the table for the Empty Bowls' project. It might be evidence."

"Of what?" I asked.

Before Lucinda could answer, my mother responded, "That's what we're about to find out. We've got to see if any of the other pieces from those shelves were dated the same time as Sharon's piece. Then we'll know who was working here at the time and what they might know about Sharon. Or if something happened four years ago and that's why Sharon quit."

I sounded as baffled as I looked. "Huh? I thought most of those people were . . . well, you know, deceased."

"They're not all dead. Like I told you before, people leave clubs for all sorts of reasons. You just need to figure out Sharon's. Anyway, we've got work to do. Start with those smaller bowls Lucinda put on the side counter. Meanwhile, she and I will work together on the ones we put by the big kiln."

By the time I knew what was happening, the evening had disappeared and, with it, my nice swim back home. Instead, I had to listen to my mother and Lucinda play "Did you know that person?" as we studied the dates under each of the pottery pieces.

Most of the jars, bowls, and assorted objets d'art were made within the past two years, but there were three pieces dated from the time Sharon's bowl was formed. The first was some sort of wall sconce made by Henrietta Arnold. Lucinda turned to my mother and sighed. "Poor woman. Passed away last year. Only ninety-three. Emphysema."

"She lived a good life. Now put that thing down and let's have a look at the last two pieces Phee found."

One was a lovely vase, bisque. With the right glaze, it would look nice in any kitchen or dining area. Unfortunately, the only notation carved into the clay was the date. Not so much as an initial or even a smiley face.

"That leaves this monstrosity," my mother continued. "It's either a very small platter or a large ashtray. It's almost as obnoxious as that greenware urn we wrestled off the back shelf. That thing must have been here for a century. The plastic was even brittle. So, getting back to this piece, what do you think, Lucinda? Platter or ashtray?"

"Platter, I believe. An ashtray would be bound to have those little indents and—"

"Good God! Does it really matter?" I was one step away from insanity. "What does it say on the bottom? Read the bottom."

My mother turned the item over and read the name. I was sure I heard it right the first time but had her read it again.

"Mario Aquilino."

Chapter 22

"So, let me get this straight," Marshall said the next morning as he tossed a wadded piece of paper in the trash. "You helped your mother and Lucinda at the clay club last night and found two pieces of pottery that proved Sharon Smyth and Mario Aquilino had been members of that club four years ago."

Nate, who was standing a few feet away by the copier, looked up. "Wasn't that the guy from the Lillian who was seen leaving her apartment at an indecent hour a few weeks ago? It's in my notes. God knows, every little thing is in my notes. I can tell you who uses sugar and who uses the blue packets or the pink packets. Maybe I should have another chat with him."

"Um, don't!" I waved a hand in front of my face and, for an instant, he and Marshall gave me blank looks. "I don't think that's such a great idea. I mean, those residents are already freaked out. I was going to speak with Mario Aquilino about the incident that took place in his apartment a few weeks ago. The wall paintings? Remember? Around the time of the petty pilfering? Then Sharon Smyth got murdered and everything changed."

Nate raised an eyebrow and gave Marshall a semi-nod.

"Phee may be right. Last thing we need is to get the residents riled again."

He stepped away from the copier and walked toward me. "Since you're already familiar with the Lillian, it might not be such a bad idea if you were to have that conversation with this Aquilino fellow. Find out what he knew about Sharon Smyth."

"You mean, find out if he might have had a motive for killing her?"

"Not in so many words, but yeah. And you can't be clumsy about it, kiddo."

"Clumsy?"

"You know what I'm saying. You can't simply ask him. You've got to eke it out of him like you would with a five-year-old who was snitching cookies."

"Both of you are going to owe me big time, you know."

Nate laughed and gave Marshall a poke on the arm. "Can't be any worse than Rolo Barnes. Phee doesn't cook."

I was aghast. Or at least pretended to be. "Hey! I've been known to work my way around the microwave, and don't just stand there, Marshall, help me out."

"She, uh, I mean—"

"Never mind. I'll call Mario Aquilino and see if he would be willing to meet with me this week. And by the way, hasn't the sheriff's department come up with anything yet? DNA? Fingerprints?"

The men shook their heads in tandem and all they said was, "They're sifting through evidence."

My mother was right. I pictured the evidence file bulging at the seams without one solid theory in place.

"Hey, don't look so dejected," Nate said. "Forgot to tell you. I got a call a little while ago from a Gila County deputy sheriff. Seems our own sheriff's department was quite convincing regarding those coordinates you and your aunt tracked down."

"Really?" I was astonished.

"Now, don't go getting yourself all excited about this, because it's a long shot. A really long shot. Empty water bottle or not from the Lillian, it wasn't as if any crimes were committed in the high desert. Still, the deputy said he and his partner were going to have a look-see. I faxed him a copy of Quentin's John Hancock from that jar, squiggly lines and all."

"Promise you'll let me know the minute you hear anything."

"*I'll* let you know," Augusta shouted from across the room. "The call's got to come in here first."

Marshall tried not to laugh. "We can't win. If this was the sheriff's department, I would say we deputize both of them and get it over with."

When the men had left the room, Augusta offered to call Mario Aquilino and set up an appointment for me.

"I can make it sound as official as you'd like," she said.

"Thanks, but I don't want it to scare him off. If he thinks it's official business, he might shut down and refuse to say a word. I'd better call him myself and come up with something."

Twenty minutes later I got up the nerve to call the man. I told him I was a friend of Gertie and Trudy and went on to explain how they contacted me regarding the room thefts and the other improprieties. Then I asked if he would be willing to chat with me for a few minutes sometime next week.

"Make it this afternoon. I'm in my eighties. I could be dead by the end of the week."

He agreed to meet me in the lobby at five forty-five. Enough time for him to finish dinner and more than ample time for me to get to the Lillian from work. Other than my brief conversation with Mr. Aquilino, it was a pretty uneventful day.

That was, until Kimberlynn Warren called me at a little past three.

"Miss Kimball? I hope I'm not interrupting anything, but I wanted to get back to you regarding those petty thefts. The Lillian may have a murder on its hands, but at least some of the pilfering can be explained. Not that I'm equating both of them, I'm just saying—"

"I understand. It's all right. So, what can you tell me?"

"After the sheriff's department and your office interviewed the residents, two of them came to see me. Apparently my staff wasn't as discreet as I would have liked and that's a matter I have to deal with. Nonetheless, some staff members apparently spoke with residents regarding the disappearance of those little items. That's what prompted Clive Monroe and Emily Outstrader to speak with me."

I tried to remember what items had been removed from their residences but couldn't remember if it was tuna, olives, yarn, or something else.

"Yes, um, go on."

"Mr. Monroe wanted me to know he found his Elks Club pin. Apparently it was still on the lapel of his sports jacket. He was positive he had returned it to his top dresser drawer, but when he went to take out his jacket, he saw the pin on the lapel. And as far as his tissues go, the box was just about empty and he thinks he might have tossed it out."

"That's one mystery solved," I said.

"Emily Outstrader's missing tuna is the other one. She had forgotten she placed those two cans into the collection box for the food pantry. When she remembered, she was totally embarrassed. Especially since she made it a point to let everyone know about the would-be theft."

"Yeah, I can see how that would be embarrassing."

"Anyway, if I hear of anything else, I'll be sure to let you know. I seriously doubt we'll see much more of that sort of thing."

"Oh?"

"We've added hallway security and locker checks for our employees."

"Is that legal?"

"Certainly. Security is never an issue and since the lockers belong to the Lillian, they're not considered personal property. I truly don't believe the staff is responsible for those missing items, but one never knows."

I thanked her and told her I appreciated her call. Then I immediately picked up the phone and called Gertie. No answer. Same for Trudy. I figured I'd buzz them once I got to the Lillian later in the day.

Some of those thefts were really quite inconsequential, if they were thefts at all. Whoever bought the Snickers bars probably ate one and forgot about it. And as for the missing pen and paper clips, that wasn't theft, it was a fact of life. Heck, I could start out with half a dozen pens and a zillion paper clips in my desk and wind up with one bent clip and no idea where the pens had gotten off to. Sometimes I could find three or four pens in my bag and other times I was lucky if I found a half-chewed pencil.

As for the five dollars . . . well, that might not have been stolen, either. People had been known to spend money without thinking and then open their wallet or purse only to find the twenty dollars they thought they had was gone. Maybe that was the case with Norma O'Neil.

It still didn't explain the missing purple ball of yarn or the jar of olives, but I half expected those items to turn up. The yarn probably rolled under a dresser and as far as those olives . . . well, maybe Warren Bellis stashed them with his toiletries or something. People had been known to do that sort of thing.

What really concerned me wasn't so much the missing items but the rifling through dresser drawers. Gertie and Trudy said it happened to them and again to someone else. Not underwear, a sock drawer. What kind of person did that sort of thing? And why on earth would someone go to the trouble of reversing Mr. Aquilino's paintings? Was there a more sinister motive in mind? Like making the tenants so uncomfortable they'd leave? And if that wasn't working, would they take it one step further and commit murder?

It was a struggle to stop concocting scenarios and focus on the monthly billing. Last thing I needed was to make a mistake. Especially one where money was involved. I pushed all thoughts of the Lillian to the back of my mind, took a deep breath, and pulled up the accounts. It was almost five when I finished. I rapped on the door to Marshall's office and poked my head in.

"I've got to get a move-on. Mario Aquilino asked me to meet with him right now. Said he's old and might be dead if I wait too long."

"Hmmph, I think I'm going to start using that line. So, I guess we'll have to hold off on seeing each other until to-morrow night."

"Looks that way. I'll call you later."

"Sounds good. Hey, be careful, huh?"

"I'm only going to the Lillian."

"It's still a crime scene, and just because that guy is old, doesn't mean he isn't dangerous."

"Don't those residence hotels conduct background checks on their tenants?"

"Cursory at best. Like arrest records, outstanding war-rants, and credit scores. They haven't come up with an 'unstable person' check, to the best of my knowledge. So again, be careful."

"Watch it—you're sounding like my mother."

Marshall shot me a dirty look as I winked and left the building.

Chapter 23

Walking into the Lillian at exactly five forty-five, I witnessed the lengthy exodus from the dining room. The lobby was teeming with people waiting in line for the elevators, and the ground floor corridors reminded me of "passing time" at my old high school. Loud voices and the occasional foul words. The only thing missing was the slamming of locker doors.

Mario Aquilino must have spied me the minute I walked through the main door. I could hear his voice in the crowd but wasn't sure what he looked like. I stood still, my back to the fountain, and waited. Like the parting of the Red Sea, the people in front of the elevators stepped aside so he could make his way toward me, one foot at a time behind a large walker. My eyes were fixed on the yellow tennis balls that he had placed on the walker's legs. Probably for traction.

The walker looked like it weighed more than he did. The man appeared slight and fragile, with wisps of graying hair and a thin white moustache. He plodded his way past the crowd and motioned for me to take a seat near the fountain.

"You must be the spinster sisters' friend. I think they went up to their apartments already."

"Nice to meet you. I'm Phee Kimball. I won't take up

much of your time, but I promised Gertie and Trudy I'd look into some of the thefts and unusual things the residents have noticed."

"You can say it out loud. The intrusion into our privacy. What's next? A video camera in our showers?"

"Um, it may turn out to be easily explained. Like maybe an unscrupulous worker or a resident who's—"

"A whack job?"

"Well, that's getting to the point."

The crowd in front of the elevators had dwindled down considerably. Unlike the last time I was in the building, the elevators seemed to be working flawlessly. Mario Aquilino watched as the elevator door closed on the last six or seven people.

"What kind of nut job goes into someone's apartment and messes with their paintings?"

I shrugged. "Has anything turned up missing?"

"No. And believe me when I tell you, I checked everything. Look, you need to see for yourself. Follow me up to my place and I'll show you those paintings."

"Oh, er, no need to do that. I believe you."

"Seeing is believing. You need to see what they did."

It didn't take a rocket scientist to understand the concept of two paintings being switched on a wall, and the last thing I wanted to do was go into some strange man's apartment. Granted, he was as frail as they come, but still, I'd learned never to underestimate anyone.

"That's okay. Really it is."

"No, it's not. You've got to take a look."

Then he pushed his head back and raised his brows. "Oh, don't tell me you're one of those women who refuse to be seen going into a man's apartment. What the hell can I do at my age?"

"Um, uh, it's not that, it's just—"

"You can prop open the bloody door if that makes you feel any better. Come on. I'm not getting any younger sitting here."

No red flags or alarms were going off in my head. He was right. I was being silly.

"All right, but only for a few minutes."

It took at least five of those minutes for him to make it to the elevator. As I walked in front of the fountain, the blondes, Tanya and Tina, were staring into their computer screens. They didn't seem to notice me.

One push of the button and the elevator opened. When we got off on the third floor, we only had to walk a few steps. Mario Aquilino's apartment was adjacent to the lift. He unlocked the door and stepped inside.

"You can grab that folding chair and use it to prop open the door."

I was beginning to feel more than a little foolish, but I did as he said.

One look at his apartment and my mouth dropped open. I'd never seen such an immaculate place. And that included my mother's house. From the carefully placed cushions on his couch to a kitchen that was practically beaming, I made a note to go home and run the vacuum cleaner, no matter what time it was.

"This is the living room–kitchen combo. My bedroom's off to the left and the bathroom is next to it. Those paintings are on that wall between the living room and my bedroom."

Other than a large framed picture of the Southwest desert that hung directly over his couch, the two paintings in question were the only other ones in that room. They were small paintings, each smaller than an eight-by-eleven piece of paper. I walked over and took a close look. They were framed watercolors of birds—a roadrunner and a quail. Everything looked normal to me.

"I switched them back. It was unnerving."

"Because someone had done this," I said.

"Because the damn birds were facing the wrong direction. It's jarring to have two birds facing away from each other. Someone was trying to upset me and they did."

Another glance at his apartment and I knew exactly what he meant. Mario Aquilino was beyond being a perfectionist. Borderline obsessive-compulsive when it came to space and order. I took a quick breath and nodded. "Nothing else was disturbed?"

"Only the paintings."

I took another look. The wall on which the paintings were hung had an air-conditioning vent on the top near the ceiling. Not so much as a single cobweb. The smoke alarm was on the opposite wall across from the kitchen area. *A place for everything and everything in its place.* I looked again and remembered something. Something about Arizona air-conditioning.

"Thank you, Mr. Aquilino. This gives me a good idea about what we're dealing with. I promise I'll get back to you as soon as I have some information."

Then I broached the topic I was really interested in, Sharon Smyth. "Ordinarily, these kinds of things are dealt with by the management in conjunction with the authorities, but I imagine, given that awful murder, everyone is focused on finding the killer."

Not that I thought the man could so much as swat a fly without getting winded, but I studied his reaction. No sign of discomfort whatsoever.

I pressed on. "Did you know her well?"

"Not that well. I thought she was one of the more normal ones. Until she bought that Quentin Dussler clay jar. You would've thought it was made of gold or something the way she carried on. First, she made a big deal telling everyone about it, then she wondered why it got stolen. Hells bells. A Quentin Dussler jar. She hated the guy. Go figure."

"Wait a second. She knew him?"

"Unfortunately, yes. He made her life miserable a few years ago when she was in the clay club. Berating her, criticizing her work. She was in a damn club for crying out loud, not medical school."

"So you knew her from the clay club?"

"Yes, along with the thirty or forty other members. I used to be in that club, too, but molding clay when you've got arthritis is impossible. I had to give it up. Sharon had a real talent for it, in spite of what Quentin Dussler used to say."

I brushed a strand of hair from my brow. "You don't suppose . . . ?"

"That she killed him?"

"I wasn't going to phrase it like that."

Mario lifted his walker and gave it a thud. "How many ways can you phrase it? Killed? Offed? Murdered? Wasted? Polished off? And no, I don't think she did it."

"How can you be sure?"

"I can't."

I decided not to press it. "Uh, about that clay club . . . my mother and one of her friends joined recently. In fact, they roped me into going over there last night to sift through all the unclaimed pottery pieces and get them ready to donate to charity. I guess that's something they do a few times a year."

"Last night? You went last night?"

I swore the man almost looked stunned. "Usually they do the clean-outs in July and October. Must be they changed the schedule or the racks were getting overloaded. Damn snowbirds with their unfinished stuff. Clogs up space for everyone else."

"Especially that back closet," I said. "I don't think you would've appreciated seeing it. Or smelling it, for that matter. I guess that's what happens when someone wraps plastic on the wet clay and sets it in there."

"They cleaned out the back closet, too? All of it?"

"Um, yeah. Why? You've been in the club. Weren't they supposed to?"

Mario scratched the back of his neck with such force I thought his skin would peel off. "Only if the pieces didn't have WIP signs under the plastic."

"WIP?"

"Work in progress. It means leave it the hell alone."

Thinking back to last night, I remembered seeing some of those slips of paper. They had fallen out of the plastic and gotten tossed into the garbage.

I made some sort of weird grimace and swallowed. "I don't think the ladies knew what those slips of paper meant. All of the pieces were set out in the front room to be fired. I imagine they started today and will continue firing the greenware this week."

"Aargh. No one ever pays attention to anything."

"It wasn't intentional."

"Never is."

I was hoping to find a way to ask him what he was doing in Sharon Smyth's apartment that night (or day, depending upon how you looked at it), but there was no graceful way to slip it into the conversation. In fact, I wasn't even sure the man actually *was* in her apartment. After all, I had heard it from Trudy and she heard it from "a very reliable source," whoever the heck that could be. I might as well have picked up that little morsel of information at the monthly Bagels 'N More brunch with the book club ladies.

Worst of all, Nate was counting on me to find out something. And he didn't want me to be clumsy about it, either.

Well, you can't have it both ways. "There's no tactful way to say this. Well, maybe there is, but—"

"Say it already. I'm not getting any younger standing here and gabbing."

"Were you and Sharon Smyth involved romantically?"

Mario's jaw dropped. "It's that crazy Yolanda from the fourth floor, isn't it? Old bitty can't keep her yap shut about anything. Maybe people show up at other people's doors when they run out of laxative or need a damn pain pill."

"So you and Sharon weren't involved?"

"For your information, Miss Kimball, I stopped swapping saliva with women when I moved into this place. Last thing I needed was to have a heart attack. Does that answer your question?"

I stood there, momentarily dazed before I could mutter a word. Finally, I said something coherent. "Well, er, um, thanks again for meeting with me. I'll be sure to keep you posted."

I returned the folding chair to the corner of his living room and closed the door behind me. I didn't know who was more embarrassed, Mario Aquilino or me. And as far as my boss was concerned, I planned on telling him I handled the matter with a certain amount of finesse. My next stop was the reception desk. I had one more issue to deal with.

Tanya and Tina were conversing with each other as I exited the elevator. I walked over and leaned against the desk. "Hi! I'm hoping you can help me out. Can you tell me where the house manager resides?"

Tanya looked up. "His apartment is on the ground floor, immediately to the right of the elevators, but if someone needs service, they're supposed to fill out a form or contact us if it's an emergency."

"Thanks. I'll go let them know."

I headed to the elevator and took it one floor up. Then I used the stairwell to get back to the ground floor. The house manager's residence was easy to spot. The sign on his door could be read from a thirty-foot distance. MICHAEL MELROY, HOUSE MANAGER. I knocked and waited.

"Mr. Melroy?" I asked when he opened the door. "I need a minute of your time."

He smiled and shook his head. "You can't possibly be a resident here. So, whose daughter are you?"

Tiny Mike was enormous. Tall. Wide. Muscular. I figured he had worked years in construction.

"Actually, I'm here on behalf of an acquaintance of mine. Mario Aquilino."

"Hmm, I was in his place not too long ago. Everything should be fine."

"Um, yeah, that's just the thing." I leaned an elbow against his door frame. "Did you happen to change the filter in his air-conditioning unit?"

"As a matter of fact, I did. I try to do that sort of thing when the residents are in the dining room or attending a major function. Why? Is he having trouble with the AC? He didn't say anything."

"No, not the AC, but the paintings under the unit were disturbed. No damage, but put in the wrong place. You wouldn't happen to know anything about that, would you?"

"Oh crap. Of all things. I should've left a work tag on his door. I ran out of them when I got to his floor and didn't feel like going back to get them."

"Work tag?"

"When I enter a residence to do maintenance, I leave a

tag on the door to let the tenant know I was there. I should've realized Mario would know someone was in there. Even if everything was completely intact. That guy has some sort of radar. I swear, he can tell the minute he walks in the place. Don't ask me how."

"So something did happen?"

"I accidentally bumped into the wall with my ladder and the two paintings fell. I checked them over carefully and nothing was broken. I even made sure to wipe them with a cloth so there wouldn't be any fingerprints. Then I put them back. Even. Perfectly even."

"But you didn't put them back in the right order. The birds face each other."

"Oh brother. Is he pitching a fit up there?"

"He was worried someone with not such good intentions entered his residence."

"Oh holy crap! I'd better speak to him. I'm surprised he didn't report it to the management."

"Um, from what I hear, the residents are kind of wary reporting anything to the management."

"Yeah, I can't explain it either, but there's a weird vibe going on."

Vibe. I hadn't heard that word in years. "Anyway, you'll talk to him, right?"

"I'll buzz his place right now. Hey, you don't suppose he'll complain to the management about me, do you? I'd hate to get in trouble over this."

"I kind of doubt it. He seems like a nice guy. I think he'll be relieved it was you who entered his apartment and not some 'whack job.'"

"Yeah, that sounds like him. I appreciate you letting me know. Thanks, Miss . . . ?"

"Oh. Kimball. Phee Kimball. And you're welcome."

I went back up the stairs and down in the elevator in case the blondes got suspicious. The L'Oréal sisters, as Taylor called them, were still fast at work on their computers.

"Have a nice day," I shouted, but neither of them bothered to look up.

Chapter 24

"Mario Aquilino wasn't dangerous." I phoned Marshall later that evening. "He was cranky and ornery but harmless. Oh, and here's the best news of all. I solved the mystery of his switched paintings."

I went on to tell Marshall about the entire evening, including Mario's take on Sharon Smyth and my brief conversation with Mike Melroy (aka Tiny Mike), the house manager. I was about to mention the odd comment the guy made about the vibe at the Lillian when Marshall beat me to it.

"I can't put my finger on it, but there's kind of an unsettled feeling at that place. And I'm not talking about the murder. When Nate and I interviewed the residents, most of them were feeling as if something had changed, or was about to change, but they couldn't quite explain."

"Yeah, I know. Gertie and Trudy said the same thing. Oh geez, I probably should call them and let them know about Mario's paintings. That's one less thing they have to worry about."

We ended the call, finalizing our plans for tomorrow night—trying out the new Greek restaurant in Surprise and maybe a moonlight swim back here. I immediately dialed

Gertie as soon as I said good night to Marshall. She sounded more annoyed than relieved.

"So that's all it was? Tiny Mike forgot to leave a work tag on the door? He should know better. And of all the apartments here, it had to be Mario Aquilino's. Do you have any idea how fastidious that man is?"

"Um, yes."

"Tanya and Tina from the front desk posted a letter on all the residents' doors a little while ago. It was regarding those thefts that have been going on. Kimberlynn Warren wrote it herself. Very official. She said some of those thefts weren't thefts and that the items have been located. Not all of them, but most. I suppose, from now on, no one will believe us about anything. They'll think we're just a bunch of old dolts."

"I wouldn't say that. There's still the matter of someone going through people's drawers and, of course, the murder. I imagine that will be an ongoing investigation for a while. Anyway, will you please let your sister know I called?"

"She's sitting three feet away from me, poking my arm. It would be hard not to let her know you called."

In the background Trudy said, "Hurry up, *NCIS* is coming on."

Gertie thanked me for calling and I told her I'd keep in touch. Finally, I could kick back and turn on the TV, too. No sooner did I grab a tangerine from the fridge and start to peel it when the phone rang. Now who? I had been with my mother and Lucinda yesterday, so it couldn't possibly be her. *Hopefully.* I glanced at the caller ID and lifted the receiver. It was my aunt Ina.

I hadn't spoken to her since our escapade in the high desert last Sunday. Perhaps she was calling to find out how the investigation was going.

"Phee! Louis remembered something about Quentin

Dussler and thought you should know. It was a few years ago. Before Louis and I met. Louis was still working for that cruise line. Bless my Louis, he has the memory of an elephant. I'll get right to the point. A last-minute traveler came on from Zeebrugge to Fort Lauderdale. A special boat had to take him to the ship because cruise lines don't dock in Belgium. The big transatlantic ports are Amsterdam and Copenhagen. Anyway, the guy was Quentin Dussler. For some reason, he decided to take a transatlantic voyage back to the States instead of flying. And he wouldn't take a plane to one of the ports."

"All of a sudden Louis remembered that?"

"Not all of a sudden. He was taking out the recycling and noticed the headline about Quentin's murder. That'll serve him for letting the newspapers pile up without reading them. But you know how musicians are, their minds are always elsewhere. Well, the paper had an old photo of Quentin and Louis recognized him."

"Louis came across thousands of passengers. Why on earth would he remember Quentin Dussler?"

"I asked him the same thing. Seems your uncle was at the bursar's office waiting to make a withdrawal from his account. You know what a gambler he was. Anyhow, this Quentin Dussler arrived and insisted the bursar stop everything and get him a safe deposit box. And not just any box. One reserved for passengers whose contents are so valuable they require additional security."

"And Louis remembered all of this?"

"It's hard to forget when you've got an itch to gamble and are forced to wait while some pompous buffoon—your uncle's words, not mine—stands between you and the millions you're about to win."

"I see. So, uh, does Louis have any idea what Quentin Dussler might have been guarding?"

"It wasn't gambling money. Louis never saw him in the casino. And believe me, your uncle would have noticed."

"Was that the only time he saw him? At the bursar's office?"

"Yes. And it begs the question. What was Quentin Dussler securing?"

I wanted to tell her that some people traveled with lots of jewelry. Expensive jewelry. But from what little I knew about this highly temperamental artist, I seriously doubted he was one of them.

"Hmm, that's fascinating," I said. "How many years ago was it?"

"Hold on."

My aunt screamed for Louis and Louis screamed back, "Five!"

"Thanks, Aunt Ina."

"Tell me. Do you think this Quentin stole some priceless piece of art and didn't want to risk taking it on a plane?"

That thought had crossed my mind, too. And I was one step ahead. What if he *did* steal something and the real owner tracked him down and killed him? It was as good a motive as any.

Before I could respond, my aunt went on. "Have the sheriff's deputies checked out those coordinates yet? I didn't figure as much since I hadn't heard from you."

"No, not yet, but they will. Nate managed to convince our county sheriff's department and they said Gila County was cooperating. I don't know what they expect to find, though."

"Let me know. Oh, have you seen that hideous piece of artwork your mother made? That god-awful bowl or whatever it is with the dog's picture on it? She's planning on entering it in the Creations in Clay contest. Heaven help us all!"

"When is that thing, again?"

"June thirtieth. And if I were you, I'd mark it on my calendar if you haven't done so already. Your mother's becoming quite obsessive about that show."

I rubbed my temples with my free hand. "I won't forget. And thanks again for letting me know about Quentin."

My iPad was resting on the coffee table in front of me. I flipped the cover and went into Safari search under "art thefts." In a matter of seconds, I pulled up the National Stolen Art File, as well as international listings of stolen art. Nothing in that time frame for Belgium. But that didn't mean Quentin couldn't have been in a neighboring country. This was massive. Massive enough for an entire FBI department. Way out of my league. Not that I had a league. But I knew someone who did.

Marshall must have been sitting on top of his phone because he answered it immediately. "Is everything okay?"

"Everything's fine."

I quickly told him about my conversation with Aunt Ina and Louis's recollection of Quentin Dussler boarding that ship and insisting on a highly secured valuables safe. I was becoming more and more animated.

"It's worth a shot, isn't it? Rolo Barnes could track down that stuff in a matter of hours."

"And how fast can you track down the next sophisticated piece of kitchen gadgetry he absolutely has to have?"

"I'll split the bill if it comes to that. So, please?"

"Relax. I'll give Nate a heads-up. Seven thirty still good for you tomorrow?"

"Wouldn't miss it."

I sank back into the couch and stretched. Finally, I could

look forward to an evening with Marshall that wouldn't be interrupted.

Our seven-thirty dinner date started out wonderfully the next night but suddenly went awry. I thought I'd seen enough of the clay club room to last me well into the next century, but apparently, I was wrong. We had barely finished our salads at Zorba's New Greek Cuisine when Marshall got a text from Nate.

"Good God, no!" were the only words he muttered as the phone was thrust into my hand.

I stared at the message. "I can't believe it. A possible break-in at the clay club room and they want you guys to get over there?"

"That's what happens when two or more agencies work a case together. They want reps from all parties. Guess what's next is up to you. I can take you home and drive to Sun City West or you can be part of the fun. If we get out at a reasonable hour, there may still be a burger joint open."

The words left my mouth immediately. "Clay club and burgers it is."

Marshall motioned for our waiter, paid the guy in cash for our salads, and raced out of there with me at the other end of his arm.

"Why would anyone want to break into the clay club?" he kept muttering as his foot got heavier on the gas pedal. We were only five or six miles from the Bell Road turnoff to the complex and I couldn't figure it out either. None of it made sense.

"One thing is for sure. It's certainly not to steal my mother's creation. Or Lucinda's, for that matter. Unless, of course, it was to abscond with them and spare everyone from seeing them."

"They can't be that horrible."

I laughed so hard I nearly choked. "You'll see for yourself. Unless they got destroyed, those pieces were supposed to go into the kiln yesterday for their first firing."

Two Maricopa County sheriff's cars were blocking the main entrance to the recreation center, their blue and red lights flashing. Marshall pulled up behind them, leaving enough space to pull out in the unlikely event another vehicle decided to park behind us. Nate's car was clearly visible off to the left under one of the large parking lot lights.

With the exception of some animated voices at the end of the corridor by the club room, the recreation center complex was absolutely still.

"How did they know there was a break-in?" I asked as we got closer to the room. "It's a Saturday night and there's no night custodian on duty."

"Good question. We're about to find out."

Nate spied us from where he was standing, in front of the large glass window that had been shattered. "Another fun-filled evening in Sun City West. Watch you don't step on the glass. They've got a maintenance crew coming in to clean up as soon as we're done."

A few feet away was a deputy sheriff taking photos.

"Alarm system go off?" Marshall asked the officer.

"There is no alarm system," was the deputy's response. "Someone phoned the posse station and reported it."

I immediately charged toward my boss. "Who? Did they say who? Did they track the call?"

"Whoa! Good to see you, too, kiddo. A man and his wife had left the aquatics building and were walking through the club area courtyard because, according to him, 'the wife just had to show me some enameling display.' That's when they saw the broken glass in front of the clay club room and called the posse. Needless to say, a posse volunteer drove over to check it out, notified maintenance, and, well, you can see the rest."

"The rest" consisted of three more deputies scanning the room for evidence. I walked past Nate and looked inside. Nothing appeared to be disturbed. No broken pieces. No signs of disarray. The sign-in sheets by the door were still on the counter and the binders where they kept the membership information were still shelved. A cooling rack for the recently fired pieces stood off to the right of the kilns. I cringed. The horrible Streetman platter was intact. Same for Lucinda's jar.

"My mother will sleep easy once she hears about this. Her artwork remains untouched." *Unless someone accidentally trips and falls near those bisque pieces. Bite my tongue.*

"This beats the heck out of me," one of the deputies shouted. "Sheer vandalism."

I walked over to where he was standing. "Were any other club windows smashed? The porcelain painters? The copper enameling? The basket weaving?"

"This was the only club room, ma'am," he said.

"Ma'am." I absolutely abhor that word. It makes me feel as if I'm eighty instead of in my forties. I felt like opening my mouth and saying something but instead I walked quietly to the back room, where Lucinda, my mom, and I had cleaned out that closet. I switched on the light and glanced at the empty shelves. Everything was as we had left it. Then I walked to the counter area where we had placed the greenware for firing.

Some of the pieces, like my mother's, had been fired already, but the others were still wrapped in plastic, waiting for someone to put them in the kiln. I took a cursory glance at the items and realized something wasn't quite right. The large urn-like bowl I had moved from the closet was no longer there. And it wasn't sitting alongside the bisque pieces.

Watching my step, I walked to the counter. That was when I heard a soft crunch underneath my foot. Thank God I was wearing Skechers with decent treads. It was glass. Broken glass. Small pieces. Not enough to be visible, even with the overhead light on.

"I think I found out why someone smashed that window."

Everyone stopped talking at once and moved toward me. I was beginning to feel more than self-conscious. "I was here the other night," *unfortunately,* "with my mother and we were sorting clay greenware for firing. One of those pieces is missing. A large bowl that sort of resembles an urn. I think whoever broke that window came here to get that bowl."

"That makes absolutely no sense," the deputy said. "Those things are a dime a dozen. And you said yourself it was still greenware. Doesn't that mean it's still a piece of molded clay?"

"It does. But I think there's more to it. I wish I knew what."

Chapter 25

"Are they going to be dusting for fingerprints?" I asked Nate and Marshall as the three of us left the "crime scene" to the deputies.

Nate shook his head. "Probably not. Too many prints in the room and a minor theft. They'll notify the club president, maintenance will clean up, and that's that."

I couldn't believe what I was hearing. "But, but . . . what if the thief is the murderer?"

Marshall gave my arm a slight squeeze. "According to the deputies, these kinds of smash and grab crimes are fairly common. And they're not about to waste time and resources tracking down an unfinished clay bowl."

"But, but—"

"Let it go, Phee," Nate said. "There are other leads that may be more productive as far as the murders go."

We had crossed into the parking lot and our voices seemed to echo in the semidarkness.

Nate took a step toward Marshall and me and spoke softly. "Quentin's bank records, his business dealings, and his background. It's extensive. And thanks to your aunt Ina, this new piece of information about the guy's transatlantic trip. Hey, that reminds me, weren't you going to speak with that Aquilino guy about the other murder?"

"I did. Last night. He said he knew Sharon from the clay club and that's pretty much the extent of it. Although, I did get the idea he was well-enough acquainted with her to borrow assorted digestive aids and pain meds from time to time."

Even in the quasi-darkness I saw Nate grimace. "Ugh. No need to go there."

It was nearly eleven by the time Marshall and I got back into the car. Both of us were wired and exhausted. A strange combination. And neither of us felt like eating a meal.

"I've got ice cream in the freezer. Neapolitan. You can scoop out all three flavors or dive into the chocolate like you usually do," I said.

"This is scary. You're really getting to know my bad habits."

I kicked off my shoes as soon as I entered the house and heard them thud against the wall before landing on the shoe mat. Marshall glanced down as he did the same, only his shoes landed directly on the mat. "Got a broom handy? Looks like we tracked in some pieces of glass."

Sure enough, small shards of glass were visible on the black rubber mat. I imagined they'd gotten trapped in the treads of our shoes and had fallen out when the shoes bumped against the wall. Normally I didn't worry about tracking in dirt. Not that I was a total house slob, but I wasn't fanatical like my mother, or worse yet, like Mario Aquilino. But, in this case, I certainly didn't need Marshall or me to wind up cutting the soles of our feet.

"You get the ice cream out of the freezer and let it warm up for a bit while I grab a dustpan and brush," I said.

"Sure thing."

Marshall's voice trailed off as I opened the closet by the front door and removed a small dustpan and brush from its hook. Bending down, I shook each shoe, let the remaining glass pieces drop, and swept them into the dustpan. It was surprising how many slivers of glass we had tracked in.

"You may want to vacuum your car mats," I said as I continued sweeping.

A small pebble-like piece of glass rolled slightly and I gave it another brush. It kept getting caught up in the bristles, so I grabbed it and was about to toss it in the dustpan when I realized it was partially covered in clay. My fingers accidentally slid across it, but, oddly enough, I didn't cut myself. I walked it over to the light above the kitchen sink. Marshall was standing a few feet away.

"Would you look at this for a moment? It was on the bottom of one of the shoes. I don't think it's glass."

By now, most of the clay had fallen off the shard and I could see I was holding a small, perfectly shaped gem.

"Don't drop it." I placed it in Marshall's hand. "What do you think?"

"Unless window manufacturing has changed over the years, we're not looking at a piece of broken glass."

"A diamond?"

He shrugged. "Maybe. Or maybe some sort of imitation, but, whatever it is, it's been faceted. Take a good look. It's all set to be mounted in a ring."

"My God. That thing had clay on it. It came off on my fingers when I picked the piece up. Real or fake, it must have been buried in that greenware bowl. That's why someone broke in and stole it. I mean, who in their right mind would smash into the clay club and take off with an unfinished piece of pottery?"

"Someone who knew exactly what they were looking for."

"But why now? Why all of a sudden?"

Then it dawned on me. The night before, I had mentioned cleaning out the clay room when I spoke with Mario Aquilino. And I was more than certain he seemed a bit alarmed. Then again, his reaction might have been a normal one, given his personality quirks. And besides, the guy was barely ambulatory. Not likely he'd manage to drive to the clay club, smash the glass picture window, climb in, and secure that piece of greenware.

Marshall reached for a coffee mug and set the small stone in it. "Didn't you say something about slips of paper for pieces that shouldn't be put in the kiln?"

"Uh-huh. 'Works in progress.' Why?"

"If what we've got here is a real diamond and not a zircon or whatever those synthetic diamonds are, and it was carefully hidden in the molded clay, it would be destroyed the minute that piece got fired. I read that in a scientific journal a while back. The diamond would vaporize. So much for it being harder than all the other gems."

He picked up the mug and stared into it. "Want to know what I'm thinking? That clay bowl was harboring more than one gemstone. And it was the perfect hiding place. Tucked back on a shelf in a musty old closet, wrapped in plastic with a note that virtually protected it from being shoved into a kiln. If I were hiding diamonds or other gems, that would be the perfect place."

"Yeah. Perfect. Until my mother and Lucinda decided to help with the spring clean-out."

"Listen, I know you're probably exhausted and the ice cream's melted by now, but I need to give Nate a call. We've got to go back to the clay room and see if any other gems wound up on the floor. Or worse yet, in some garbage can the maintenance guys used."

"I'm going to take a quick look at the mat and the dustpan. I didn't dump the dustpan yet. Maybe we tracked in more gems."

I didn't find anything else by the door or in the treads of our shoes. We even took a flashlight to look at the car mats but didn't turn up anything. Still, one possible diamond was enough to send us, Nate, and two deputy sheriffs back to the clay room.

The maintenance men were finishing up when we arrived. A large sheet of plywood now covered the open window. Thankfully, the deputies had gotten there in time to prevent the workers from dumping the small garbage cans into a dumpster out back. Diamonds or no diamonds, I made a vow never to go dumpster diving again, having suffered through an awful humiliation when I first came to Sun City West to help my mother track down an alleged book curse. In order to find a key piece of evidence, I wound up headfirst in a larger-than-life garbage bin.

In a matter of minutes, Nate and one of the deputies had spread a large piece of construction paper along one of the counters. The other deputy lifted the first of two garbage cans and dumped the contents on the cardboard. Thankfully, one of the supplies he had in his sheriff's van was a box of disposable gloves that we put to good use.

It was a slow and tedious process. At least the garbage was limited to shards of glass, paper products, and some empty coffee cups. Nothing that would cause any of us to gag. We weren't as fortunate with the second can. It must have been sitting in the clay room for a few days because it really smelled ripe. Sure enough, we discovered the remains of a banana, a few yogurt containers, and, my personal favorite, a half-eaten fiber bar.

While the men poured through the contents on the counter, I took Marshall's flashlight and went back to the closet, where that bowl had been resting comfortably until the day before. I stared at the racks as the light flickered. Bits of dried clay were still on the shelves. I looked around the room and spotted a small, empty wastepaper basket. Using the edge of my hand, I slid the clay particles into the basket and, like the men in the front room, dumped the contents on the small counter in back.

It took me less than a minute to unearth another possible gem.

"I've got one!" I screamed. "Not as big but the same thing."

One of the sheriff's deputies placed it in a small plastic bag and labeled it, along with the larger gem Marshall and I had turned over to them.

"My theory's beginning to add up, huh?" Marshall gave me a wink.

Nate, who was busy sifting through the glass debris, looked up. "Keep working."

I wondered if this was what it felt like panning for gold. At least we weren't on the ground with our feet in some shallow stream. Each of us scanned a particular area on the counter, taking our time to touch every little piece of dried clay we came across.

An hour later we unearthed the last of the treasures—a gem that was slightly larger than the one I had found on my shoe mat. Perfectly faceted, ready to be set.

"These could be worthless pieces of synthetic junk or the real deal," Nate said.

"We'll know soon enough," one of the deputies said. "Tomorrow's Sunday, but I'll put a call in for someone in our lab to take a look. With the right equipment, determining whether or not something's a diamond shouldn't be rocket science. Heck, a good jeweler could do that."

I started to giggle. "So could my aunt Ina, but let's stick to the county lab."

As we cleaned up the place and turned off the lights, Nate pounded on Marshall's shoulder. "Unless there are dead bodies strewn all over the floor, don't call me." Then he turned to me. "I don't suppose there's any way your mother or Lucinda would remember whose bowl that was?"

"They might. My mother was complaining about having to remove a large greenware urn from the closet. I'll give her a call tomorrow."

Nate was about to say something when I finished his thought. "Don't worry. I'm not going to breathe a word about the diamonds or whatever they are."

"I wasn't worried about that. I was more concerned she'd invite me to that clay club celebration. If she does, tell her I'm going to be out of town that weekend."

I quickly turned to Marshall in case he'd follow Nate's lead. "If I have to go, so do you."

Chapter 26

I awoke to the aroma of freshly brewed coffee. It was one of the nicest things about having Marshall at my place in the morning.

"I can't believe it's after ten." I sauntered into the kitchen and poured myself a cup. "What a night."

"Yeah, what a night. My head hit the pillow and that's the last thing I remembered before waking up. One of these nights we'll have to do this right."

I stepped behind him, leaned forward, and planted a kiss on his neck.

He grabbed my arm, pulled me closer, and responded in kind. "Hey, there's nothing I'd rather do than spend the rest of the day with you, but, Sunday or not, I've got a ton of work waiting for me and it can't wait until tomorrow. I've got to finalize reports on that fraud case and the Casa Grande abduction. I've been so busy with these two murders, I haven't been able to catch up."

"No problem. At least I can follow through on that clay urn. My mother or Lucinda might remember if there were any markings underneath it."

"Clever, huh? I mean, if those stones do turn out to be diamonds, who in their right mind would ever look in a musty old clay club closet?"

"Whoever made that piece did it a long time ago. The plastic was brittle and the clay had dried up. It must have been a former member. None of the active members would leave their artwork sitting around that long. Nope, that urn was made for one reason only—to hide something valuable. Oh my gosh! The diamond industry. Mary Melhorn said she thought Quentin's wife worked in the diamond industry when they were living in New York. We've got to find out if that's true. Because if it is . . ."

"Whoa. Slow down. Get the reins back on that horse of yours. First of all, the lab needs to make a determination. And we're not sure who made that urn. It could've been someone who had nothing to do with Quentin Dussler."

I shook my head. "Nah, I like my Dussler theory. What if his wife was really a diamond thief and, little by little, she amassed a fortune in gems? Not right away. Over the years, so it would be off the radar."

"Got news for you. Stealing diamonds is never off the radar. And help me get this straight. Which Dussler theory is that brain of yours working on? Because last night you practically hog-tied me to get in touch with Rolo Barnes. Art theft. After talking with your aunt, you were convinced Quentin was sneaking stolen art into the country. Look, let's take this one step at a time. We'll see what the lab says and you'll find out if your mom or Lucinda knows who signed that urn, deal?"

"It'll have to be."

Two coffees later, Marshall left for the office. At least it would be quiet on a Sunday. No one to interrupt him. The same couldn't have been said for my place because the minute he left, it seemed as if the phone wouldn't stop.

The first, and strangest of all, was my aunt Ina, but that shouldn't have surprised me.

"Phee! There are only three nail salons in the valley that

can do that iridescent holographic glitter coat and wait till you hear the cost. It's over four hundred dollars. My mind was so preoccupied with Louis's recollection about Quentin I completely forgot to tell you about this when we spoke on Friday."

"Um, hi, Aunt Ina. Are you calling to tell me you want your nails done that way?"

"Don't be ridiculous. I've never been a huge fan of glittery nails. And four hundred dollars . . . True, my Louis wouldn't bat an eyelash, but it got me thinking. What kind of bartender can make that much money? Especially out in the desert boondocks. Yet, there she was, fancy nails and all."

"Maybe she has a friend who did them. There are nail salons up north in Payson."

"Tsk. Tsk. None that know how to do that style. I got a listing of that city's salons and called them."

"Why are you so concerned about that lady's nails?"

"Because I can spot a fake when I see one and she had 'imposter' written all over her. I didn't want to say anything at the time because you had enough to worry about."

"Why would someone pretend to be a bartender? And if she was pretending, she did a really good job."

"I know. Now we have to figure out what else she was doing up there."

"I'm sure if there's any suspicious activity, the Gila County Sheriff's Office will find out. Nate said they're going to check into those coordinates."

"Good. And they have us to thank for pointing them in the right direction. Oh, was that a pun? Did I just make a pun? Usually Louis is the clever one."

It was a good thing we weren't on Facetime or she would have seen me grimace.

"Um, well, yeah."

I told my aunt the county lab would be testing the water

bottle, and I also informed her about the break-in at the clay club. I stopped when it came to the diamonds, or would-be diamonds, depending upon the outcome. Marshall was right. I needed to take things one step at a time.

"Maybe whoever killed Quentin Dussler was looking for something and didn't find it in his house. The next logical place would be the clay club room. Shall I write this all down for your boss?"

"Gee, uh, no. I think he's already on top of things."

The next interruption was a brief one—my friend Lyndy. Calling to see if I wanted to go for an evening swim. I said yes and we agreed to meet at the condo pool at eight. I was about to take a shower when the third call came in.

My mother sounded as if she was being choked. "The most horrible, horrible thing happened. Someone broke into the clay club room last night. I was going through my e-mails this morning when I saw the note from the club president. They smashed the window to get in."

"Hi, Mom! I was just going to call you. I know about the break-in. I was with Marshall when he got a text about it. We both went over there."

"You did? And you didn't tell me? Why didn't you call? What did they steal? The note wasn't too specific."

"They only took one item. Like I said, I was going to call to tell you—"

"I knew it. I knew it. Some miscreant simply *had* to have that platter of mine. That's the trouble with creating unique art. It's all one-of-a-kind and once someone sets their sights on it, there's no stopping them."

"They didn't steal your piece of artwork."

"Oh." The disappointment in her voice came through.

"Sorry, Mom. The only thing they took was that large

greenware urn or bowl thing we dragged out of the back closet."

"That grotesque thing? Who would want that?"

"Exactly. Nate and Marshall need to know. Sheriff's department too. That's why I was going to call you."

"How would I know who would want something that ugly? Besides, it hasn't even been fired yet. Which reminds me, when you saw my platter, had it been fired?"

"Yes, yes. You can relax. Lucinda too. So, tell me. Was that urn signed on the bottom? The two of you were scrutinizing everything. Was there a signature carved in it?"

"Hmm, offhand, I don't remember, but I'll call Lucinda and see if she does. She'll be happy to know her jar is still there."

"Great. If I don't answer, leave me a message. I'll be in and out."

I heard a faint yip in the background. "Streetman wants a snack. It's his munchy time. I've got to run."

Munchy time. Oh brother. "Fine, catch you later."

Monday morning seemed to arrive in the blink of an eye and I found myself back at my desk sifting through accounts. Marshall had some follow-up work to do, which meant he'd be out of the office most of the day. Nate's schedule was pretty similar. It felt as if all of us were at a standstill regarding the murders.

No news yet from the sheriff's department and no calls from Rolo Barnes. Marshall had broken down and put him on the case as well. As for the forensic lab at the sheriff's department, they'd take their own sweet time. As far as Rolo was concerned, it was definitely a crapshoot.

At a little past one, Nate rapped on my door frame.

"Your mother can relax, kiddo. Sharon Smyth's note wasn't a hit list. The forensic crew that cleaned out her apartment found the other half of the note. Seems she tore that half off to write a grocery list on the back. They found it clipped to a pile of coupons in one of her kitchen drawers."

"Wow, that's a relief. What did it say?"

Nate read me the note verbatim and I was stunned. "What? She never let on that she still taught at the clay club. And that note. My God! That's worse than a hit list. We can't tell my mother what that note really said. She's better off thinking someone's gunning for her and Lucinda. You know how she is."

"Eventually she'll find out."

"Yeah, well, let her find out from someone other than me. Or you. What about Quentin's note?"

"That, I'm afraid, just had the names on it. Hard to say if it's the same thing or not. Hey, don't look so forlorn."

"What do you expect me to look like? It feels as if everything is stalled."

"It always does. And then the proverbial you-know-what will hit the fan and you'll wish we were back to waiting."

While it wasn't exactly a fan blade wobbling from a direct hit, Rolo Barnes did call Nate about an hour later and, once again, my boss shared that conversation with me.

"Hey, kiddo, you'll be happy to know things are coming together."

"Huh? What? When?" I automatically saved the program I was working on and shoved my chair back from my desk. "Tell me everything. Did the Gila County deputies find anything in the high desert?"

"Not that I know of. Not yet, anyway. But your favorite cyber sleuth did."

"Rolo! What did he find?"

"Probably his way into my bank account, but, seriously,

he tracked those numbers from Quentin's inventory. We were right. They were bank routing numbers. But not easily recognizable ones. It would have stymied the sheriff's department. The numbers were encrypted."

"How do you encrypt a number?"

"By using algorithms, but that's all I know."

"Ew. My math skills are limited to standard accounting procedures. So, what did he find out?"

"Mind if I pull up a chair? I've been running around all day and my feet are worn out. Anyhow, Rolo faxed me the information and Augusta's putting it together. He didn't want to e-mail it, and it was too long to relay over the phone. Plus, he has this thing about phone conversations. He's pretty certain the National Security Agency is listening in."

"Uh, why does Augusta have to put it together?"

Nate rolled his eyes. "Because Rolo sort of encrypted that, too. Only he gave me the code to decipher it."

"Yikes. How long will that take?"

"Hold on."

Nate leaned his chair back and shouted, "Augusta, how are you coming along with that fax?"

"Almost done. Be right in."

At that moment, the main office door opened and I heard Marshall's voice. He and Augusta were speaking. Within seconds, Marshall walked into my office and handed Nate the papers. He slid another chair closer to the desk. Our eyes were glued to Rolo's discovery.

"I made you three copies, Mr. Williams," Augusta shouted. "Two for the investigators and one for Phee, so she won't be leaning over your shoulders."

"Thanks a heap," I shouted while everyone laughed. Then I took a closer look at the sheet in front of me. "Holy cow! Look at the locations. How would someone in the

United Arab Emirates have heard of Quentin Dussler? Or the Turks and Caicos islands, for that matter? I can't imagine what made that guy's pottery so coveted."

"That seems to be the question of the hour," Nate said. "Along with why someone would want to kill him."

Marshall lifted his head. "Take a look at the second to last name and location on this list."

We were all silent for a minute. Long enough for it to sink in. I blinked and stared at the paper again. Then I grinned. "At least we won't have to go to the United Arab Emirates or somewhere in the North Atlantic Ocean to have a conversation with one of those buyers."

My boss stretched out his arms until his shoulder blades met. "Nope, only a half hour jaunt to the Lillian."

"Shouldn't you notify the sheriff's department or something?" I asked.

He smiled and looked at Marshall. "Eventually."

The two men scrambled to their feet and nearly knocked each other over as they bolted to the door.

Nate shouted, "Lock up, Phee," and Marshall added, "I'll call you later."

Suddenly my spreadsheets looked tedious and boring. I wanted to go with them, but I wasn't about to act like a petulant child about it. "Fine. Have fun."

Chapter 27

Augusta was standing at my doorway in a matter of seconds. "Those two hit the road like the devil himself was after them. Only one name was local. I suppose that's where they were headed, huh?"

"Yep. They couldn't wait to get there."

"That Rolo Barnes certainly doesn't make things easy for anyone. I was about to tell Mr. Williams about something else I noticed, but the phone rang and I got tied up with a new client. Now it's too late."

"You can always tell them tomorrow."

"I know. But I wanted to save them some time. Take a look at the third name on the list. I'll bet they looked at the location first and ignored the name."

I grabbed the paper and read it out loud. "Marque Living."

Augusta grunted. "That's the biggest damn retirement conglomerate in the Southwest. They run independent living, assisted living, and all sorts of living. If you can call it that. Seeing their name on that list kind of makes me wonder. What would they want with a piece of pottery?"

"Same as the first name, I guess. It doesn't strike me as being all that odd. I mean, those places spend a lot on decorative items for their residences. You should see some of those resort retirement communities. Fresh cut flowers, gourmet meals, fancy movie theaters . . ."

Again that "tsk" sound from her. "Flowers don't break. Those elderly people bump into things all the time. Why risk breaking a thousand-dollar item" If you ask me, I'd wager whatever they bought is sitting in someone's fancy living room and not in one of their residences."

"My gosh, Augusta. You're beginning to sound as suspicious as my aunt Ina. She's gotten herself in a tizzy over that Punkin Center bartender's nail polish."

"Ain't going there. Don't know a thing about nail polish."

"Augusta, getting back to that fax from Rolo you deciphered, is there any chance we can figure out if there's a name associated with Marque Living?"

"Nope. When that Dussler guy sold his piece of pottery, the buyer was Marque Living. End of story."

"Maybe. Maybe not. They have a corporate office in Scottsdale. Want to know how I know?"

"You'll tell me anyway, so go ahead."

"At one of those annoying brunches from my mother's book club, the topic of senior living came up. Hey, don't look at me that way. It was a better topic than their usual stuff. Well, seems the ladies were all talking about what they would do when they reached their nineties, and Marque Living came up. And none of them had anything favorable to say."

"Bad reputation? Senior abuse? Filthy housing?"

"No, no. Nothing like that. They just see it as another one of those corporations that have been buying out the little guys. You know, the independent retirement communities. Like the Lillian and the Monte Carlo, for example. They're not part of a chain."

"I get it. Who wants to eat at some franchise when a family-owned restaurant is right around the corner?"

"Uh-huh. Too bad that office is in Scottsdale. I'm tempted to take a drive over there myself. Guess I'll have to offer up this new tidbit to Marshall."

"Yeah, well, don't forget to tell him where the tidbit came from."

"Don't worry, Augusta. He'd figure it out even if I didn't tell him."

"By the way, that Rolo Barnes sounds as if he isn't off the grid, he's in his own grid. The cover sheet that came with his fax is a doozy."

"What do you mean?"

"See for yourself. I probably should've shown it to Mr. Williams but I was too engrossed in figuring out how to interpret the information."

Augusta handed me the cover sheet and I read it out loud.

" Still working on the Klingons. Expect another fax to-morrow. R "

"See what I mean?" Augusta said. "Klingons. Like in *Star Trek*. Those techie guys are so far into that sci-fi stuff it scares me. What do you suppose he's going to be faxing Mr. Williams? Whatever it is, it'll probably take me all morning to put it together."

"Yeesh. I haven't got the slightest idea. When Marshall calls later, I'll let him know."

"You know what baffles me? The amount of money those buyers paid for that pottery. I don't think an original Michelangelo sold for that much."

I looked at the sheet again. "I see what you mean. I think those numbers with the decimal points next to the banking numbers reflect an amount based on one million. So, this one, for some buyer in California, says one point oh three.

That must mean he paid one million, thirty thousand for it. Is that what you're thinking?"

"Yep. I could buy an estate in Belize and a new car for that amount, and unlike that piece of pottery, I wouldn't have to worry about it breaking."

"Hmm. At first I thought Quentin's pieces were selling high. Like in the thousands. But now, after seeing this, I'm absolutely astonished."

"Astonished or not, I've got a pot roast in my slow cooker and it'll fall apart if I don't get home to eat it."

We locked up the office at a little past five and headed to our respective homes. I gave Lyndy a call the minute I stepped in the door and convinced her to take a quick swim with me at seven. Thank goodness Lyndy was flexible about time. By nine, I should have been fully relaxed, only I hadn't heard from Marshall. Nothing on my answering machine and no voice mail on the cell. I figured he and Nate's investigation had gone longer.

Finally, at a few minutes before ten, he called.

"Sorry it's so late, hon, but we had a hell of a time with something that should've taken us an hour at most."

"Stopping by the Lillian always takes longer than you expect. I'm surprised the management didn't mention purchasing something from Quentin. Augusta and I figured out what they paid. It was close to half a million for that piece, wasn't it?"

"Sure was. Too bad Nate and I never found Kimberlynn Warren to ask her about it. When we got to the Lillian, those two blondes told us she had gone home early for the day. Took our best persuasive skills to get them to tell us where she lived. Festival Foothills. Of all places. Another nine miles down the road."

"So, did you get a chance to speak with her?"

"We might have, if it wasn't for those Gertrude sisters.

They spotted us at the reception desk as they were coming out of the dining room. The minute they saw us, they flew into a panic. One of them shouted, 'My God! Is there another murder?' and the next thing we knew, we had a crowd of octogenarians surrounding us and bombarding us with all sorts of questions. It was impossible to get away. And I swear, those blondes at the desk were snickering behind their computer monitors."

"That sounds horrible."

"It was. Believe me, it was. To make matters worse, today was apparently the day when Sharon Smyth's apartment got cleaned out. The sheriff's department was done with their forensic investigation and the management was anxious to re-rent the place. Nate and I had to hear all about that as well."

"Oh no."

"Yeah. One guy kept muttering, 'Like it never happened. Like it never happened.'"

"I think that's the slogan for one of those restoration service companies."

"That would explain it. Anyway, by the time we got out of there, it was much too late to drive anywhere but home. I picked up a take-out order from Jack in the Box and ate most of it on the way. Tomorrow, Nate and I will go straight back there to have that conversation with their director."

"You think she used the Lillian's money to buy that clay creation for herself?"

"I'm not sure about that, but the banking numbers indicate the Lillian. An independent business. Not a corporation or an individual. So, it begs the question, who authorized that sale? And personally, I'd like to see that half-a-million-dollar piece of pottery. Business dealings gone bad can be motives for murder, but this is way over the top. It makes my head spin."

"I think Rolo is going to make it spin more. Augusta had the cover sheet for his fax and it said he was working on the Klingons and would get you that information tomorrow. What the heck? Klingons? The guy's been beamed up one time too many, if you ask me."

Marshall choked back a laugh. "'Klingons' is a term Rolo uses for information that literally clings on to something else. In this case, he's tracking down any other accounts that might link to the ones he's found. You know, like a savings account linked to checking. Or, most likely, accounts that show frequent monetary transfers back and forth."

"Do you think Kimberlynn Warren was transferring money from the Lillian's account into her own?"

"If she did, Rolo will spot it."

"There's one more thing Augusta noticed."

"If Augusta keeps this up, we're going to have to give her a raise. What was it?"

I told him about Marque Living and he agreed with me. Either he or Nate would have to have a chat with them sometime this week. Of course, there was no crime in purchasing decorative artwork, but if a deal went bad, as Marshall had pointed out, it could be a motive for murder.

"Okay, then," he said. "I'll catch you tomorrow. Let me know what your evenings look like so we can get together. And unless hell freezes over, save next weekend for me."

When I arrived at work the next morning, Marshall had already left for the Lillian with Nate to hunt down Kimberlynn Warren. Augusta was sitting at her desk with a scowl on her face and Rolo's latest fax in her hand.

"I had to wait for the second fax to come in so I could figure out the first one. No wonder I have to touch up my roots all the time."

"What does it say? Rolo was going to see if any of the accounts were linked to other ones or if there was unusual activity. According to Marshall, 'Klingons' refers to anything that clings."

Augusta adjusted her glasses and took another look at the sheet of paper. "We've got the English language. It wouldn't kill him to use it."

"So, let me see. Do any of those accounts stand out?"

"Uh-huh. Just as I suspected—Marque Living and that one from the Lillian. Also, a third one, from California."

Just then the phone rang and she picked it up. I waited by her desk as she took the call.

"Yes, I'll let him know." The instant Augusta hung up, she turned to me. "That was the sheriff's office calling Mr. Williams. The lab confirmed those things were diamonds."

"Wow. I thought as much."

"There's more. They were substantial enough to have serial numbers. Damn government. Everything's got to be numbered these days. Next thing you know some imbecile in Washington will want us to have bar codes on our arms."

"Only really, really expensive diamonds have laser serial numbers. I read about it a long time ago. I think it's to prove the diamonds aren't conflict diamonds. Did the sheriff's office tell you anything else? Did they tell you who they were registered to?"

"Nope. Said for Mr. Williams to call them."

"Bummer. I was hoping we'd find out where they came from."

"Mr. Williams will find out, and he'll let us know."

"Yeah, yeah. But that could take hours. Who knows how long he'll be at the Lillian."

Augusta shrugged and I stood there momentarily.

"Geez," I said. "I don't know what's wrong with me. I've

got a ton of work to do and all I really care about doing is solving those murders."

"Good thing you work for a private investigator and not the county coroner. You'd be wanting to perform an autopsy."

"Ugh."

Nate called at a little past ten to tell Augusta he'd be running a tad late for his appointment with a new client at eleven. He also mentioned something about Marshall meeting with one of the deputies at the sheriff's office. Maybe they'd tell *him* where those diamonds came from.

Then another call came in. One I'd been anxious to get ever since Aunt Ina and I traipsed over to Punkin Center. It was the Maricopa County Sheriff's Office relaying some information from its counterpart in Gila County. With my door wide open, I heard Augusta's end of the conversation and marched myself into the front office.

The second she hung up, I put both hands on her desk and leaned forward. "So, are you going to tell me? Are you going to tell me?"

"You sound worse than my eight-year-old great-niece. There's nothing to tell you."

"What do you mean?"

"What I mean is they were as closemouthed as they were the first time they called today. You'll just have to wait for Mr. Williams to get back and call them."

"Aargh. This is so infuriating. Could this investigation possibly move any slower?"

"Look at the bright side. When you got up this morning, you didn't know those stones you found were really diamonds. Now you do. If you ask me, you know a lot more than you think. Do you want me to put this thing together for you or would you rather stand here whining?"

"My God! Diamonds. Stolen diamonds. They had to be stolen, right? Only a thief would hide gems in a piece of greenware. But there's been nothing on the news about stolen diamonds. Nothing that I can—wait a second. Wait a second."

Augusta thumbed the desk. "I'm waiting. Hell might freeze over, but I'm waiting."

"A while back, I was fiddling around with a news app and they mentioned some update on a diamond heist that took place in Europe a few years ago. I really wasn't paying much attention. And then this weekend my aunt Ina called and told me about Quentin Dussler taking a transatlantic voyage from Belgium to Fort Lauderdale. That was a few years ago, too. And he acted really funny about having to have a special safe. Oh my God! You don't suppose? Because I do. It's been staring me in the face all this time. Quentin Dussler must have stolen those diamonds in Belgium. Probably Antwerp. That's the largest diamond district in the world. It's a square mile. That's why Quentin made his way to Zeebrugge and took a cruise ship to Florida. Less conspicuous that way. Don't you see, Augusta? He stole diamonds, snuck them into the United States, and buried them in the greenware. It's so obvious. The real owner found out and murdered him. It wasn't his wife who was stealing the diamonds. It was him."

"Slow down. You lost me. What about the wife?"

"I heard she worked in the diamond industry in New York. But it wasn't her. It couldn't have been."

I was rambling on, a mile a minute, and tapping my feet at the same time. "I figured out the motive. And I might have solved an international jewel theft. Do you have Rolo Barnes's phone number handy? Marshall was going to ask him to look into possible art thefts. My theory, too. Only I was wrong. About that. But not this."

"Slow down. You're giving me a headache, and should *you* be the one calling Rolo Barnes? Not that I'm telling you what to do, but—"

"You're right. You're right. This is so darn frustrating. We'll have to sit around all day and wait for Nate or Marshall to get back."

"Or we can actually earn our paychecks. . . ."

"Very funny. We'll catch up at lunch. Let's call out for something."

"Fine with me."

It wasn't until quarter to four when Nate and Marshall got back to the office. I couldn't wait to tell them my theory. Especially since I was 100 percent certain I had it all figured out. They listened attentively and then poked more holes in it than a slice of Swiss cheese. I was furious.

"What? That can't be right. Are you sure? Is Rolo absolutely sure? Did you have him double check?"

I was leaning against Augusta's desk and literally felt like picking up her stapler and heaving it across the room. Marshall walked toward me and gave me one of those patronizing pats on the shoulder, but it wasn't working. Meanwhile, Nate stood a few feet away rubbing his chin.

"It's the best theory we have." I stared at my boss.

"That may be the case, but it's still wrong. Look, the timeline doesn't add up. Quentin Dussler boarded that ship in Zeebrugge a week before a major diamond heist took place in Antwerp. Whatever he stowed away in the ship's safe wasn't from that heist."

"But, but . . ."

"Rolo located the ship's manifest. Quentin boarded it from Zeebrugge. The dates don't lie. About a week later, thieves stole diamonds valued in the millions from a secured diamond house in Antwerp."

Augusta cleared her throat. "Couldn't have been *that* secured."

Nate continued. "But you are right about one thing, kiddo."

"What's that?" I asked.

"The diamonds that you and Marshall found in the clay club room came from that theft in Antwerp. If that doesn't put us in high gear, nothing will."

"I don't understand."

Marshall raised an eyebrow and let out a slow breath. "It's an international jewel theft. That means the FBI and Interpol will be contacting the Maricopa County Sheriff's Office if they haven't done so immediately. We'll be mired under with protocols and paperwork. Not to mention those agencies usually don't like to work with us local investigators."

I couldn't believe what I heard. "Yikes. I get it. That diamond heist comes under their jurisdiction, but what about the murders?"

Marshall continued. "If that piece of greenware can be linked to Quentin, they'll consider his murder part of the case. As far as Sharon Smyth's death is concerned, there's no definitive evidence that would cause them to get involved."

"You're absolutely sure about the timeline?"

"Give it up, Phee," Augusta said. "The dead guy wasn't your thief."

Chapter 28

"Ah-hah! I still think Quentin was behind all of this," I said. "Stolen diamonds were found in a piece of pottery. In Sun City West, no less. And what about those bank routing numbers from his inventory? How did Kimberlynn Warren explain what the Lillian was doing on that list?"

Nate walked to the Keurig, selected a flavor, and popped it in the machine. "According to her, the company that manages the Lillian purchased the piece for its aesthetic beauty, as well as an investment. She said it was a common practice for resort residences."

"Fine. So where is it? Where is it being displayed?"

"Now we get to the sticky stuff," Marshall said. "The clay piece in question fell from its display area and shattered."

Augusta cleared her throat to the extent that the sounds she made were downright obnoxious. "Grr. Hrrumph. How convenient is that?"

"Convenient enough to collect insurance money," was Nate's reply as he added creamer to his coffee. "Kimberlynn showed us the insurance claim. Documented with a before and after photo of the jar in question."

"Something's rotten in Denmark," I said. "Or should I say Antwerp?"

"I think the complete Shakespearian quote is 'Something

is rotten in the state of Denmark,'" Augusta said. "But I'll wager the Lillian was the first stop on the corruption train. Phee and I noticed another buyer in the Phoenix area—Marque Living. They've got a Scottsdale office."

Nate looked at Marshall, then Augusta and me, and finally back to Marshall. "How'd we ever manage to conduct an investigation without these two?"

"Why do you think it took us so long?" Marshall asked. "Marque Living was on our radar. We read that list of Rolo's and didn't miss a trick. Paid a lovely visit to their corporate headquarters. Remind me that if I ever get old enough for one of those places, you'll stand me up by the side of a barn, take out a pistol, and shoot."

I swallowed. "Pretty awful?"

"Oh, not their places. I'm sure they're fine. The independence you have to give up. We read one of their contracts. Might as well sign over your brain so someone else can do all the thinking for you."

"What about their Quentin Dussler purchase? Did they admit to it? Do they have it on display or did it—"

"Oh yeah. It did. Met with the same mishap as the one from the Lillian."

Nate took another sip of coffee and gave Marshall a nod. "Do I dare tell them?"

"What more can you tell us?" My voice suddenly got louder.

"Marque Living collected beaucoup bucks from their insurance claim. Same company as the Lillian, too. Both places paid for a special collectibles addendum."

"Doesn't that strike you as a bit odd?"

Before either of them could answer my question, the phone rang and Augusta picked it up. "It's for you, Mr. Williams. Deputy Ranston from the Maricopa County Sheriff's Office."

I know it's technically impossible, but my skin began to crawl. Deputy Ranston and I didn't have the best relationship. Heck, we didn't have a relationship. He was one of the investigating deputies, along with his partner, Deputy Bowman, when a dead body was found at the Stardust Theater last winter. A dead body that belonged to someone in one of the Sun City West plays. I was sort of "working the scene" because my mother was in that play. Unfortunately, Deputy Ranston thought I'd overstepped my bounds on more than one occasion.

Forcing myself to be still, I listened to Nate's end of the call, but couldn't ascertain much. The only words he said were "yep," "uh-huh," "no kidding," and "thanks."

As soon as he hung up, he got as far as "Got a report from Gila County" when two people walked in the door. My mother and Shirley Johnson. All of us froze, with the exception of Augusta, who immediately busied herself at her desk.

"Mom! Shirley! What are you doing here?"

Nate and Marshall managed to say hello or something to that effect when my mother cut in. "Shirley and I decided to have afternoon tea at the Victorian Teahouse in the historic district. And since your office is on the way home, we thought we'd drop in and pay a visit."

Pay a visit? We aren't a historical site. "And?" I stood perfectly still, waiting for the other shoe to drop.

"And, since we're here, I'd like to know if any progress has been made on that note with Lucinda's and my name on it."

I opened my eyes wide and gave Nate the look that could only mean one thing—do not tell her there was more than one note. And if you do, don't tell her what Sharon Smyth's note really said.

He winked, walked over to my mother, and placed an arm around her. "It'll be all right, Harriet. I know how disconcerting this must be for you. But rest assured, it's probably something inconsequential."

My mother wasn't buying it. "Can you say without hesitation that a crazed killer isn't about to make Lucinda and me the next victims?"

"I seriously doubt it. Of course, that doesn't mean taking any foolish chances like leaving your car or house unlocked."

"She's got a watchdog," Shirley said. "And a screamer device."

"Okay, then," I said. "It's all settled. The dog will bark, the screamer will go off, and all will be right with the world." *Unless the dog pees on himself again.*

My mother glared at me. "No need for sarcasm."

"You're right. I'm sorry. The minute Nate or Marshall hear anything, I'll call you."

My mother took Shirley by the arm and led her out the door. "Nice seeing all of you. And as for you, Nate, make that note a priority. Understand?"

The men were grasping for words as the door closed behind the women.

I watched as they walked away. "Wow. That was unexpected."

Nate nodded. "And unnerving. This day keeps getting more and more unpredictable. At least we might have a real clue from your escapade to Punkin Center. Deputy Ranston informed me the Gila County Sheriff's Office found some evidence by that outcrop of rock you discovered."

"What? What was it?"

"They were able to match up the squiggly lines from Quentin's signature to the layering formation on the rock.

220 *J.C. Eaton*

Quentin, as you recall, used arrows on some of those squiggles."

"So? What did they find?"

Augusta, who had stopped for a moment to glance at her computer monitor, looked up. "You'd better tell her, Mr. Williams, before she has paroxysms. That's Greek for having a fit. It was in today's crossword puzzle."

Nate started to open his mouth but wound up laughing to the point that Marshall had to take over. "They followed the terrain and located the entrance to an old copper mine. A few feet inside they found two more empty water bottles from the Lillian."

"That's it? Water bottles?"

"One of them had lipstick along the edge. They sent it to their forensic lab to see if any DNA could be extracted. Of course, that could take months."

"Did they find anything else?"

"Too dangerous to venture inside."

"So now what?" I asked.

"Gila County Sheriff's deputies will be monitoring the area for unusual activity."

I shrugged. "So that's it, huh? More water bottles and the banking account information Rolo found?"

"That's all we've got, kiddo," Nate said. "The Lillian, Marque Living, and that third place in California. What was the name of it again?"

"Serenity Brook," Marshall said. "Also a resort retirement complex. But their Quentin Dussler piece is alive and on display in the lobby of their Palm Springs location."

I shook my head. "Not for long, it isn't. Doesn't anyone think it's more than coincidental that two luxury retirement places bought original pieces of art only to have them break? And don't tell me it was because of the insurance money. I mean, why pay an exorbitant amount of money for a clay jar only to collect the same amount from the insurance? Both places showed you the claims, right? They weren't lying about the amount they paid."

Marshall gave me one of his adorable smiles that creep partway up from his lips. "What are you getting at, Phee?"

"There has to be more to it. And if Augusta can stop looking at her monitor long enough to hand me the phone number associated with Serenity Brook, I'm about to find out."

"Move over, Miss Marple," Nate exclaimed. "Give her the number, Augusta. I'd like to see this. But not on our line. Chances are they have caller ID. Get her one of those prepaid cell phones from the file cabinet."

"We have burner phones?" I asked. "I thought that was only in the movies."

"You need to visit Walmart more." Augusta handed me a phone and smiled.

I tapped the numbers and glanced at Nate. "Don't make me laugh."

The director's name was Dean Carlington, and I hoped my little ruse would work. No sooner did I hear the words, "Serenity Brook Resort Retirement, how may I direct your call?" than I launched into my "collection agency" voice. I had used it from time to time in Mankato when people were delinquent with bill payments.

"Please connect me with Mr. Carlington's secretary," I said. "It's regarding action on their recent purchase of a signed Quentin Dussler piece."

Within seconds, I was on the line with an Eric Ansley. As soon as he introduced himself, I wasted no time. Mainly because I thought I would lose my nerve.

"Mr. Ansley, our office hasn't heard from you. Have you

destroyed the Dussler piece and reported the casualty to your insurance company? We expected word of it at least a week ago."

I kept my voice low and stern. Then I waited. Someone once told me silence was a very valuable negotiating tool. I prayed they were right. Nate, Marshall, and Augusta were all staring at me, and I couldn't afford to lose my focus. After what seemed like minutes, Eric Ansley spoke. I held the phone away from my ear so everyone could listen.

Eric sounded jumpy. "It will be taken care of this week. Mr. Carlington will phone you as soon as the claim is filed. When can we expect delivery?"

I froze. The silence at my end made Eric Ansley more nervous and his voice cracked. "You have my word. Expect our call within the week."

I took a long breath and spoke slowly. "Since you have procrastinated, *we* will call you. Expect our call no later than Friday. Once we've ascertained the piece is no longer viable, you'll receive further instructions."

"Er, um, uh . . . Call Mr. Carlington's cell. The 818 number, not the 747."

I clenched my fist and took a breath. "This is troublesome. We have the 747 in our records."

"Please. Call 818-374-8421."

I reached across Augusta's desk for a pen, but she had beaten me to it and was writing the number on the first piece of paper she could get her hands on, a candy wrapper.

"Thank you, Mr. Ansley, you've been most cooperative. We shall be in touch."

I pushed the delete icon before Mr. Carlington's assistant, or whoever Eric Ansley was, said another word.

Nate slapped the side of his cheek and stared at me. "Holy crap, kiddo. No wonder the Mankato Police Department sicced those delinquent accounts on you. That voice scared the hell out of me."

"Yeah, well, it's giving me cause for alarm, too. I'm the one dating her," Marshall said.

I flashed him a smile and chuckled. "You have nothing to worry about. But now, do both of you believe me? Quentin Dussler had to have been behind this. Somehow he stole the diamonds and planted them in greenware pieces until he was ready to move them to his hiding spot in the desert. His greenware was safely stashed in the back of the clay club closet and left undisturbed. Until my mother came along.

Once buyers purchased his over-the-top completed creations, they were given information that allowed them to decipher a code embedded in the piece. That code led them to where their diamond or diamonds were hidden, but they had to destroy the clay creation first so the embedded code couldn't fall into anyone else's hands. It wasn't artwork they were buying, it was stolen diamonds."

"I have to admit, Mr. Williams and Mr. Gregory, Phee's got a point. I imagine she read a lot of Nancy Drew as a child," Augusta said. "This Carlington fellow is expecting to find out where his treasure has been stowed. And I'll wager it's in Punkin Center. In a creepy old mine, to be precise."

"It all makes sense," I said. "The Lillian water bottles were there because someone from the Lillian went to that area to pick up their diamond. Or diamonds. Water bottles were the last thing they were worried about."

Nate listened carefully, rubbing his chin the entire time. "Let's say, for a moment, Phee is right about the jars being used as treasure maps, for lack of a better term. Who's going to put Mr. Carlington's diamond in that mine now that Quentin Dussler is dead? Assuming Quentin was the one doing this. And since Mr. Ansley must know about Quentin's death, he didn't seem at all worried. So, who's running the diamond ruse?"

"Whoever killed Quentin," I said. "And I know one surefire way to find out."

Chapter 29

"Please don't tell me what I think you're about to tell me," Marshall said. "That you plan on setting up some sort of 'sting' operation. Worse yet, with your aunt Ina. Because it's a good way to get yourself killed."

"Oh, no way. Not me. I'm not that crazy. I figured it was something you and Nate could do."

Marshall stifled a laugh and Nate shook his head. "Not without full cooperation from two sheriffs' departments. You may be on to something, kiddo, but they'll still stick us with that timeline thing."

"Maybe Quentin had a partner," I said. "Everyone keeps talking about his niece. What about her?"

"No one can locate her. Of course, it doesn't help matters since we don't even know her name. I got so exasperated, I turned to Rolo. I'm going to owe that guy a fortune. He'll be able to build his own damn veggie-paleo-grain restaurant by the time we figure out these murders."

"But you *will* talk to Deputy Ranston about this, won't you?" I asked. "Or Bowman. At least he doesn't scowl all the time."

"Rest assured, kiddo. We're a regular tag team these days."

Augusta stood up and stretched. "I don't know about the rest of you, but I have work to do before we close. And I can get a lot done in the next twenty-five minutes if you'd all skedaddle."

I walked to my office. "Um, yeah. I'd better finish a few invoices I started."

"Guess you and I are the only slouches," Nate said to Marshall. "We'd better fix that."

I spent the next twenty minutes finishing up the invoices. Then I heard the phone ring followed by Augusta shouting for me. "It's Gertie from the Lillian for you. Says it's important."

"Okay. I'm picking up."

"Miss Kimball, thank goodness you're still at work. The most distressing thing happened a few minutes ago. Tanya killed a scorpion."

"Um, uh, you're calling to tell me the receptionist killed an insect?"

"Not an insect. A scorpion. A horrible, harmful creature. It was enormous. Trudy and I were just coming back from dinner when we saw the thing scuttling across the lobby. They're fast, you know. Anyway, we weren't alone. Others were leaving the dining room, too. Someone screamed 'Scorpion!' and next thing I knew, Tanya raced from the back of the desk, grabbed one of those floral pillows from the nearest chair, and held it over the thing. Too bad everything is electronic on that front desk or she could've used a book. Anyway, it took forever, but Tanya wouldn't give up. She applied so much pressure the dreadful scorpion didn't stand a chance. Everyone applauded when it was over and done with."

"I see. Is that what you wanted to call me about?"

"No. I called for another reason. Hold on. Trudy's yelling about something."

I heard Trudy's voice in the background, getting louder. "Tell her about the broccoli. Tell her about the broccoli!"

"Miss Kimball doesn't have time to hear about the damn broccoli."

"Tell her to make time. I think it's important."

I made a face she couldn't see, obviously, and told Gertie I didn't mind hearing about the broccoli.

"Fine," she said. "I'll put Trudy on."

"Miss Kimball? This is Trudy. I thought you should know someone's been tampering with our food."

"Tampering with your food? What do you mean?"

"Cream of broccoli soup is always served at the salad bar. But now it's different. The broccoli is normally cut crosswise so it forms lovely florets. Well, not anymore. A few days ago they began to cut it lengthwise into these ugly stringy pieces. I don't like eating stringy things."

For the life of me, I had no idea why Trudy thought this was so urgent, but I let her continue until I thought I was going to lose my mind.

I tried to be tactful. "Maybe they hired a new cook. Or got a new recipe. Ask your server to speak with the chef the next time you go to the dining room. Or better yet, see if the chef would be willing to come to your table."

"It won't do any good. Don't you understand? Something's not right around here. A scorpion in the lobby and badly cut broccoli. I'm telling you, something's going on. Maybe Sharon Smyth knew what it was and that's what got her killed. Anyway, here's Gertie."

"Well, nice talking with—"

"Miss Kimball? It's me again. Gertie. Forget about the broccoli. I overheard something this afternoon and thought you should know about it. And don't tell me to call the sheriff's department. I'm calling you."

"Um, er . . . fine. What is it?"

"I had a hankering for cupcakes this morning. It was after breakfast and I didn't feel like waiting for lunch, so I sort of helped myself to a few of them. They always have them for guests in that small waiting room off the director's office. No one saw me go in there. One of the blondes was working on her computer and the other one was probably in the restroom."

"Uh-huh. Then what?"

"I had finished off a velvet cream cupcake and had just wrapped two vanilla ones in a napkin and put them in my pocketbook when I heard an argument in Kimberlynn's office. I recognized Kimberlynn's voice but not the other lady's, so I tiptoed to the door and slid it open ever so slightly. No one noticed."

"What were they arguing about?"

"Money. That's what people always argue about. Kimberlynn said something like, 'How fast can you get it done? The buyer is getting anxious, and I want this over with. Last thing we need is the feds crawling all over this place.' And then the other lady said, 'Because you were sloppy. You should've found out where she kept her notes before you—'"

"'Before you' what? What did she say?"

"I couldn't hear the rest. Some old fart came to the front desk and he was really loud. Probably forgot to charge his hearing aid. By the time I heard the women again, it was only one word."

"What word?"

"Friday."

"Gertie, did you see what that other woman looked like?"

"Of course I did. I already told you I opened the door and peered in."

I had all I could do to stop myself from screaming, "Get on with it!" Instead, I lowered my voice, taking great care to keep it as gentle as possible. "Please describe her for me."

"She was young. Maybe your age. Long blond hair with

a reddish hue. I think they call that strawberry blond. I like that term better than dirty blond. Dirty blond always makes one think they haven't washed their hair."

I bit my lip so I wouldn't groan. "What else did you notice about her?"

"I don't remember if she was wearing pants or a skirt. But her blouse was short sleeved and beige. Button down. Oh, this probably isn't important, but her arm was dangling over the chair. Her left arm. She wasn't wearing a wedding ring. And that nail polish! Who wears nail polish like that?"

"Like what? What do you mean?"

"Looked like something someone would expect to find on a Las Vegas showgirl. All glitzy and glittery. It nearly blinded me. The colors looked as if they were jumping off her nails. Violets and lavenders. Some blues, too."

For a moment, I was stunned. Gertie had just described the iridescent holographic glitter coat my aunt Ina and I had seen on that bartender in Punkin Center. If my aunt was sitting here next to me, she'd poke me in the arm and say, "I told you that girl got her nails done elsewhere."

"It was good you called me," I said. "What you overheard could be very important. Please, whatever you do, don't say a word to anyone."

"I already told Trudy."

"I mean, other than Trudy."

"I won't. That Kimberlynn is up to no good. Maybe Sharon found out and Kimberlynn killed her. Oh no! Oh no! What if she saw me? What if she plans on killing me next?"

"Relax, please. Calm down. You said no one saw you, right?"

"One of the blondes did. She nodded as I left the waiting room."

"I wouldn't worry if I were you. Listen, Gertie, I'll let my boss know. Um, to be on the safe side, don't wander anywhere in the building alone. Like the laundry room or even into the elevator."

"How can I with Trudy breathing down my neck complaining about broccoli?"

I promised to get back to her in a few days. The second I was off the phone, I pushed my chair back from my desk, stood, and made a beeline straight for the front office. I rapped on Nate's door and then Marshall's. Loudly.

"Is the cavalry coming?" Augusta asked.

"We are the cavalry," I said.

"What's going on?" Marshall was out of his office and facing me as Nate opened the door and walked toward us.

"We've got to do that sting thing because I think the Lillian may be linked to the diamond thefts. Gertie overheard something. And she saw something. Someone, actually. The bartender from Punkin Center. I'm sure it was her."

"I'm locking the door," Augusta said. "It's after five and I don't want any interruptions while I hear Phee's story."

I was all but flailing my arms. "It's not a story. It's a break in the case."

For the next five minutes, I told them everything Gertie had told me, but didn't mention her sister's observations. Following one train of thought was hard enough without nebulous ramblings about broccoli and "something not right" at the Lillian.

"You're pretty certain the description matches up to that bartender?" Nate asked.

"Oh yeah. How many strawberry blondes with iridescent, holographic, glittery nails can there be?"

"None, if I had my way," Augusta muttered to herself.

I had to restrain myself from biting one of my own nails. "So, now what do we do? Plant a fake diamond near that outcrop and have the sheriff's deputies arrest whoever shows up to claim it?"

"Hang on, kiddo. The diamond drop is one thing, but from what Gertie told you, I don't think Kimberlynn's issue had anything to do with that. She used words like 'feds crawling all over *this* place.' I take it to mean the Lillian. And 'buyer getting anxious.' We know it's not our guy from California because you had to coax him over the phone. So, either we're dealing with another diamond buyer who purchased one of those Dussler pieces or it's something entirely different."

"Drat! We really need to know who made that greenware urn. My mother was supposed to ask Lucinda. Oh phooey! That means I've got to call her."

Augusta reached out her arm and pointed to the phone on her desk as if she was auditioning for a melodrama.

"Fine," I said. "She should be home by now."

I picked up the receiver and dialed. My boss, my boyfriend, and my coworker watched as if I was about to perform some sort of magic trick.

"Hey, Mom, I forgot to ask you something."

Augusta reached across the desk and hit the speaker button.

"You don't have to yell, Phee. I can hear you. What did you forget?"

"Did you ever get a chance to ask Lucinda if she remembered seeing anyone's signature on that urn? You know, the one that was stolen."

"I thought I told you. Wait a second. I told Shirley, not you. Lucinda did see someone's initials etched into the clay. But it won't help you. It said 'Mom.' Isn't that sweet? Someone's mother was making an urn for one of her children. Too bad she never finished it. Now it's gone. Of course, it was quite the monstrosity, so I really don't understand who would have stolen it."

"Um, yeah. Did Lucinda remember anything else on that urn?"

"Nope. Just 'Mom.' In capital letters. I think I might do something like that the next time I make a bowl or plate for Streetman."

Augusta, who had just swallowed some water from the bottle she had on her desk, turned away and nearly spat it out on the wall behind her.

"Not funny," I mouthed.

"What did you say, Phee?"

"Oh, sorry. I was only clearing my throat."

"While I have you on the phone, I thought I'd ask if you and Marshall would like to come over for dinner on Wednesday. It's potluck. The book club ladies will all be here to plan for our upcoming year."

I turned to Marshall and ran my index finger across my throat. "Um, er, I'll check our schedules and let you know. Anyway, thanks for the info."

"Let me know the minute you hear anything about that note."

"I will. Catch you later."

"She's making bowls for the dog?" Augusta slid the phone toward her.

"Probably an entire place setting," Marshall replied. "Guess we can rule Quentin Dussler out. That stinks. Worse yet, the signature on that urn isn't going to get us any closer to figuring out who buried the diamonds inside it."

I nodded. "Yeah, 'Mom' could be anyone. Think of how many things are signed 'Love, Mom.' Gifts, letters, notes, postcards . . . Oh my God! Postcards! Quick! Augusta, hand me that phone."

I pressed those number keys furiously and prayed my aunt was home. "Aunt Ina! Is that you?"

"Of course it's me. You sound stressed, Phee. Is everything all right?"

"Yes, yes. Everything's fine, but I need to ask you something. Remember when we were in that bar? You know, the one in Punkin Center."

"Of course I know. Why?"

"Remember when you pointed out that postcard from some market in Antwerp?"

"The Grote Markt. Not a market. It's the town square in the heart of Antwerp. Don't tell me you plan on going there. Are you going with Marshall? When? Don't go in the summer. Too many tourists."

"No, I'm not going. We're not going. I have to find out what was on that postcard. You said someone's mother sent it. How did you know?"

"Honestly, Phee, they signed it, 'Having fun, Mom,' in some god-awful white pen across the Silvius Brabo statue. Who does a thing like that?"

"Maybe a murderer. Maybe a diamond thief. Thanks, Aunt Ina. Send my love to Louis."

I shoved the phone back to Augusta. "MOM! This has to be the connection! Antwerp. Diamonds. Greenware. Whoever 'Mom' is, she must have broken into the clay club and stolen the jar. Her jar! She's the thief. When she found out the place was being cleaned out, she couldn't wait for the next day. But the bartender and Kimberlynn are much too young to be moms. And Sharon is much too dead. Then who?"

"Slow down, kiddo, before you drive all of us crazy. Maybe 'Mom' has nothing to do with parenting."

Chapter 30

The whole thing was one giant mess and, the more I tried to make sense of it, the worse it got. Obviously, Quentin Dussler had sold his high-priced special glazed pottery for an outrageous price because he was really selling coded maps to stolen diamonds. But, according to the timeline from that diamond heist in Belgium, he couldn't possibly have been the master thief. Unless, of course, he wasn't working alone.

"Whoever 'Mom' is, she had to be Quentin's accomplice," I said. "That's the only thing that makes sense."

Nate put his arm on my shoulder and gave it a squeeze. "Quite possibly, yes. Look, I'll touch base with the sheriff's department, find out what, if anything, they've gleaned in the last few hours, and I'll fill them in on what we've discovered."

"I've got a few odds and ends to go over with Rolo, so I'll get going on that. It shouldn't take too long." Marshall took a step toward me. "How about if I pick up something for us to eat when I'm done with Rolo? Probably an hour or so at most."

"I can get something on my way home. It'll be quicker."

"Great. Surprise me."

* * *

Marshall arrived at my house at a little past seven. We were both starving and tore into the assorted wraps I bought from the deli. Once we'd washed them down with iced tea, the conversation immediately turned to the investigation.

"Rolo wanted to double check on something before he called us, but he's pretty confident about Quentin's niece."

I tossed the paper plates into the trash. "He located her? What's her name?"

"Quentin Dussler doesn't have a niece. Rolo went through family records, tax records, you name it. There is no niece."

"But that's impossible."

"Not really. Think about it. Where did you first learn he had a niece?"

I bit my lower lip and tried to remember. "From my mother, I guess. Oh, and then from Cindy Dolton in the dog park. Later from Lon and Mary Melhorn. They were the couple Cindy said knew Quentin."

"Did anyone actually meet the niece?"

"Um, come to think it, the Melhorns never said they did."

Marshall shrugged and plopped himself on the couch. "Maybe I should be doing some digging on those two. Meanwhile, I've got more news from our favorite cyber sleuth."

I could tell from the look on his face the news wasn't going to get anyone any closer to solving the murders. He rubbed his temples and groaned. "Rolo said there's a money dump going on at the Lillian."

"A what?"

"Sorry. I keep forgetting not everyone knows Rolo's terminology. When he started poking into the bank routing numbers from Quentin's inventory and saw the Lillian, he couldn't help but pry further. That's when he discovered something fishy. So, he checked the other two resort retirement residences and noticed similar patterns. All very recent."

"What patterns?"

"The residents have individual accounts at these places. It's like a buy-in, but their principal remains in place. The interest accumulates and goes directly to the facility, along with a fixed amount the residents pay from their own resources."

"Is that typical for those continuing care communities?"

"I'm not sure. But the point is, the principal is supposed to stay fixed, but it's shrinking. Rolo discovered a slow pattern of monetary leakage, so to speak. Small, at first, but growing. At this rate, the residents' buy-in monies will disappear."

"My God! Did he notify the attorney general for Arizona? What about the FBI?"

"Phee, Rolo operates under the radar. You know that. If he notified anyone, he'd be arrested."

"Aargh."

"Nate and I will have to find another way around this."

"But don't the residents see that their money is disappearing?"

"Not necessarily. They may only get interest statements from their resort retirement residence company, like the Lillian or Marque Living. And the statements may just indicate the original principal. Think Bernie Madoff, but slightly different. When people perceive things are going well, they don't question it. Especially very elderly seniors."

"Did Rolo figure out where the money was going?"

"Mainly offshore accounts. A bear to track down."

"Poor Gertie and Trudy. It's all the money they have. What will happen when it's drained?"

"I'm thinking whoever is behind this has it figured out. The money will disappear around the same time the residents pass away. Let's face it, when you're in your nineties, how many more years do you expect to live? They'll never miss the money. Their beneficiaries will. Simply put, the resort residence will inform the next of kin that their beloved relative exhausted his or her monies."

I folded and unfolded the napkin in front of me. "That's unconscionable."

"Scams like this usually are."

"Geez, so now, not only do you have to deal with two unsolved murders but also a corruption case."

"Not so fast. We can't jump into that one without revealing how we found out about it. Right now, the murders are the priority, which brings me back to the conversation Gertie overheard. Something's going to happen on Friday. Nate thinks it involves the Lillian since Kimberlynn said 'feds crawling all over this place,' but that doesn't eliminate the 'drop-off' spot out in Punkin Center and the likelihood there'll be a diamond buyer showing up."

"Not Mr. Carlington. I sort of strung his assistant along on that phony call."

"You told him you'd contact him no later than Friday. He's expecting your call and, once he gets it, he, or his representative, will race to that spot in the desert to claim their stolen diamond. They already have the map. When he arrives at the spot, he'll be met by the Gila County Sheriff's Office. They'll question him until they find out who's behind all of this. That is, of course, if Nate and I can get all of this coordinated tomorrow. So far, we're working with two sheriff's departments—Gila and Maricopa. That's bad enough. We've got to get this done before the feds muck it up and Interpol makes it worse."

"What??? You're using my idea after all? Is that what you and Nate talked about when I left the office?"

Marshall had that cute sheepish look on his face but didn't say a word. Instead, he leaned over, put his arm around my shoulders, and kissed me.

"Don't think your amorous advances are going to get you out of admitting I was right," I said.

"I'll take any excuse to kiss you."

"Seriously, a sting? Will you be going? Will Nate?"

"No. We'll help coordinate, but it will be up to the sheriffs' departments. It's the Lillian we're more concerned about. Come on, right now we've got better things to do."

He planted another kiss on my lips. Slower. Softer.

"The hell with the sheriffs' departments. You're right. We do have better things to do."

I didn't give the sting operation or the Lillian another thought until the phone on my nightstand rang relentlessly in the middle of the night. I fumbled in the darkness to lift the receiver. Marshall immediately tossed the covers off and sat up.

"Hello?" I mumbled.

My heart was pounding and I prayed it wasn't my mother calling to tell me something awful had happened.

"Miss Kimball? This is Mario Aquilino. You're going to want to hear what I have to tell you."

"Mr. Aquilino, do you know what time it is?"

"Of course I do. It's twenty to six. The sun's been up for a half hour. And early breakfast is about to be served."

Marshall had gotten out of the bed and opened the plantation shutters. Hazy sunlight illuminated the room. I rubbed my eyes and yawned into the phone. "Tell me, what's going on?"

"I'll tell you what's going on. Sharon Smyth snuck in here and left me a letter sometime before she was murdered. It was balled up in one of my socks. She must have rearranged my sock drawer when she left the thing. All rolled up like some kind of missive. I didn't notice it until now because that drawer was for my dress socks, not my everyday socks. I suppose you'll want to know why I decided to wear dress socks today, huh?"

"I, uh, er . . ."

"Forgot to do the damn laundry, does that answer your question? And I wasn't about to pay to have the Lillian do it. There. Are you satisfied now?"

"Um, sure. So, about the note. What does it say?"

I motioned for Marshall to move closer to the phone and held it out so both of us could hear what Mario had to say.

"I'm holding the note. It's a damn long thing. I suppose you could call it a letter. Do you want me to read it now?"

"Yes," I practically screamed.

"It says, 'Mario—I found out the Lillian is about to be sold. Right under our noses. I left my mail on the reception desk counter for a second in order to get something out of my eye. When I picked up my letters, the other one must have been under it. It was addressed to Kimberlynn, but I didn't realize it until it was too late. I had already opened it. Long story short, some company by the name of Wolters Stork is buying them out. I thought about destroying the letter, but I think it's a crime to tamper with the mail. I'm going to confront Kimberlynn. If something happens to me, you'll know why. Sharon Smyth. P.S. I was going to put letters in the Gertrudes' drawers, but they're a mess. Especially Trudy's.'"

"Mr. Aquilino, put that letter in a safe place and wait for me. I'm driving right over."

"Don't hurry. I want to digest my breakfast."

"When you're done in the dining room, wait in the lobby. And please don't say a word to anyone."

Mario Aquilino's call was stronger than any caffeine boost I'd ever had. Still, I made Marshall and me our usual K-cups before washing up and throwing on some clothes.

"Let's take a long, relaxing shower tonight," Marshall said, "but, for now, that deodorant will have to do. Come on, we'll take my car. It's not as if we're going to wind up in separate places tonight. Admit it, we should be spending our off hours together."

He was right. About the deodorant, the car, and our relationship. Marshall wanted to spend more nights in my casita than his own rental place, and I wondered if we'd reached the point where we were ready for the next step. Needless to say, I didn't have time to dwell on it. We were out the door and in his car before I knew it.

"Yikes, I've never moved so fast in my life. Most likely Mario is still in the dining room giving the waiters a hard time."

Marshall chuckled. "Yeah, he sounds like a character all right. But why do you suppose Sharon Smyth decided to leave a letter in his sock drawer?"

"They knew each other from the clay club. I guess she figured she could trust him. She must have felt the same way about Gertie and Trudy."

"Do me a favor since I'm behind the wheel, and call Nate. Give him a heads-up."

"I already took out my cell phone."

"Good. When you're done, I need you to place another call."

"Don't tell me. Rolo?"

"Uh-huh. Use my phone. He's on speed dial. Next car I get will have a hands-free phone with Bluetooth. Meanwhile, I've got you."

"You sure do. Give me a second."

Rolo answered the call on the second ring, thinking it was Marshall.

"Sorry to disappoint you," I said, "It's Phee. Phee Kimball."

"I know. I recognize your voice. Is Marshall in one piece?"

"Yeah. He's right here. Driving. Wait a sec. He's pulling over so he can talk to you."

"Hang on. I'm toasting some quinoa for my dried acai berries."

The silence at his end of the line lasted a few seconds. By that time, Marshall had pulled the car into a plaza and I handed him the phone.

"Rolo, I need you to check on something right away. Look up Wolters Stork. It's a Dutch company. Find out if the Lillian, or those other two places, are funneling money into one of Wolters Stork's accounts. It's really important."

Whatever Rolo said, Marshall replied with, "Try to detangle it fast. It may be linked to a murder."

He ended the call with a couple of "uh-huhs" and "I'll take my chances with the white death."

He tossed the phone on the console and got back on the road.

"The white death?" I asked.

"Yeah, sugar."

Chapter 31

Surprisingly, people were out and about when Marshall and I pulled into the side parking lot at the Lillian. There were a few dog walkers and one lady in a pink jogger's outfit walking slowly down the block.

"It's early," I said. "The blondes don't start working until seven. Unless they're really diligent, they won't stroll in here for another fifteen minutes or so. And the director isn't about to arrive until eight or nine."

Marshall reached for his sunglasses. His car didn't have Bluetooth, but it had a neat little drop-down tray next to the visor. "Everything's starting to add up. Let's hope it doesn't stall. Sharon's letter to Mario confirms what Rolo observed—money is being moved. And if my suspicions are right, whoever is orchestrating this operation may be using the residents' own monies to buy out the place. But that wouldn't provide enough money. So, how else is Wolters Stork being paid?"

"My guess is a hefty down payment from those stolen diamonds. That little encounter between the bartender and Kimberlynn had to be more than coincidence. It's like some crazy circular maze, only I can't tell where it begins."

"Too bad you can't tell Gertie and Trudy who the real

underwear drawer perpetrator turned out to be. At least, according to her own confession."

"You're right. It wasn't some creepy nutcase. It was Sharon Smyth, trying to figure out the best spot to hide her letter. Maybe when all of this is over we can let the Gertrudes know."

Mario Aquilino was in the lobby, seated in a floral chair off to the side of the fountain. The reception desk was vacant, except for a bowl of candies and a sign instructing people to call the house manager after hours.

"Psst! I'm over here!" Mario shouted.

Marshall and I hurried over and dragged two chairs closer to the larger floral one. Mario reached in his pocket, pulled out the letter, and thrust it at Marshall. "Quick. Before anyone gets suspicious."

I wanted to ask "Suspicious of what?" but decided not to. "Um, thanks, Mr. Aquilino. This is really helpful."

"So, are you going to arrest that witch?"

"Arrest? Witch?"

"Kimberlynn Warren. If I didn't think my butt would go numb waiting in this chair, I'd watch you do it."

Marshall leaned closer and kept his voice low. "We don't have the authority to arrest anyone. I'm an investigator, not an officer of the law. Besides, the letter provides circumstantial evidence of a possible wrongdoing, not definitive proof of malfeasance."

"You sound like a thesaurus. I'll tell you what it proves. The management at the Lillian is selling us out."

I tapped Marshall on the shoulder and motioned for him to step away for a second.

"We'll be right back, Mr. Aquilino," I said. "I just need a moment with Mr. Gregory."

When we were out of earshot, I said, "Mario doesn't know about the money dumping. No one does. Not yet.

He's shaken up because of an alleged buyout, but he may think his investment money is at stake. We need to reassure him before things get crazy around here."

"Hon, his investment money *is* at stake. At least according to Rolo. But you're right. No sense starting a frenzy. I'll see what I can do."

Marshall and I returned to our seats, trying to look nonchalant as a few of the guests meandered through the lobby. For the next three or four minutes, he used a combination of diplomacy and child psychology to reassure Mario of our intentions to pursue the matter.

"So, you see, this letter provides us with a valuable link into Sharon's murder and quite possibly, a questionable business dealing. Rest assured the appropriate authorities will work with this new evidence to expedite the case."

"I want to be notified when Kimberlynn is going to be arrested. I can bring my special seat cushion to the lobby."

"We can't make any promises, Mr. Aquilino, but we'll keep you informed. And please don't say anything to anyone about the letter."

"Fine. And don't you lose it, either. I didn't get a chance to make a copy."

Marshall and I shook his hand and were out of the building before the blondes arrived.

"It's five minutes to seven," I said. "Talk about cutting it close. I really didn't want them to see us."

"Then walk fast. I think that's them getting out of the red Mazda."

We stopped for another cup of coffee and some pastries at a Dunkin' Donuts and brought a dozen back to the office.

"If I know Nate," Marshall said, "he probably hasn't eaten anything. Of course, this stuff would send shock waves through Rolo, but it's one of the four food groups as far as Nate's concerned."

I laughed for a brief second. "What about the letter? Now what?"

"Once we make a copy, Nate or I will drive the original to the sheriff's station. They'll want to have a word with Kimberlynn Warren regarding any role she might have had in Sharon Smyth's death. And since we procured this new evidence, Williams Investigations will be along for the ride. I'm sure by now Nate's already called Deputy Ranston."

Marshall was right.

The minute we arrived at the office, Nate grabbed Mario's letter and a maple glazed donut, not in that order. He said something about "too many cooks coordinating Friday's plan" and darted out of the place. "If Deputy Ranston calls here," he yelled, "tell him I'm on my way."

Augusta shouted back, "You got it, Mr. Williams," before asking if there were any Bavarian cream donuts in the box. Meanwhile, I had to put all of my sleuthing aside and work on the billing. Marshall was hoping for a quick response from Rolo, but given the magnitude of the situation, it would take days, if not longer.

Then again, I forgot whom we were dealing with.

Suddenly, I remembered something. It was Wednesday. Potluck Wednesday at my mother's house and she had invited Marshall and me to join the book club ladies. Pushing myself back from my desk, I stood up and walked into Marshall's office. The door was wide open and he was staring at some notes he had taken.

"Hey, sorry to interrupt, but I forgot about my mother's invitation to join the book club ladies for potluck dinner tonight. It's early. I can always make an excuse."

"We should go. We should absolutely go."

"Huh? What? Are you delirious?"

"I'm being proactive. Let's face it. Half of what we figure out emanates from bits and pieces of conversation those women dredge up. By now, one of them has heard something about the murders. I'm not about to discount anything. So, yeah, give her a call and tell her we'll head over after five."

"You're a glutton for punishment. You know that, don't you?"

"I'm an investigator who's learned not to question his sources. Or his girlfriend's choice of donuts."

Marshall had a full schedule with client meetings and phone calls, while Nate was stuck in some planning session with the sheriff's deputies. Augusta called out for deli sandwiches around midday, and we helped ourselves. No earth-shattering news. No new leads.

Then, at a little past three, Nate returned to the office with an interesting development. I had just stepped out of my office when he went straight to the remaining donuts, bit into one, and, with a mouth half full, asked Augusta to "get Marshall out here."

"Great," Nate said. "You're all here, so I don't have to repeat this. The sheriff's department got the lab work back on that piece of plastic bag they found near Sharon Smyth's body. It was a plastic bag from a spa in Fountain Hills. Fortunately, a tiny part of the logo was still visible and somehow they figured it out."

"Fountain Hills?" I didn't realize how loud I was until I saw Nate taking a step back. I immediately lowered my voice. "That's off the Beeline to Payson near that huge casino. Fort McDowell. And the Beeline shoots over to Punkin Center. What spa? They must have a nail salon. Find out if they do that holographic glitter thing. My aunt Ina said only three places in the valley do that. Oh my God! The bartender. She's the murderess. It all makes sense."

"Want me to take notes, Mr. Williams?" Augusta asked. "Before Phee forgets her train of thought?"

I glared at Augusta. "My train of thought's fine. Listen, Gertie overheard a conversation between Kimberlynn and the bartender. It *had* to be the bartender. The description was a perfect match. The bartender accused Kimberlynn of not finding someone's notes. That someone had to be Sharon. And then, the bartender said Kimberlynn was sloppy and shouldn't have done something before finding those notes first. I'm thinking the 'something' was the murder."

"I thought so, too," Nate said. "Of course, Gertie didn't hear the entire conversation and her recollection might not have been accurate. Still, it was close enough for me to convince the sheriff's deputies to track down that bartender. Remember, the Gila County deputies have coordinated their own setup for Friday. That's the date we believe a "pickup" is going to happen in the high desert. So, no one wants to spook the bartender first. If she's involved in any of this, she might tip off her cohorts."

There was so much to take in and it all seemed to be happening at once. I brushed that same annoying strand of hair from my forehead and groaned. "What's the plan? What's going to happen exactly?"

"We're still finalizing it. Marshall and I have a breakfast meeting tomorrow morning in Sun City West with Deputies Ranston and Bowman. We should know more after that."

"Geez, seems like all they do is meet and strategize."

"Yeah," Augusta said. "And eat donuts."

Nate brushed off some crumbs from his shirt and laughed. "Got to admit, there are a lot of strings attached to that bartender. Like her relationship with Kimberlynn, for starters, and the fact she's working so close to an alleged drop-off spot for some stolen diamonds. Wish we could find a way to link her to Quentin Dussler, but, so far, there's nothing. We don't even know her name, but that's an easy fix. Those Gila County deputies have lots of contacts."

Marshall rubbed his hands together and then wiped them on his pants. "Tomorrow's Thursday already. Not a whole lot of time to put this together. And I don't think those deputies have anything solid in place yet. Think we should have Phee contact Dean Carlington at Serenity Brook and tell him the delivery is set for Friday? I'm wagering the guy has a private plane so he wouldn't even bother with needing to book a flight to Phoenix."

"Too soon," Nate said. "She spoke to the assistant yesterday. We'll have her place the call tomorrow. And yeah, Carlington's the CEO of a mega company. If he doesn't own his own plane, he's got company planes at his disposal."

"Um, what if someone else shows up for the diamonds?" I asked.

"They'll be arrested, too," Marshall said. "And everyone will be questioned about Quentin's murder."

I returned to my desk and the spreadsheet I was working on. It felt good to immerse myself in something straightforward. The next hour and a half flew by. I heard Augusta turning off the copier and realized it was time to head to my mother's.

"Should we stop and pick something up for the potluck?" Marshall asked once we were in the car.

"I'm sure there'll be gads of food, but picking up a cheesecake never hurts."

We made a quick stop at a little Italian bakery before driving into Sun City West.

"So, who's going to be at your mother's tonight?"

"The usual crew—Shirley, Lucinda, Myrna, Louise, and Cecilia. The snowbirds are gone and Aunt Ina had tickets to the Phoenix Symphony. Oh, and Streetman. He probably has his own place setting."

Chapter 32

The usual Buicks were lined up along my mother's street. Marshall parked on the opposite side in front of the only shade he could find—a jacaranda tree in dire need of trimming. As we approached my mother's house, I warned Marshall to watch for the dog.

"Why? Will he snap?"

"No. He might escape and you'll wind up spending the rest of the night tracking him down. He's really fast. Then again, he may just hide under the nearest piece of furniture."

Fortunately for us, that was exactly what Streetman did when we got to the door. Our knock scared him sufficiently to stop begging, according to my mother, and dart under the couch.

She ushered us inside and shut the door. "Don't worry. He'll be out in a minute. Sit anywhere. What can I get you to drink?"

"Whatever you've got." Marshall greeted the ladies, who were already seated in the living room. Myrna, Louise, and Cecilia on the couch, Shirley in one of the floral chairs, and Lucinda next to her in an armchair. I motioned for Marshall to take the wing chair while I commandeered the other floral one.

"The food is on the counter in the kitchen. We can all help ourselves," my mother said. "And look, Phee and Marshall brought a giant cheesecake." Then she looked at the dog, who'd finally crawled out from under the couch. "If you're good, you can have a tiny bit of cheesecake."

I nudged Marshall in the arm and whispered, "See what I mean about the dog?"

"So," Lucinda said, "any news yet on those murders? Or the note? Harriet and I had nothing to do with the victim and yet he had a paper with our names on it."

Thank heavens you don't know who else had one.

"Probably something to do with the clay club," Marshall said. "We're still—"

"Working on it. I know. I know." My mother sounded more matter-of-fact than irritated.

Casseroles, salads, and assorted appetizers filled the entire counter. I helped myself to a seven-layer nacho dip and some raisin and carrot salad. Then I added a deviled egg to the mix. Marshall took a little of everything and managed to balance it as he made his way back to the living room.

"Feel free to sit at the kitchen table or the patio table," my mother called. "You'll be more comfortable."

"Come on." I led Marshall out to the patio. "You'll get used to this."

We were joined by Louise Munson and Myrna Mittleson at the small round table. Streetman was frantically running back and forth between tables, hoping to gobble up anything that accidentally fell to the floor.

"Only a few weeks until the Creations in Clay," Louise said. "Your mother is hoping her piece wins an award. This is so exciting."

I grabbed my iced tea and swallowed. "Uh-huh."

"Have you seen the piece?" she asked. "All your mother would tell us is there's nothing like it."

Again, I took another swallow. "Uh, yeah. Nothing like it."

Then Myrna spoke. "It's really too bad some of the original members are no longer active in the club. I remember going to that show a few years ago and was astonished at the talent. I'm trying to remember the name of that woman who made those glorious cookie jars. Oh yes, Mary Olsen. That was her name. Of course, that must have been a good seven or eight years ago. Maybe nine. The clay club was one of the original Sun City West charter clubs."

Marshall tapped my arm. "Wasn't one of those acquaintances of Quentin's named Mary? I seem to recall you saying something about that when you first met with Cindy Dolton in the dog park."

Lon and Mary Melhorn. That's where I learned about the niece. The nonexistent niece. And there was more. Mary had mentioned having once been in the clay club.

"Mary Melhorn told me she and her husband used to be in the clay club. Years ago. That's how they knew Quentin. Holy cow! You don't suppose Mary Olsen is really Mary Melhorn? Lon could be her second husband. And if that's the case—"

"I know. You've got to have another conversation with her. It has to be you."

Louise cleared her throat and leaned forward. "What are the two of you talking about? Did we miss something?"

"I'm sorry," I said. "Marshall and I can't get our minds off this investigation, and when Myrna mentioned Mary Olsen, it reminded me of something."

Myrna bit off part of a deviled egg and wiped her mouth with a napkin. "I don't know much about Mary Olsen. I'd only seen her at the shows, but I can tell you this much— that woman has spectacular taste in jewelry. It's not easy to forget tanzanite and diamond earrings or those Pandora bracelets that cost a fortune. Her clothing wasn't off the rack, either. Imagine having money and talent. What a combination."

When I'd met Mary Melhorn, she was wearing expensive Hidalgo designs. And that company only produced eighteen-karat gold.

Myrna popped the remainder of the egg in her mouth and swallowed. "Add a wealthy husband to the mix, and you've got it made. I'm not sure what he does, but it's enough to keep her in baubles."

Baubles. Designer jewelry. Clay club. It couldn't be a coincidence. I got up from my seat and charged into the kitchen. This wasn't a crack in the case; it was a downright earthquake fault. "Mom!"

"What, Phee? What happened? Did Streetman eat the spicy nachos?" My mother leaned into the patio and looked for the dog.

"No. Look behind you. He's in the living room by the armchair. Listen, this is important. Do you have any pictures of the clay club members going back seven to nine years? Maybe in an old brochure or something?"

"I don't save that stuff. If I want to look at pictures, I pull up their Web site."

"The clay club has a Web site?"

"Of course. All the major clubs do."

"Oh my God! Quick! I've got to get to your computer. Sorry, everyone. This should only take a few minutes. Come on, Marshall. You can finish eating later. The computer's in the spare bedroom. Let's go."

Marshall got up from his spot on the patio and followed me into the back bedroom. The computer was an ancient relic, compared to mine, and seemed to take forever to boot up. I entered the password immediately, since it was my mother's name. Then I Googled "Sun City West Clay Club." In seconds, I was directed to their site.

"Oh look! There's a whole ribbon on top. 'Events, Empty Bowls, Virtual Tours, History, Sales.' It's got to be with 'History.'"

Even though Marshall was standing directly behind me, I was talking to myself as I scrolled through a never-ending collection of club members engaged in all sorts of activities. It was a mindless blur as I scanned images of people sitting at the pottery wheels, stuffing themselves with food at picnics, or holding up their creations for the camera. Finally, I got to a section labeled "Officers."

The photos were displayed in descending order, starting with the current year. I held on to the mouse and kept scrolling. Nine pictures later, I had the answer I was looking for. And possibly the murderess.

"It's her! It's her! Take a good look. I'll get out of your way."

I all but shoved Marshall into the chair. He put his elbows on the desk, clasped his hands, and rested his chin on his knuckles. "Which one of those ladies is she?"

"The one in the middle." Her hair wasn't quite as gray but, other than that, she looked the same. Stylish and clad in tasteful jewelry. "The names are listed below, but they're too small to read. Wait a sec. Let me see if I can enlarge the picture by zooming."

"Unbelievable. Mary Olsen, Treasurer," Marshall said. "And now, Mary Olsen Melhorn. MOM!"

"What a clever scheme to hide those stolen diamonds in a piece of greenware. She knew it would be safe in the back of that closet. It was the one place where things were left alone. Until my mother and Lucinda decided to do some extra cleaning out."

"She certainly threw everyone off the scent by fabricating that story about Quentin's niece. Still, we have no idea what Mary's involvement was with that heist or with his murder. But I do know something that can get us closer. Hold on."

He took out his cell phone and tapped it a few times. I didn't hear what he said, or whom he called, because, at that precise second, my mother shouted, "We're cutting the cheesecake. Streetman is getting antsy. The computer can wait."

I motioned for Marshall to stay put and continue with his call.

"I'm right here, Mom. Marshall will be out in a second. Give the dog a biscuit or something."

When I walked into the kitchen, most of the ladies had already helped themselves to a slice of cake and Streetman was eating his portion as well. I shuddered and got plates for Marshall and me.

"What's going on?" Myrna asked. "One minute we're talking about Mary Olsen's jewelry and the next minute you're out of the room."

"Um, er, uh, it made me think of something about the investigation, and I had to get on Mom's computer."

"Well, forget the investigation and enjoy the cheesecake. The giant sampler was a great idea. My favorite is the caramel swirl."

Just then Marshall walked back into the kitchen and I handed him a plate. "How did it go?"

"It went. I'll tell you about it in the car. I also gave Nate a buzz."

We sat back down at the patio table and finished our desserts.

"Now we're going to get to the interesting part of the evening," Louise said. "We need to set up the reading list for next year. Your aunt couldn't make it, but she e-mailed everyone her suggestions."

"That's our cue to get out of here," I whispered to Marshall.

We thanked my mother for inviting us, promised to call her if we got any new information about the murders, and said our good-byes.

"Have fun selecting books," I said as I closed the front door. "Especially Aunt Ina's." Halfway down the walkway, I grabbed Marshall's wrist. "Tell me. Did you call the sheriff's department about Mary?"

"No. I called Rolo instead. Hacking into government sites is one of his favorite pastimes. He couldn't wait to check out passport information."

"You mean?"

"Yeah. Given the information your uncle Louis had about Quentin's transatlantic voyage, we don't need Quentin's passport dates. We know when he left Belgium. What I need Rolo to find is passport information for one Mary Olsen Melhorn. Date of entry and exit. And any Klingons. We need to know who was with her."

"How fast can he work?"

"Depends. I've known Rolo to go forty-eight hours straight on something. Especially if he's wired up on a new diet craze."

"And what about our end?"

"That's a two-prong nightmare. Tomorrow, you'll make the call to Dean Carlington and set that in motion for Friday. Just think, if we hadn't come here tonight, we never would've realized who 'MOM' was. I'm telling you, those women are a wealth of information."

"If you can sift through the hearsay, rumor, and gossip."

"Who do you suppose is the other diamond buyer? The one Kimberlynn alluded to when Gertie overheard her speaking with the bartender?"

"Not sure. And Nate and I aren't sure if that conversation

was about the diamonds. It could've been something else. We'll only know on Friday when all of this is set in motion."

"So, you and Nate are going up to Punkin Center?"

"One of us will. Nate has a feeling something may happen at the Lillian. I think it had to do with that conversation of Kimberlynn's. So, one lucky party gets to stay in town."

"I wonder what kind of plan the sheriffs' departments have in store for Friday."

"Me too. And we're supposed to be in the loop. Meanwhile, I'd rather think about our plans for tonight. How about a warm swim before getting under some cool sheets?"

"You've got it backward but count me in."

Chapter 33

"You sure that's all you want for lunch?" Augusta asked. "A toasted bagel from the deli?"

"I'm not that hungry. My stomach's all in knots wondering about tomorrow. I keep thinking I'm forgetting something, but I don't know what."

"Relax. Nate and Marshall know what they're doing, even if they're dealing with your least favorite deputies. Be thankful the FBI hasn't shown up yet with some doofus from Interpol."

"I suppose you're right. As soon as the men get back to the office, I'm supposed to call Dean Carlington and finalize the arrangement."

"Looks like that'll be sooner than you think. Here comes the boss now. He's crossing the street. Parking's impossible this time of day. Sure you don't want me to pick up anything else for you to eat? I'm on my way out now."

"No, a bagel's fine."

Nate had filled his stomach before returning to the office from an early meeting in Sun City West. Marshall was with a new client in Peoria and wouldn't be back for a bit. Augusta grabbed her bag, walked to the door, and muttered a few words to Nate before taking off for the deli.

"How'd the morning go?" I asked him.

"Everything looked good on paper."

"Meaning?"

"Who the hell knows? I'm going to need something stronger than Rolaids to deal with all those protocols. It's almost one. Ready to place that call?"

"Sure. Let me get the number Eric gave us. I left it on my desk."

"Might as well sit at your own desk and be comfortable. I'll be right in."

I lifted the candy wrapper from underneath my pink flying pig paperweight and stared at the number. Nate walked in, handed me a new burner phone, leaned against the wall, and gave me a thumbs-up. I bit my lower lip. "What if Dean Carlington didn't break the jar and call the insurance company?"

"Don't worry, kiddo. He did. I guarantee he wouldn't risk losing a million-dollar diamond. Go ahead. Call him."

I closed my eyes and pretended I was calling about a delinquent account. Dean Carlington picked up on the second ring.

"Mr. Carlington, you may proceed as planned. We shall deliver the package to the designated location by nine tomorrow morning. I trust that's satisfactory for you."

"Yes. Yes. I've taken care of everything. Um, how long will the package remain before it's too late for pick-up?"

I started adding up the amount of time it would take to fly from Palm Springs International Airport to Sky Harbor in Phoenix. Then the drive up north. I didn't want to make it too easy, but I certainly didn't want the plan to crash and burn before it began. "Five and a half hours. I'd plan for an early start, if I were you. Good luck, Mr. Carlington. It's been a pleasure doing business with you."

My fingers hit the end button before I could take a breath.

"That was wonderful, Phee," Nate said. "Tomorrow's going to turn out to be one hell of a day."

The plan was clear-cut. In less than twenty-four hours, Marshall would meet with a team of Maricopa County deputies at their station in Fountain Hills. From there, the crew would connect with the Gila County deputies at Jake's Corner, a tiny dot on the map near Punkin Center. According to Nate, the deputies were going to stash a fake gem and fan out in the high desert. They'd be close enough to the outcrop to zoom in on whoever showed up for the prize. My money was on Dean Carlington, but the sheriff's department was certain he wasn't the only buyer. At least with Dean in play, they'd have someone to bring in for questioning. Thank goodness I managed to be so convincing on the phone with the guy when I spoke with him today.

"Will Ranston and Bowman be part of the sting tomorrow?" I asked.

Nate shook his head. "Not directly. They've got to have deputies who can ride dirt bikes without killing themselves. Ranston and Bowman, along with some Gila County deputies, will be stationed along the road once the operation gets underway."

"You mean they'll show up once Dean Carlington is already on the footpath."

"Exactly. But there's one glitch."

"What?"

"Like we talked about before, there may be another player. And, we don't know if any of these buyers are armed. Let's face it, we're dealing with a bizarre diamond heist that may or may not have something to do with the Lillian. I'm still not comfortable with that conversation Gertie overheard between Kimberlynn and that bartender."

"So you believe that woman was the bartender?"

"I believe you. *That*, and the fact the signed postcard

from Antwerp had the same name, 'MOM,' as that signature from the stolen urn. The bartender had to have known Mary Melhorn."

"Speaking of which, why can't the sheriff's department search Mary's house?"

"Not enough evidence for a warrant. But don't fret. If my suspicions are right, Mary Melhorn may be paying a visit to Punkin Center tomorrow as well."

"What about the Lillian? Do you really think something's going to happen there tomorrow?"

"Wish I knew. I can't seem to get that expression out of my mind. 'Feds crawling all over the place.' Only thing I can do is plant myself over there tomorrow. Got it all set. I'll be with a deputy, and we'll ask the residents some follow-up questions regarding Sharon Smyth. It should appear seamless."

No sooner did I finish discussing tomorrow's rendezvous with Nate than Rolo called to tell him the astonishing news. Mary Olsen had indeed been in Belgium, Antwerp to be exact. She'd arrived ten days after Quentin Dussler left the country. And she didn't arrive alone. She was accompanied by her daughter, Carolyn Olsen, a former gymnast.

"Holy cow!" I said.

"Oh, it gets better. Rolo's e-mailing me Carolyn's passport photo. I don't know how he does this stuff, but I'm not stopping to ask. Heck, that photo's probably in my in-box by now. Hold on."

"I got your bagel, Phee," Augusta announced. "It was a zoo at the deli. You'd think they were giving food away. And I picked up one for you, too, Mr. Williams, in case you're still hungry. Toasted with cream cheese."

"Thanks. I'll know how hungry I am as soon as I check my e-mail."

Nate rushed into his office with Augusta and me on his heels. We charged over to his computer monitor as if it was about to deliver the holy grail. As Nate scrolled through his messages, I held my breath.

"Yep, here it is," he said. "Under 'Vacation Photos.'"

The picture was somewhat pixilated but absolutely recognizable.

"That's her!" I shouted. "Carolyn Olsen. The bartender."

Nate looked away from the screen. "Where'd you say you put that bagel?"

Augusta handed him a small brown deli bag.

"Excuse me, ladies. I've got to place a few calls. And, Phee, you were right all along."

Rolo's revelation forced the office into a tailspin. It meant Nate would have to accompany Marshall tomorrow to Punkin Center in order to "have a chat" with Carolyn. Assuming she was still tending bar. A clever scheme to cover up her real intentions. The deputies, according to Nate, weren't able to "switch gears" without "hours of planning and copious notes."

"I'm not comfortable with this change in plans," he told me when he had finished delivering Rolo's information to the Maricopa County Sheriff's Office. "I've got an uneasy feeling about the Lillian. Nothing definitive. Nothing that would warrant having an officer on duty. To make matters worse, the deputy who was going to join me there tomorrow had a change in his schedule."

"I don't mind stopping by in the afternoon. I could say I'm there to see Gertie and Trudy. What do you say?"

"I'm not sure."

"Honestly, Nate, it'll be fine. Sounds like all the action will be in the high desert by Punkin Center. You're the ones who have to be worried."

"Yeah, but we're armed. Look, go ahead and stop by, but if anything, and I mean anything whatsoever, strikes you as odd or uncomfortable, get out of there and call the posse. Got it?"

"Sure. But first you'll have to define 'odd.'"

"Very funny."

Marshall returned to the office a little while later and caught up with the latest series of events. Due to tomorrow's schedule, he decided to sleep in his own place tonight. "No sense in both of us losing sleep."

I tried to hide how nervous I was feeling.

"You have nothing to worry about, hon," he said. "Everything will go off without a hitch tomorrow. Sure, they've got big guns blazing, but that's for show. We're dealing with diamond thieves. Not wackos."

I thought back to that awful hostage situation in Casa Grande where Marshall was lucky he wasn't ambushed. "Call me as soon as they take Dean Carlington into custody. And Carolyn. And maybe her mother, if she's there, too."

"It'll be okay. You be careful at the Lillian. And don't go into anyone's apartment. Even Gertie and Trudy's. And especially not Mario Aquilino's. No matter what they may want to show you."

"What about Kimberlynn Warren? Shouldn't someone be taking her into custody?"

"She's not going anywhere. Once the operation in Punkin Center is completed, I'm sure the sheriff's department will have lots of questions for her. Meanwhile, the less she suspects the better."

Marshall called me twice that evening. Both times to reassure me. That made me even more nervous. All I could picture was one of those god-awful Westerns with men shooting guns all over the place. Then I remembered something. That day we trekked up to the high desert, my aunt insisted I was being followed by a man with a gun.

More than likely it was her imagination. But what if, in addition to the diamond heist gang, there was a real wacko traipsing about? I called Marshall back, but it went to voice mail and I fell asleep before trying again.

Chapter 34

I got into the office earlier than usual. I didn't mind working every other Saturday and, frankly, as worried as I was about the situation, it gave me something to do other than housework. Besides, I'd had a lousy night's sleep and I was really edgy. I hadn't had a miserable night like that in months. I fell asleep without a problem but woke up a few hours later unable to get back to sleep. No matter what I did, my mind wouldn't shut off.

There were so many tentacles to the case it made it impossible for me to rest. In retrospect, I should've gotten up, written down my thoughts, and gone back to bed. But instead, I let my mind weave a complicated spiderweb, beginning with Mary Olsen Melhorn.

If she wasn't the mastermind, she was certainly a key player. I was positive it was her greenware urn that was used to hide the stolen diamonds. And, she'd been in Antwerp at the time of the theft. Then there was her daughter, the bartender. Why on earth would someone stick around an isolated place like Punkin Center unless she had other motives? Obviously, she knew about the drop-off spot in the high desert. And what about that text message she sent when Aunt Ina and I were in the bar? Carolyn must have been alerting those off-roaders to our presence.

Then there was Quentin Dussler. His clay jar "road maps" led buyers to a secret location where they could obtain a stolen diamond or diamonds. I imagined every time a buyer contacted him, he notified Mary. She would then go into the clay club, presumably to check on her piece of greenware, but, in reality, to remove one or more of the stones. Didn't my mother tell me some of the members kept their greenware wet so if they wanted to alter it in any way, they could do so before it dried?

The three of them, Mary, Carolyn, and Quentin, had to have been in cahoots. But maybe one of them got greedy and decided it was time to get Quentin out of the picture. If Mary and her daughter were working together, they could have easily killed Quentin. The same way Sharon Smyth was murdered. A plastic bag over the head. In her case, they removed the bag and stuffed linens and towels around her. In Quentin's case, it was clay. Clay that molded to his face.

Quentin's murder was the first and the killers must have been really careful to remove the evidence. Their plastic bag. They weren't so fortunate with Sharon. And why Sharon? She had nothing to do with the diamonds. And her clay jar "road map" was long gone before she was.

I leaned my elbows on my desk, bent my head down, and ran my fingers through my hair. The sound of Augusta unlocking the office door made me jump.

"I'm in here," I shouted. "Got in real early so I kept the door locked."

Augusta marched inside my office. "You doing all right? I've seen old photos of refugees coming through Ellis Island who looked better than you do. And that was after crossing the Atlantic."

"If you must know, I probably didn't get more than two or three hours of sleep last night. I don't know how Nate and Marshall deal with this stuff all the time. I like things to be clear-cut and simple. You know, like a balance sheet."

Augusta rolled her eyes and trounced over to the coffee-maker. "So, did you come up with a theory yet?"

The words spewed out of my mouth. "Quentin. Mary. Carolyn. Sharon. Diamonds. Clay."

"Uh-huh, got it so far," she said. "What about that Kimberlynn woman? The one whose conversation with Carolyn, the bartender, got Nate to thinking the Lillian might be involved."

"I'm not sure. That's where it gets all murky for me. There's nothing that links her to Quentin, the clay club, or those Antwerp diamonds. Still, she and Carolyn were having more than a tête-à-tête."

"But Sharon Smyth was one of her residents. And Sharon had suspicions about the markings on that stolen clay jar of hers."

"True. Hey, you don't suppose—"

"That Kimberlynn stole Sharon's clay jar? It wouldn't have done her any good. Sounds as if the diamonds get put into circulation, so to speak, once the jar is destroyed and the insurance company is notified. Then the buyer goes and picks up his or her treasure. The map's good for one round only. And Sharon's jar wasn't insured."

"So, what do you think's going on between Kimberlynn and Carolyn?" I asked.

"Whatever it is, I wager it has to do with those resort retirement places. Don't you think it's awfully fishy that the diamond buyers seem to have connections with those places? And if any of my relatives decide to stick me in one of those, they'll have to get past Mr. Wesson and Mr. Glock."

"Your lawyers?"

"My guns."

I helped myself to a cup of coffee, too, a new K-cup flavor I'd been meaning to try. Chicory blend. "Hey, before

I forget, I promised Nate I'd drop by the Lillian today. Like you said, he had a feeling something is in the wind over there. I'll scope things out with the Gertrudes."

"I keep bear spray in my desk if you need it."

"I'm visiting a retirement place, not Yellowstone National Park."

I went back to my desk and pulled up last month's billing. Augusta had a ton of work, too. She was revising the new client contract agreements for Nate and had some tax records to look up. With the exception of a few sporadic phone calls, it was a quiet morning. At one point I asked her if any of those calls were Nate or Marshall, but I knew better. She would have yelled for me if they were.

Five and a half hours was a long window for Dean Carlington and I wondered if I shouldn't have made it three or four. The wait was making me anxious. I figured the Lillian might take my mind off Punkin Center and whatever impending disaster might be out in that high desert.

"I think I'll head over to Sun City West. I'll stop at a hamburger place for an early lunch on the way. Call me if anything comes up. I'll keep my ringtone on high."

"You got it," Augusta said. "See you later."

Everything looked normal at the Lillian when I pulled up a short while later. The May heat made it uncomfortable for people to be out and about at midday, but I spied a few ladies heading to their cars. I nabbed a spot in the side lot and went straight to the front door. A blue Toyota RAV4 was parked near the delivery vehicles. A magnetic sign on the driver's side door read GREATER PHOENIX MOBILE NOTARY SERVICES. Yep, the Lillian provided for everything.

No one was in the lobby when I walked inside the building. Then I remembered it was lunchtime and the residents would be in the dining room. I stepped over to the reception desk, expecting to see the blondes, but instead, Taylor was there.

"Hi! I was so used to seeing the blondes I forgot you worked on Saturdays," I said.

She looked up from the computer screen and smiled. "Yeah, those two are going boonie cruising today. It's always something with them."

"Boonie cruising?"

"You know, off-roading. It's a passion of theirs. Along with kayaking, target shooting, and snowboarding. Their lives totally revolve around entertaining themselves. That's when they're not being pampered at a spa or paying an obscene amount of money for a manicure. Tina called me to ask about something, and while I was on the phone with her, I heard Tanya shouting, 'I'll need a massage and an herbal wrap when we're done riding.' Can you imagine?"

"Um, no. I've never had that kind of money."

"They invited me once to go with them to some fancy salon in Fountain Hills, but I couldn't afford to blow a week's salary on nails or a facial. Frankly, I don't know how they do it. I mean, the Lillian pays well, but not that well."

"Taylor, do you know where they go boonie cruising?"

"Up north. Especially this time of year. You'd have to be insane to go anywhere below Phoenix in this heat. I'm figuring east of the I-Seventeen in the Tonto National Forest. Lots of cool places to check out. What's the matter? Did I say something wrong?"

"Um, sorry. I was just thinking, that's all. By the way, is Kimberlynn in?"

"She was. I mean, she still is, but not in her office. She was in the middle of signing some papers with a mobile notary when Mr. Aquilino from the third floor called the desk. He was insistent she go to his apartment. I don't think it had anything to do with maintenance or he would have called Tiny Mike. Anyway, the notary's still back there. She ushered him into the small reception room. Probably didn't feel comfortable leaving him alone in her office. At least it's chocolate chip cupcake day. Want one? They're the best."

"Thanks, but I'll pass. I can always—"

Just then, the man I recognized as Vernon McWellan from one of my earlier visits rushed over to Taylor.

"We've got a situation. She said not to call the sheriff. Said she could handle it, but I'm telling you, she'll be face-down in the laundry room if you don't do something. Got a whole crowd from the early lunch shift up there, too."

"Who? What?" Taylor asked.

Vernon leaned over the counter and shouted, "The director of this place. Kimberlynn Warren. She's being held hostage in front of the laundry chute by that old curmudgeon Mario Aquilino. I had to go back upstairs to my apartment because I forgot my Pepcid AC. The second I opened my door into the corridor, I saw them. Tell you one thing, that Mario sure has guts."

Taylor leaned forward. "I'm not sure I understand. What's going on exactly?"

"I'll make it real easy for you." Then he turned to me. "And to the nice visitor. Mario's got Kimberlynn shoved against the laundry chute with his walker. If either of them makes a sudden move, she'll do a backflip to the basement. Is that clear enough?"

I suddenly remembered about the laundry chutes. In fact, it was Taylor who had explained it to me when we first met. It sounded as if the design was an accident looking for a place to happen, but, in this case, it was a weapon.

"Taylor," I said, "you've got to call the sheriff's posse."

"Kimberlynn's not going to be too happy about that," Vernon grumbled. "But go ahead. Ain't me who'll lose my job."

I glared at Vernon. "Fine. I'll make the call."

"No need," Taylor said. "I can do it. We've got the

nonemergency number right here. If I call nine-one-one, they'll send an ambulance and a fire truck."

As she placed the call, I asked Vernon if he knew what prompted Mario to corner the residence director against a swinging laundry chute.

"How am I supposed to know? All I can tell you is Mario kept yelling, 'No buyout. You can't pull this crap.'"

"Relax, I called the sheriff's posse," Taylor said. "They'll send someone over. Uh, maybe I should call maintenance. Have them go upstairs."

I gave her a nod. "Good idea. I'll head there, too."

Taylor reached for the phone again and froze. Her eyes were glued to the computer monitor in front of her. "Oh no. This is bad. Really, really bad. Someone posted a YouTube video. Someone from here. I didn't think the residents knew about YouTube. The video's on Facebook. Wow. That was fast. I never would have seen it if I wasn't juggling between screens before you got here, Miss Kimball. It makes the time go faster."

Suddenly my phone rang. It was Augusta. In less than three seconds, I forgot about the video and jumped to Nate and Marshall. I backed away from the counter. "Excuse me a second. I've got to take this."

I couldn't tell if Augusta was laughing or choking. "What, Augusta? What? Are they okay?"

"I should be asking you that question. Don't know about them, but you've got a hell of a show going on at the Lillian. I was scrolling through Facebook when I saw it. It's my break time. I don't scroll when I'm working. Do you need backup?"

My God! Is the whole world on Facebook? "No, no. I think everything will be under control. The sheriff's posse is sending someone."

"Okey-dokey."

Taylor looked out the front door. "I think it's too late. There's a news van pulling up. KPHO. They're downtown. How the heck did they get here so fast?"

Vernon groaned. "For two people who've got their noses stuck in those electronic things all day long, I'm surprised you didn't know about the grand opening across the street. Pet World. Lots of senior discounts. Big hoop-dee-do. KPHO is covering it. It was on last night's news. The van was right across the street."

"That still doesn't explain how they knew what was going on here," I said.

This time it was Taylor who answered. "KPHO's on Facebook, too."

Chapter 35

Elevators could be notoriously slow when you were in a hurry. They could also get stuck. I opted for the stairs. Thank God they were carpeted and wide. I managed to reach the third floor only slightly out of breath. In front of me was a long hallway that was quickly filling up with onlookers.

I tucked my bag under my arm as if it was a football and I was the quarterback. Forcing myself to take long strides, I headed right for the end zone. Or in this case, the laundry chute near the elevators. Kimberlynn Warren had her hands pressed against the wall, inches from the swinging door. Mario had her trapped with that walker of his and wasn't about to budge.

"Admit it!" he yelled. "You killed Sharon Smyth. Admit it! Admit it! You killed her because she found out you embezzled our money and had to sell this place."

"That's not true. I didn't kill her," Kimberlynn cried. "I swear."

Using my elbow, I wedged myself through the growing crowd. "Mr. Aquilino! Stop!"

"I'll stop when this witch admits what she's done."

"Pushing her down a laundry chute isn't going to get you any answers."

"Want to bet?"

Mario gave the walker another nudge and Kimberlynn gasped. Unlike traditional laundry chutes, the one at the Lillian was designed to make things easier for senior citizens. It consisted of a rubber door that swung back and forth, not like the kind that resembled a double-hung window. One wrong move and Kimberlynn would go backward. Mario didn't seem to care.

"I can prove Kimberlynn's a murderer," he said. "It's all in the letter Sharon left me before she was killed."

So much for him not telling anyone. Maybe Marshall should have gotten that agreement in writing.

Suddenly the hallway got brighter. It was a light from the KPHO camera crew. We were being filmed. Before I could say anything to Mario, I heard the newscaster's voice. "This is one heck of a day in Arizona, folks. First the wildfire in the Tonto National Forest near Payson, and a bizarre hostage situation, of sorts, playing out at the Lillian, a resort retirement hotel in Sun City West."

My stomach began to tighten. As if my guts were coiling.

The newscaster went on. "At least the Lillian's situation is limited to a hallway, not the high desert. We'll skip to that wildfire video in just a moment but, meantime, let's find out what's going on here."

Thoughts of Nate and Marshall getting trapped by a wildfire flashed through my mind. The newscaster didn't say *where* in the Tonto National Forest it was, only that it was near Payson. Lots of places were near Payson. I didn't have time to dwell on it because the next thing I knew, the newscaster had made his way to the front of the melee and was holding a microphone in front of Mario Aquilino. "Sir, can you tell us why you're holding this woman hostage?"

"Holding her hostage? What the hell would I do that for? I'm holding her in contempt. And if she doesn't admit to what she did, I'm sending her straight down the laundry chute. Anyone make a move toward me and that's where she's going."

The newscaster stood absolutely still. "For the sake of our viewers, can you please give us your name and the name of your hosta—I mean the name of the woman?"

Kimberlynn lifted her head up. "I'm Kimberlynn Warren, the director of the Lillian, and the gentleman is Mario Aquilino, one of our residents. It would appear as if Mr. Aquilino has been under quite a bit of stress lately."

"Stress my you-know-what," he went on. "Sharon was wise to your scheme, so you murdered her."

The conversation, live and on the air for the Greater Phoenix community, continued. And just as I was on the verge of finding out what Kimberlynn was about to say, my phone rang.

"Phee, it's Augusta again. Rolo faxed us some information. You'll never guess who used to be on the board at Wolters Stork."

"Dean Carlington?"

"No. Alonso M—"

"What? I can't hear you. I'll have to call you back. It's a circus over here."

"A what?"

"Circus!" My voice had gotten louder to compensate for the noise in front of the laundry chute, but as soon as I said the word "circus," everyone quieted down as if on cue.

Then, two sheriff volunteers from the posse stepped out of the elevator. Taylor didn't request deputies, only posse volunteers.

"Arrest that man!" someone in the crowd shouted, pointing to Mario. "He's liable to kill the director."

Mario looked as if he really was going to give her a shove.

"I mean it," he said. "Admit you killed her. Time's up!"

Kimberlynn must have noticed that expression, too. "Wait, Mr. Aquilino. Wait! I didn't kill Sharon, but I know who did."

"Damn!" someone shouted from behind me. "We just blew a bulb. Hey, Eddie, got an extra in your bag?"

While the camera crew was fumbling to change light-bulbs, Kimberlynn spoke. "If Mr. Aquilino agrees to give me some breathing space, I'll explain."

I put my hand on Mario's shoulder. "I don't think she's going anywhere. At least give her an inch or two."

Mario took a step back but kept the walker in front of him like a shield of armor.

Kimberlynn caught her breath. "Mr. Aquilino's partially right. About selling the Lillian. The management and maintenance costs were so high there was no way out. You see, I'm not only the director, I hold the majority of shares in the company. And then a few years ago we were approached with a unique opportunity."

"Did you get that on film?" I asked, turning to the camera crew.

A man who looked to be in his early thirties answered. "Sorry. We had to shut it down temporarily. The video feed from that wildfire up north is probably on the air. We're working to change the bulb."

I detected a slight smile on Kimberlynn's face. None of this was being recorded.

She continued as if she was giving directions or reciting a recipe. "Other resort retirement hotels were struggling, too. Wolters Stork, a major Dutch enterprise, learned about us and offered to incorporate us into their conglomerate. Not buy us out, as Sharon Smyth might have thought, but merge with us. And add other resort hotels. The only trouble was our bleak financial picture. We couldn't afford the buy-in price. And that's when an old friend of mine,

Carolyn Olsen, came up with a plan to get us the capital we needed."

"The Antwerp Diamond Heist?" I asked.

"How did you know?"

"I work for an investigator. And I'm a good listener. So, tell me about Carolyn."

"She studied architectural design in Italy, art history in Italy and France, and found the time to be a practiced gymnast. All skills needed to mastermind that heist. The only trouble was how to sell those stolen diamonds. And not just any diamonds. Rare blue diamonds."

That explains the price tag. "And that's where Quentin Dussler came in?"

"Uh-huh. Carolyn's mother was one of Quentin's protégées in the Sun City West clay club."

"Mary Olsen Melhorn, right?"

"You certainly have done your homework, Miss Kimball."

Just then Mario interrupted us. "If we don't get those blunderheads to change that bulb pretty quick, she'll deny everything."

"I wouldn't worry about that," I whispered. "Look at all the witnesses behind you. Let her continue."

"Don't come complaining to me when she clams up. And my walker and I aren't moving from this spot until that deputy over there arrests her."

"He's a posse volunteer, not a deputy. If he wants her arrested, he'll have to call for the nearest MCSO deputy."

"Fine. Fine." He turned back to Kimberlynn. "What about Mary? Speak up."

"Mary and Quentin devised a clever plan. Once the diamonds were safely out of Belgium, Mary hid them in an unbaked clay piece. Her work wasn't as noticeable as Quentin's, so no one would give her pieces a second look. As each diamond was sold, she removed it, gave it to Quentin for distribution, and returned the clay piece to the storage closet or whatever they call it. The profits were split among all of the parties. The distribution angle was the most ingenious of all."

"Using GPS coordinates and specialized designs on the finished products?" I asked.

"Uh-huh. How did you know?"

"Let's just say the staff at Williams Investigations is on top of everything." *Especially Augusta.* "But you still haven't explained who killed Sharon. You said you knew."

"I'll get to that. Give me a chance."

At that moment, the two posse volunteers approached Mario and tried to convince him to put his walker on the ground and let Kimberlynn step away from the laundry chute.

"The hell I will. Not until she admits to killing Sharon or tells me who did. And if you don't have the authority to arrest her, then I'm not budging."

Kimberlynn coughed a few times to clear her throat. "If I'm guilty of anything, it's carelessness. I left a letter from Wolters Stork in plain sight and unfortunately Sharon inadvertently read it. That meant she was privy to information that would have compromised our operation. It was too risky for everyone involved. The diamond buyers, the management at Wolters Stork . . ."

"So one of them killed her?" I asked.

"I'm afraid so."

"Um, before you go any further, I'd like to know how those diamond buyers were solicited to purchase the gems in the first place. Not like you could put them on Craigslist."

Kimberlynn half smiled. "That was the easy part. Ever hear of the Darknet market? It's the Internet mecca for illegal goods. In this case, we stuck to buyers who had interests in senior resort residences. It made it cleaner that way."

"I'm sure the residents at the Lillian will be glad to hear that," I said.

"And we're back *live* from the Lillian," came a voice from KPHO, "where one of the residents has cornered the director and is refusing to let her go."

One of the posse volunteers, a stout man in his late sixties or early seventies, sucked in his stomach and stood directly in front of the camera. "We made a call. The sheriff's office is sending over a deputy who has the authority to make arrests."

I tapped Mario on the arm again. "It's not worth getting arrested for creating a disturbance or kidnapping."

"Kidnapping? Have you lost your mind?"

"I'm not sure if that's the right word, but why take a chance? Put the walker down and go back to your apartment. She'll have enough to answer for. I can assure you."

My God! "I can assure you?" Why on earth do I say those things? I can't assure anyone of anything.

"You'd better keep your word. I know where you work," he said.

Then, as if he was simply out for a little stroll down the corridor, Mario Aquilino stepped away from the laundry chute and walked the ten or twelve feet back to his apartment. No one tried to stop him. The "hostage scene" at the Lillian fizzled in front of the cameras.

"Looks like the hostage situation is over at the Lillian," one of newscasters announced. "We'll be sure to follow the story and keep you apprised of any new developments. Meanwhile, we'll go back to the station for that ongoing wildfire coverage up north. Who says life in the desert isn't interesting?"

One of the crew members shut off the light and wound the cord around his shoulder. They walked to the elevators.

"We were trying to save this place." Kimberlynn was

now leaning against the wall, a good five or six feet from the laundry chute.

I took a step forward. "You know who did it, don't you?"

"I'm not saying a word without speaking to my lawyer."

Meanwhile, the crowd dissipated. One by one, they walked to the elevators or back to their apartments on the third floor. I heard snippets of their conversations.

"I hope the murderer isn't anyone we know."

"How many diamond thieves do you know?"

"If this place is sinking, I'm moving to the Monte Carlo."

"If they can refund your investment money."

"Someone needs to call *Sixty Minutes*."

"Too bad he didn't give her a shove down that chute. We'd be on every channel."

"You'll need to go downstairs," one of the posse volunteers said to Kimberlynn. "The deputy should be here any minute."

Kimberlynn walked to the elevator, flanked by the two men. Then I took the stairs to the lobby, pausing to send texts to Nate and Marshall.

Kimberlynn Warren confessed to her role. Are you near the wildfire? Call me.

My palms were sweating and my pulse was racing. There was a good chance Nate and Marshall were in a far more dangerous predicament than staving off an octogenarian with a walker.

Taylor was no longer at the reception desk when I got to the lobby. Instead, she was standing in front of the fountain staring at the parking lot. The KPHO van had just pulled away. I moved to the farthest corner of the room, plunked myself down on a cushy chair, and pushed the KPHO app.

In seconds, I read the "Breaking News" that was scrolled across my screen in a bright red ribbon.

AREA SHERIFFS' DEPARTMENTS EVACUATE RESIDENTS
IN THE HIGH COUNTRY. GILA AND MARICOPA
COUNTY DEPUTIES CALLED TO RESPOND.

Chapter 36

The story beneath the scrolling ribbon wasn't good. A wildfire had started somewhere south of Gisela, near Payson, and was quickly heading south to Jake's Corner. That wasn't too far from Punkin Center, and it was where Nate and Marshall's rendezvous with the deputy sheriffs was supposed to take place. To make matters worse, the winds kept shifting and that meant more evacuations. Many Phoenix residents had cabins and parked trailers in the area. Not to mention the number of campgrounds that quickly filled up this time of year. My best guess was that people would have to be evacuated northeast of Payson toward Holbrook or west near Camp Verde.

I kept telling myself to relax. Nate and Marshall weren't about to be caught up in it. More than likely, their entire operation would be canceled if things really got out of hand. I wasn't going to bother Augusta again when I heard Gertie's voice.

"Miss Kimball. We were looking all over for you. Trudy and I were barely out of the dining room when that commotion began. You didn't see us, but we went up to the third floor. Got wind of the action from Yolanda. Usually you can't trust what that batty old fool has to say, but this time she was insistent. Said Mario Aquilino threw Kimberlynn Warren down the hatch. We had to see for ourselves."

"Yes," Trudy added. "We saw all right. Mario had her cornered like a cockroach, but she was still vertical when we got there. We tried to motion to you, but you didn't see us. Then you left and we came downstairs, figuring you'd be here. So, do you think she did it? Kimberlynn, I mean? Killed Sharon?"

"I think she knows who did. Listen, I have to make a call. If I find out anything, I promise, I'll let you know."

Gertie grabbed her sister by the arm. "We'll wait by the door. When Kimberlynn gets carted out of here, we'll know. Meanwhile, I can see her over there by the counter. She's not going anywhere with those posse volunteers breathing down her neck."

I looked at the reception desk and, sure enough, Kimberlynn had two new lion tamers in front of her. Stretching my shoulders against the soft padding from the chair, I paused for a brief second. Then I took out my phone and called Augusta.

She answered before I spoke. "Still no word from them, Phee. Did you know there was a wildfire up near there? Just got an alert on my phone. What's going on at your end?"

"Kimberlynn confessed to being involved in this mess but not in front of the camera. Darn it all."

"She admitted to murder?"

"Not murder. Embezzlement and a key role in that diamond heist. But she knows who the killer is. Look, the second you hear anything from Nate or Marshall, call me."

"Phee, that boyfriend of yours will call you first. I guarantee it. He's probably questioning that Carolyn woman with those expensive nails. Bartender my patootie. She's a fancy salon girl after all. And I'm not referring to one of those Old West salons either. I'm thinking high-class nail place. What a rip-off."

"Um, most fancy salons don't think of themselves that way. They—oh my gosh. I just thought of something. I've got to go."

I hit the end icon and headed straight for Taylor. She was still standing where I last saw her, by the fountain.

"Taylor, this is important. Do you remember the name of that fancy nail salon where the blondes wanted you to go?"

"It was a spa in Fountain Hills. Like, I'm about to drive way over there for a manicure that costs more than my rent. The place was called La Tourelle and had a logo of a tower. Hold on. I left the card in my bag. You can have it. I certainly won't be using it."

Taylor took a few steps to the reception desk, reached over the counter, grabbed her bag, and pulled out the card.

"Thanks," I said.

"No problem. I'd better get back to work."

I glanced at the card and tucked it in my pocket. Two elderly residents walked past me, each one louder than the other.

"Hell of a wildfire, huh? Surprised they haven't named it yet."

"Maybe they ran out of names. They have to name hurricanes and winter storms. Next thing you know they'll be naming dust storms."

The TV in the lounge area adjacent to the lobby must have been showing the breaking news, so I walked into the room. Sure enough, a scene of burning brush and smoke took up the entire screen. The announcer, who was most probably piloting the helicopter, was trying to explain to the viewers what was going on. I seemed to have arrived just as the video was ending.

I sauntered back to the lobby in time to see Kimberlynn being escorted out of the building by a sheriff's deputy. Behind her, a small red-haired man carrying a briefcase shouted out, "We can do this at another time, Ms. Warren. I'll inform my client."

"Don't you dare." Her voice all but bounced off the walls. "I'll inform him. Don't do anything."

Just then, a text message came through on my phone. Finally. It was from Marshall.

Carlington scared off by dirt bikes. Wildfire evac trumped sting. Headed back.

I read the text twice and tried to return the call, but it went to voice mail. If I understood the message correctly, it meant Dean Carlington never secured his "diamond." For all I knew, he was on his way back to California, and probably angry as hell.

The off-roaders. It can't be a coincidence.

La Tourelle's card was in my pocket, and I couldn't get my hands on it fast enough. It was one of those ostentatious cards with frilly gold lettering that surrounded a lovely rendering of a medieval tower. The name on the bottom of the card read "Alonso Melhorn, owner." I froze. It was something Augusta had said. Something I dismissed at the time. "You'll never guess who used to be on the board of Wolters Stork. Alonso M . . ."

My God! Lon is short for Alonso. The diamond heists and the secret deal at the Lillian were being orchestrated by one hell of a family. So much for the darling Melhorns. All five of them. *No wonder those blondes can afford pricy mani-pedis and herbal cures and oh what the hell! They're probably soaking in a mud bath right now.*

"Taylor! Do you know their last names?" I was shouting, even though I was only a few feet from her.

"Whose last names? Which residents?"

"No. Not residents. Tina and Tanya."

"Sure," she said. "It's Olsen."

My mouth felt as if someone had stuffed it with cotton. Nothing came out. I nodded and hurried to my car. Again, I tried Marshall on the phone, but no luck. Same with Nate. I sent them both the same text.

Drive to La Tourelle in Fountain Hills. Got 'em.

Then I called Augusta and explained. Or so I thought.

"Phee, I don't understand a word you're saying. You're on your way to a spa in Fountain Hills? Now?"

"I know who the killers are."

I didn't give Augusta a chance to say anything else. I typed La Tourelle's address into my GPS and drove out of the Lillian faster than any resident had driven in years. I wasn't exactly sure what I was going to do once I confronted the blondes at that spa, but I'd think of something during the hour-long drive.

It was all starting to make sense. Everything had been right in front of me all along, and I never put it together. Tina and Tanya were Carolyn's daughters. And Mary's granddaughters. And Lon's step-granddaughters. Was that what you called it? And they were more than that. They were murderers.

By the time I got off the 101 and onto Frank Lloyd Wright Boulevard, I had either unraveled the entire scheme or created one that would've made Gillian Flynn proud. I followed the voice on my GPS and took the long topiary-lined driveway to La Tourelle, a breathtaking French manor house that looked as if it was magically transported to the Southwest.

Wasting no time, I parked in front, took the white stone stairs two at a time, and entered the grand reception room as if I had crossed a finish line.

"Quick," I said to a petite, dark-haired woman at the front desk. "I must locate Tina and Tanya Olsen. Family emergency."

The woman didn't blink an eye. "I'm sorry. Our guests cannot be interrupted. Who did you say you were?"

"I'm a family friend and this is urgent."

The woman lifted the receiver of her phone and made a call. Her voice was so low I had trouble understanding what she was saying.

When she hung up, she looked directly at me. "I'm afraid the ladies are in the tranquility room. Cucumber soaking baths. You'll have to wait."

She motioned to an area on the left that was reserved for visitors, not guests.

"But this can't wait."

"As soon as the ladies have exited the tranquility area, I will let them know they have a visitor."

She walked away without bothering to ask my name. At least something was in my favor. I plunked myself down on one of the leather couches and picked up a brochure. If nothing else, La Tourelle was certainly spectacular. As I thumbed through the photos of treatment and meditation rooms, a double-folded paper appeared. It was a map of the entire building. A full four-page, pull-out map.

I bit my lower lip and looked closely. The tranquility corridor was past the aroma-enhancing atrium, only a few yards from where I was seated. I waited quietly until I was certain no one would see me, especially that miserable petite woman. Then I made my way to the soaking baths.

The tranquility area was a circular courtyard that boasted its own rainforest. Small corridors branched out with signs indicating the treatment. Mud baths, eucalyptus baths, rose petal immersion baths. And all those years, I suffered with a bar of ivory soap and a shared family bathroom.

I located the sign for cucumber soaks and walked in. A tall woman in her late fifties or early sixties pointed to a locker area and handed me a white terry cloth robe. "May I have your name please, so I can note it on the schedule?"

"I, um, er . . ."

"Marisela! I need some more towels. Now!"

The woman stepped back and apologized. "I'll be right back."

The second she went into the room off to the right, I entered the only other doorway and prayed the blondes would still be there.

The old adage "Be careful what you wish for" should have come to mind, but unfortunately it didn't.

Tina and Tanya had toweled off and were wrapped in the same luxurious terry cloth robes as the one Marisela offered me.

I put my robe on a chair and took a breath. "It's over. I know who you are and what you've done."

One of the blondes, I wasn't sure which, replied, "Aren't you that Kimball woman from the Lillian? What are you talking about?"

"Diamond theft and murder. Or should I say, diamond thefts and murders?"

The blondes looked at each other and, in that brief second, I knew I was in trouble. What the hell was I doing in a room with two cold-blooded killers? I glanced around to make sure there were no plastic bags in sight. Then I took a step and prayed.

Chapter 37

"It would be a shame for someone to have an accident in here," one of the blondes said. "Imagine slipping on the floor and hitting your head on the top of the French soaker tub."

I didn't like where this was going.

Then the other sister spoke. "So you figured it out, huh? I'll give you credit for that much. Those moronic sheriff deputies were clueless."

"Almost as bad as the police back in Belgium," the other one added.

I slowly backed away from the tubs. "I can understand killing Sharon. She must have figured out the entire scheme, too, once she read that letter Kimberlynn left on the counter. She confronted Kimberlynn, didn't she?"

"Meddlesome old woman. Right, Tanya?"

"Yeah. She should've stuck to knitting or watching soap operas. When Kimberlynn told us what Sharon was going to do, we had no choice."

"Going to do?"

"Yeah," Tanya said. "That blabbermouth was going to call the TV stations."

I swallowed a lump in my throat. "So you made sure she didn't."

"Damn straight," Tina replied.

I kept backing up, inch by inch, hoping my back would eventually touch the door and I could get the heck out of there. "Okay. Fine. But what I really don't understand is why you killed Quentin. He was the one who figured out how and where to hide the diamonds so the buyers wouldn't be seen with the seller."

The sisters looked at each other. "Quentin drew up the schematics for the heist but got a little too greedy for our mother's liking. And our grandmother's. He demanded a bigger cut of the profits and that meant there wouldn't be enough money for my family's business to merge with Wolters Stork."

"So, um, Quentin was never a part of the plan to skim money from the resort retirement residents and own a part of the new business?"

"Nope. All he wanted was the money. And he threatened to go public with all of this if we didn't ante up."

Oldest story in the book. Greed. "I think your double little twist tops them all. You were the ones on the dirt bikes scaring away the buyers who followed the coordinates to that spot in the desert. Once they were gone, you took the diamonds for yourselves. And one of you was stalking me that day near the outcrop. Clever and diabolical."

"And unable to prove," Tina said.

"I'm not so sure. My guess is one of those diamonds is in this very room."

Although, if you knew it was a very clever fake meant for the latest buyer you scared off, you'd need another hour in a soaking bath to recover from the shock.

The second I said the word "room," I regretted it. Tina and Tanya lunged at me. But not before I screamed at the top of my lungs, "MARISELA! WE NEED TOWELS NOW! NOW! HURRY UP!"

If the blondes were motivated to silence me once and for all, Marisela was even more motivated to keep her job at La Tourelle. The door burst open, sending all of us toward the large soaker tubs.

"I was on my way," Marisela said, towels in hand. Then she gasped as she saw Tina and Tanya dragging me closer to the tub.

"Call the police!" I yelled. "Call nine-one-one!"

Instead, Marisela shouted something in Spanish and two other spa attendants came running. At their heels was the petite, dark-haired receptionist.

"These women are murderers," I shouted. "Don't just stand there. Get them off me and dial nine-one-one."

I'm not sure exactly what happened because I was now on the ground with my head leaning against the tub. One good thrust and I'd have a concussion that would last a century. All I remembered was the sound of a gun going off and everyone screaming.

My God! A gunshot. Is that blood running down my cheeks?

It wasn't blood. It was water. Water from the soaker tub. And the only thing the gun hit was the decorative chandelier that fell to the ground.

"No one move. Except you, Phee. You can move."

For an instant, I thought I was seeing things. It was Augusta. Augusta stood in the middle of the tranquility spa pointing her Glock or Wesson, or whatever the heck it was, at the blondes. "Think you can towel off your hair and call the police?"

"I, um, er, oh my God, Augusta! You saved my life."

"Just dial, will you?"

The Fountain Hills Police arrived at the same time Nate and Marshall made it to La Tourelle. At the sight of me, with dripping wet hair and disheveled clothes, Marshall raced over and hugged me so tight I couldn't catch my breath. Everyone in the spa was questioned, a process that seemed to last forever. The blondes were taken into custody but no diamond, real or fake, was found in the cucumber spa. The police searched their bags and every possible niche. In addition, they notified the two sheriffs' departments who were working the case.

"Maybe the diamond is in their car," one of the officers said.

Then I remembered a myth I'd heard about diamonds. Maybe the blondes had heard it, too.

"Hold on! Check their water bottles and be careful."

Sure enough, the blue Dasani bottle housed more than purified water. Given the blue bottle, it was hard to see the stone at first, but it was there, all right. Unlike a real diamond, it was easily discernable. The girls never stopped to look.

By day's end, two murders were solved and the management merger with Wolters Stork had been thwarted. It would take months, however, before the financial situation could be addressed and the monies belonging to the residents of the Lillian could be restored.

Nate and Marshall didn't know whether to be upset with me because I had taken such an incredibly stupid risk or be ecstatic because I had rooted out the real killers. But it was Augusta whom I thanked for dropping everything and racing to save me.

"I figured something was going on," she said, "when I looked up those tax reports for Mr. Williams. That bar in Punkin Center is owned by Mary Olsen. She bought it shortly after the diamond heist. It was the perfect spot for her daughter to run her operation. Too bad the grand-daughters doubled-crossed all of them."

"Wow, when you figure out how many people were involved in this operation, it's mind boggling."

"Yeah, sure is. Bound to keep lots of deputy sheriffs buried in paperwork for weeks," Marshall said. "And your mother's book club in endless chatter."

We had left the spa area and were standing in the main lobby. Tina and Tanya were escorted past us. Their hands were tied behind their backs.

"Oh no. Oh no. There's something we still haven't fig-ured out. We know why Sharon had my mom's and Lucinda's names on that piece of paper, but what about Quentin? Why did he have those names?"

Nate walked toward me. "Those blondes might know. If you hurry, maybe you can ask them before the police leave."

"Wait! Wait!" I yelled as the police escorted Tina and Tanya out of the building. "I need to ask these women something."

An officer had just opened the car door for one of the blondes when he said, "Stay back and ask your question from where you're standing. Make it quick."

I spoke loudly and succinctly. "Quentin Dussler was holding a piece of paper in his hand when you suffocated him. It had two names on it. What did that have to do with his murder?"

Tina furrowed her brow and shrugged. "Nothing. When we got to his garage on the pretense of discussing another diamond drop, he said to make it quick because he had other business to deal with. When we asked what, he held up a piece of paper and said, 'Calling these two women to tell them their pottery pieces weren't accepted for competition. The other instructor chickened out.'"

I was flabbergasted. "So that was it? Pottery pieces? Competition?"

"Yeah, why? Did you think it was a hit list?"

I opened my mouth, but nothing came out. The police cars took off and I walked back to Nate, Marshall, and Augusta. "Tell my mother it was a hit list after all. When she gets all crazy, we'll explain the murderers were arrested."

Nate rubbed the nape of his neck. "But—"

"Trust me. It's best she never finds out the truth about her pottery."

Chapter 38

"Isn't this exciting?" my mother asked. "They're about to read off the list of winners in this year's Creations in Clay contest."

It was finally June thirtieth and Marshall, Nate, and I had gotten roped into attending the annual pottery event at the Palm Ridge Recreation Center, along with my mother's neighbor Herb and her book club friends. It was the first time in weeks that we weren't stressed. I thought it would take months for things around here to settle down, like that wildfire up north that took days to contain.

Williams Investigations was credited for solving two murders and one international diamond heist. Rolo Barnes called to let us know he appreciated our business and was now remodeling his kitchen. Gertie and Trudy also called with interesting news of their own.

"That crazy Yolanda from the fourth floor was the one who stole Sharon's clay jar, along with a pair of some guy's briefs that she thought were interesting," Gertie said. "Trudy and I are seriously considering mousetraps."

As I looked around the Adobe Room, I was surprised at how many people were in attendance. The program began with a moment of silence for Quentin, long-term instructor and club member, and Sharon, former club member and intermediary instructor.

The announcer read off the list of categories and paused. "Art is constantly changing and the evolution makes for surprising new discoveries. That's why the clay club board decided to offer a new category this year—burgeoning art forms in nature. And we are pleased to announce the first-place winner in that new category for her intriguing platter. No one on our board has ever seen anything quite like it— woodland gargoyles on a lovely serving platter. The award goes to Mrs. Harriet Plunkett."

My mother all but shrieked. "Woodland gargoyles? Woodland gargoyles? Are they blind? That's Streetman."

"Shh, Mom. Just go and get the award."

As she stood, Marshall gave my hand a squeeze. "That dog sort of grows on you, doesn't he?"

"Speak for yourself."

Later that evening, when Marshall and I were back at my place and enjoying the sunset from the back patio, he kissed me lightly on the cheek and held my gaze. I wasn't sure what to expect.

"No matter how this comes out, it won't sound right, so I might as well be blunt."

It's over. He's saying good-bye. Why do I never see these things coming?

"I have a short-term lease and the one on your casita runs out pretty soon, too. So, I was thinking . . . maybe it's time for us to share our own place. I can't imagine being with anyone but you, Phee, and I'm ready to take the next step."

"I, um, er . . ."

"You don't have to say anything right now, but will you at least consider it? I mean, us moving in together in a shared place. And then, well, we could . . ."

He never got to finish his sentence. It was too hard to speak with my lips pressing against his.

Don't miss the next Sophie Kimball Mystery:

DRESSED UP 4 MURDER

Coming your way in March 2020

Please turn the page for a quick peek at this
darling new mystery where Streetman becomes
the model dog for the holidays—
all of them!

Harriet Plunkett's House, Sun City West, Arizona

"Doesn't he look like the most adorable little dog you've ever seen?" my mother asked when I walked into her house on a late Wednesday afternoon in October. Signs of autumn were everywhere in Sun City West, including pumpkins on front patios, leaf wreaths on doorways, and someone's large ceramic pig dressed like a witch. Of course, it was still over ninety degrees, but that wasn't stopping anyone from welcoming the fall and winter holidays.

My mother had begged me to stop by on my way home from work to look at Streetman's costume for the "Precious Pooches Holiday Extravaganza" for dogs of all ages and breeds. And since her dog was a Chiweenie, part Chihuahua part Dachshund, he certainly qualified. The contest made no mention of neuroses.

I tried to be objective, but it was impossible. "He looks like an overstuffed grape or something, if you ask me. And what's he doing? He's scratching at your patio door. Does he need to go out?"

"He's not a grape. He's going as an acorn. He'll look better once I get the hat on him. When he stops biting.

And no, he doesn't need to go out. We were just out a half hour ago."

"Maybe he's trying to escape because you're about to put the hat on him."

"Very funny. It's not easy, you know. There are three separate category contests, and I've registered him for all of them—Halloween, Thanksgiving, and Hanukkah/Christmas. Shirley Johnson is making the costumes. You're looking at the Thanksgiving one. I can't make up my mind if I want Streetman to go as a pumpkin for Halloween or a ghost. Goodness. I haven't even given any thought to the winter costume. Maybe a snowflake . . ."

"Right now, I think he wants to go. Period. Look. He's frantically pawing at your patio door."

"He only wants to sniff around the Galbraiths' grill. A coyote or something must've marked the tarp because, ever since yesterday, the dog has been beside himself to check it out. I certainly don't need him peeing on their grill. They won't be back until early November. I spoke to Janet a few days ago. She really appreciates Streetman and me checking out her place while they're up in Alberta. You know how it is with the Canadian snowbirds. They can only stay here for five months or they lose their health insurance. Something like that."

"Uh-huh."

"Anyway, how are you and Marshall managing with your move? That's coming up sometime soon, isn't it?"

"Not soon enough. I feel as if I'm living out of cardboard boxes, and Marshall's place is no different. We won't be able to get in to the new rental until November first. That's three weeks away and three weeks too long."

Marshall and I had worked for the same Mankato, Minnesota, police department for years before I moved out west

to become the bookkeeper for retired Mankato detective
Nate Williams. Nate had opened his own investigation firm
and insisted I join him. A year later, and in dire need of a
good investigator, he talked Marshall into making the move
as well. I was ecstatic, considering I'd had a crush on the
guy for years. Turned out it was reciprocal.

"Do you need any help with the move?" my mother
asked. "Lucinda and Shirley offered to help you pack."

*Oh dear God. We'd never finish. They'd be arguing over
everything.*

Shirley Johnson and Lucinda Espinoza were two of my
mother's book club friends and as opposite as any two people
could possibly be. Shirley was an elegant black woman and
a former milliner while Lucinda, a retired housewife, looked
as if she had recently escaped a windstorm.

"No, I'll be fine. The hard part's done. I can't believe I
actually sold my house in Mankato. Other than autumn
strolls around Sibley Park, I really won't miss Minnesota."

"What about my granddaughter? Did she get all nos-
talgic?"

"Not really. In fact, she had me donate most of the stuff
she had in storage to charity. She's sharing a small apartment in St. Cloud with another teacher and they don't have
much room. Besides, Kalese was never the pack rat type."

My mother had turned away for a second and walked to
the patio door. "Maybe you're right. Maybe he does need
to go out again. Hold on. I'll grab his leash. We can both go
out back." With the exception of the people living next door
to my mother and busybody Herb Garrett across the street,
the other neighbors were all snowbirds. Michigan. South
Dakota. Canada.

"Dear God. You're not going to take him outside in that
outfit, are you?" I asked.

"Fine. I'll unsnap the Velcro. Shirley's using Velcro for everything."

At the instant in which the sliding glass door opened, Streetman yanked my mother across the patio and straight toward the Galbraiths' backyard barbeque grill.

"I should never have taken the retractable leash," she shouted. "He's already yards ahead of me."

"Can't you push a button or something on that leash?"

"I haven't learned how to use it yet. It's new."

I was a few feet behind her, running as fast as I could in wedge heels.

Her voice bellowed across the adjoining yards as she approached the Galbraiths' grill. "Streetman, stop that! Stop that this instant!"

The dog zeroed in on the tarp and had gripped the edge of it with his teeth. My mother stood directly behind him and fiddled with the retractable leash.

"Now see what you've done," she said to the dog. "You've gone ahead and uncovered the bottom of the grill. I'll just shove those black boxes back a bit and put the tarp back down."

"Don't move, Mom!" I screamed. "Take a good look. They're not boxes. They're shoes."

"What?" My mother flashed me a look. "Who puts shoes under a grill where snakes and scorpions can climb in them?"

I bent down to take a closer look and froze. Streetman was still tugging to get under the tarp and my mother seemed oblivious to what was really there.

"Um, it's not shoes. I mean, yeah, those are shoes, all right, but they're kind of attached to someone's legs."

"What???"

If I thought my mother's voice was loud when she was yelling at the dog, it was a veritable explosion at that point. "A body? There's a body under there? You're telling me there's a body under that tarp? Oh my God. Poor Streetman. This could really set him back."

Yes, above all, the dog's emotional state was the first thing that came to my mind, too. "Mom, step back."

At that moment, she scooped Streetman into her arms and ran for the house. "I'm calling the sheriff. No! Wait. We have to find out who it is first. Once those deputy sheriffs get here, they'll never let us near the body."

"Good. I don't want to be near a dead body. Do you?"

"Of course not. But I need to know who it is. My God, Phee, it could be one of the neighbors. Can't you just pull the tarp back and take a look?"

Streetman was putting up a major fuss, squirming in my mother's arms and trying to get down.

"Okay, Mom. Go back to the house. Put the dog inside and come back here. I won't move until you do. Oh, and bring your cell phone."

My mother didn't say a word. She walked as quickly as she could and returned a few minutes later, cell phone in hand. "Here. Take this plastic doggie bag and use it as you pull the tarp away. Don't get your fingerprints on the tarp."

"I'll pull the tarp back and take a look, but I won't have the slightest idea if it's one of your neighbors. I don't know all of them."

"Fine. Fine. Oh, and look for cause of death while you're at it."

"Cause of death? I'm not a medical examiner." I bent down, put my hand in the plastic bag, and gingerly lifted the tarp. I tried not to look at what, or in this case, who, was underneath it, but it was useless. I got a bird's-eye view. Male. Fully clothed, thank God, and face up. Middle aged. Dark hair. Jaundice coloring. Small trickle of blood from his nose to shirt. No puddles of blood behind the head or around the body.

My mother let out a piercing scream. "Oh my God. Oh my God in heaven!"

"Who? Who is it? Is it someone you know?"

I immediately let go of the tarp and let it drape over the body.

"No, no one I know."

"Then why were you screaming bloody murder?"

"Because there's a dead man directly across from my patio. A well-dressed dead man. Here, you call the sheriff's office. I'm too upset. And when you're done, give me the phone. I need to call Herb Garrett."

"Herb Garrett? Why on earth would you need to call Herb?"

"Once those emergency vehicles show up, he'll be pounding at my door. Might as well save us some time."

I started to dial 9-1-1 when my mother grabbed my arm and stopped me. "Whatever you do, don't tell them it was Streetman who discovered the body."

"Why? What difference does that make?"

"Next thing you know, they'll want to use him for one of those cadaver dogs. He's got an excellent sense of smell. Don't say a word."

"You're kidding, right? First of all, the law enforcement agencies have their own trained dogs. *Trained* being the key word. No one's going to put up with all of his shenanigans. And second of all, how else are you and I going to explain how we happened to come across a dead body under the neighbors' tarp?"

My mother pursed her lips and stood still for a second. "Okay. Fine. Go ahead and call."

The dispatch operator asked me three times if I was positively certain we had uncovered a dead body. I had reached my apex the third time.

"Unless they're starting to make store mannequins in various stages of decomposition, then what we've discovered is indeed a dead body. Not a doll. Not a lifelike toy. And certainly not someone's Halloween decoration!"

Finally, I gave her my mother's address and told her we were behind the house. Then I handed my mother the phone. "Go ahead. Make Herb's day. Sorry, Mom, I couldn't resist the Clint Eastwood reference."

My mother took the phone and pushed a button. "I have him on speed dial in case of an emergency."

All I could hear was her end of the conversation, but it was enough.

"I'm telling you, I had no idea there'd be a body under that tarp. Sure, it was a huge tarp, but I thought it was covering up one of those gigantic grills. Uh-huh. Really? A griddle feature? No, all I have is a small Weber. Uh-huh. Behind the house. Fine. See you in a minute."

"I take it Herb is on his way."

My mother nodded. "Do you think I should call Shirley and Lucinda?"

"This isn't an afternoon social, for crying out loud, it's a crime scene. No, don't call them. It's bad enough Herb's going to be here any second. Maybe we should go wait on your patio. We can see everything from there."

Just then I heard the distant sound of sirens. "Never mind. We might as well stay put."

My mother thrust the phone at me. "Quick. While there's time, call your office. Get Nate or Marshall over here."

"Much as I'd like to accommodate you by having my boss and my boyfriend show up, I can't. Marshall's on a case up in Payson and won't be back until the weekend. I think he took the case so he wouldn't have to be stepping over cartons. And as for my boss, Nate's so tied up with his other cases, he certainly doesn't have time to interfere with a Maricopa County Sheriff's Office investigation."

"Humph. You know as well as I do those deputies will be bumbling around until they finally cave and bring in Williams Investigations to consult."

Much as I hated to admit it, my mother was right. Not because the sheriff deputies were "nincompoops" as she liked to put it, but the department was so inundated with drug-related crimes, kidnappings, and now a highway serial killer in the valley, that they relied on my boss's office to assist.

"If and when that happens, I'll let you know."

The sirens were getting louder and I turned to face my mother's patio.

From the left of the garage, Herb Garrett stormed across the gravel yard. "Where's the stiff? I want to take a look before the place is plastered in yellow crime tape."

"Under the tarp." I failed to mention the need for a plastic bag.

Herb made a beeline for the Galbraiths' grill and lifted the tarp. "Nope. Don't know him. Damn it. I forgot my phone."

"Don't tell me you were going to snap a photo. And do what? Post it on the Internet?"

Herb let the tarp drop and positioned himself next to my mother. "How else is poor Harriet going to sleep at night knowing some depraved killer is depositing bodies in the neighborhood? If I post it, maybe someone will know something."

My mother gasped. "Depraved killer? Bodies?"

"Herb's exaggerating," I said. "Aren't you?"

Suddenly it seemed as if the sirens were inches away from us. Then they stopped completely.

"Oh no," I said. "This can't be happening. Not again."

My mother grabbed my wrist. "What? What's happening?"

I took a deep breath. "Remember the two deputy sheriffs

who were called in to investigate the murder at the Stardust Theater?"

"Uh-huh."

"Looks like they're back for a repeat performance. Deputies Ranston and Bowman. I don't know which one dislikes me more."

Well, maybe "dislike" wasn't quite the word to describe how they felt about me. "Annoyed" might have summed it up better. Over a year ago, when my mother and her book club ladies were taking part in Agatha Christie's *The Mouse-trap* at the Stardust Theater, someone was found dead on the catwalk. And even though I wasn't a detective, only the accountant at Williams Investigations, I sort of did a bit of sleuthing on my own and might have stepped on their toes. What the hell. They're big men. They needed to get over it.

"Miss Kimball." Deputy Ranston's feet crunched on the yard gravel as he approached us from the side of my mother's house. "I should have taken a closer look at the name when I read the nine-one-one report. Seems you're the one who placed the call."

"Nice seeing you again, Deputy Ranston." I turned to his counterpart and mumbled something similar before reintroducing my mother and Herb.

"So, was it you who found the body?" Ranston asked.

I honestly don't know why but, for some reason, the man reminded me of a Sonoran Desert Toad. I kept expecting his tongue to roll out a full foot as he spoke.

"Um, actually it was my mother's dog. Streetman. He found the body."

Deputy Bowman cut in. "Just like that? Out of the blue?"

My mother took a few steps forward until she was almost nose to nose with Bowman. "For your information, Streetman and I cut across the Galbraiths' yard every day while they're still in Canada. We keep an eye on the house for them. Usually the dog is more concerned with the quail and the rabbits that hide under the bushes. He never as much as made a move toward the grill. Until yesterday afternoon. That's when he started whining to go over there. I thought a coyote might have marked it or left a deposit there."

"So you lifted the tarp up to check?" Bowman asked.

"Of course not. The dog was on a retractable leash and got to the grill before I did. He nuzzled the tarp aside, and that's when we saw the body."

Bowman gave his partner a sideways glance. "How big a dog is this Streetman that he could lift an entire tarp off a body?"

"He's less than ten pounds," I said, "but very strong."

Bowman wasn't buying it. "Look, Miss Kimball, I know you have a penchant for unsolved crimes and I'm more likely to believe it was you who lifted the tarp."

My mother responded before I could utter a word. "Only for a split second and only because she happened to see someone's legs attached to the shoes that were beneath it. And she used a plastic bag so she wouldn't get fingerprints on the material."

Then the deputies turned to Herb, and Ranston spoke. "Were you here as well when the ladies discovered the body, Mr. Garrett?"

"No. Harriet called me after dialing nine-one-one."

"I see."

Ranston wrote something on a small notepad and looked up. "The nine-one-one dispatcher gave us the Plunkett address. Would any of you happen to know the Galbraiths' address?"

"Of course," my mother said. "Something West Sentinel Drive. It's the small cul-de-sac behind us."

I could hear both deputies groan as Bowman placed a call.

"In a few minutes," he said, "a forensic team will be arriving as well as the coroner. I suggest you all return to your houses and stay clear of this property until further notice."

"Will you at least tell us who it is?" Herb asked. "For all we know, it could be one of our neighbors. Or a cartel drug lord who was dropped off here."

"Here? In Sun City West? That's what we have the desert for," my mother said.

Deputy Bowman forced a smile and repeated what he had told us a second ago. "Please go back to your houses. This is an official investigation."

"Will you be contacting the Galbraiths?" I asked.

Bowman gave a nod. "Yes."

I tapped my mother on the elbow and pointed to her house. "He's right." Then I whispered, "If you hurry, you can call the Galbraiths first."

Connect with Us

Visit us online at
KensingtonBooks.com
to read more from your favorite authors, see books
by series, view reading group guides, and more.

for sneak peeks, chances to win books and prize packs,
and to share your thoughts with other readers.

facebook.com/kensingtonpublishing
twitter.com/kensingtonbooks

Tell us what you think!

To share your thoughts, submit a review,
or sign up for our eNewsletters, please visit:
KensingtonBooks.com/TellUs.

Grab These Cozy Mysteries
from
Kensington Books

Forget Me Knot Mary Marks	978-0-7582-9205-6	$7.99US/$8.99CAN
Death of a Chocoholic Lee Hollis	978-0-7582-9449-4	$7.99US/$8.99CAN
Green Living Can Be Deadly Staci McLaughlin	978-0-7582-7502-8	$7.99US/$8.99CAN
Death of an Irish Diva Mollie Cox Bryan	978-0-7582-6633-0	$7.99US/$8.99CAN
Board Stiff Annelise Ryan	978-0-7582-7276-8	$7.99US/$8.99CAN
A Biscuit, A Casket Liz Mugavero	978-0-7582-8480-8	$7.99US/$8.99CAN
Boiled Over Barbara Ross	978-0-7582-8687-1	$7.99US/$8.99CAN
Scene of the Climb Kate Dyer-Seeley	978-0-7582-9531-6	$7.99US/$8.99CAN
Deadly Decor Karen Rose Smith	978-0-7582-8486-0	$7.99US/$8.99CAN
To Kill a Matzo Ball Delia Rosen	978-0-7582-8201-9	$7.99US/$8.99CAN

Available Wherever Books Are Sold!

All available as e-books, too!

Visit our website at **www.kensingtonbooks.com**

Follow P.I. Savannah Reid
with
G.A. McKevett